KERRIGANS

A TEXAS DYNASTY

THE LAWLESS

THE
KERRIGANS
A TEXAS DYNASTY
THE LAWLESS

WILLIAM W. JOHNSTONE
with J. A. Johnstone

PINNACLE BOOKS
Kensington Publishing Corp.
www.kensingtonbooks.com

PINNACLE BOOKS are published by

Kensington Publishing Corp.
119 West 40th Street
New York, NY 10018

PUBLISHER'S NOTE
Following the death of William W. Johnstone, the Johnstone family is working with a carefully selected writer to organize and complete Mr. Johnstone's outlines and many unfinished manuscripts to create additional novels in all of his series like The Last Gunfighter, Mountain Man, and Eagles, among others. This novel was inspired by Mr. Johnstone's superb storytelling.

All Kensington titles, imprints, and distributed lines are available at special quantity discounts for bulk purchases for sales promotions, premiums, fund-raising, educational, or institutional use. Special book excerpts or customized printings can also be created to fit specific needs. For details, write or phone the office of the Kensington special sales manager: Kensington Publishing Corp., 119 West 40th Street, New York, NY 10018, attn: Special Sales Department; phone 1-800-221-2647.

PINNACLE BOOKS, the Pinnacle logo, and the WWJ steer head logo, are Reg. U.S. Pat. & TM Off.

ISBN-13: 978-0-7860-3581-6
ISBN-10: 0-7860-3581-1

First printing: August 2015

10 9 8 7 6 5 4 3 2 1

Printed in the United States of America

First electronic edition: August 2015

ISBN-13: 978-0-7860-3582-3
ISBN-10: 0-7860-3582-X

BOOK ONE
The Testing Time

CHAPTER ONE

It was not the Comanche Kate Kerrigan feared but the three white men who rode with them.

The Comanche were on the move a mile to the south of her wagon. As was their custom, mounted warriors led the column. Behind them, also on horseback, came the young women of childbearing age. Then, walking in dust, the old people, little respected in Comanche culture. Taking up the rear, in thicker dust, staggered the slaves, mostly Mexican, but here and there were white and black faces. The slaves, about two hundred in number, were chivvied along by boys who made free use of their willow-wand whips on bent backs.

The three Comancheros, scarred, hard-eyed brutes dressed in the vaquero style then becoming popular among Texas drovers, broke away from the column, drew rein a hundred yards off, and watched Kate's ox-drawn wagon trundle past. She had a milk cow and a lanky buckskin horse tied to the rear.

Beside the wagon, his wary eyes on the Comanche column, walked old Moses Rice. His sweating face was black as obsidian and he had a huge Colt's Dragoon stuck into his waistband. At a distance of a few feet, seven times out of ten Moses could be depended upon to hit his target. "Miz Kerrigan . . ."

"I see them, Mose," Kate said. "Get the children into the wagon. Trace, Quinn, grab your rifles and stay by me."

Moses loaded Kate's nine-year-old twins Ivy and Niall and five-year-old Shannon into the wagon and told them to hush now and that he would make sure nothing happened to them. The youngsters were frightened and so was Moses. He didn't want to think how Miz Kerrigan felt.

"Ma," Trace said, "they're just sitting their horses, watching us." Like his mother Trace carried a sixteen-shot Henry rifle, a purchase that back on the Brazos had left the family broke for a three-month.

"They want what we have, Trace." She looked at her oldest son, gauging his maturity, then said, "But most of all they want me."

"Over my dead body, Ma," Trace said.

"And mine." She took the sting out of that with a smile. "The Comanche are almost out of sight. I think those three renegades will go on after them."

Quinn Kerrigan's stare reached out to the three men, his knuckles white on his .58 Springfield. "I don't think they plan on going anywhere except after us."

"Well, let's find out," Kate said. "Quinn, your Springfield can reach out far. Get into the back of the wagon. Trace, up on the driver's seat with me. And Moses, you choose where you want to be."

"I want to be back at our old place on the Brazos,

Miz Kerrigan. That's where I want to be," Moses said, looking as soulful as only an old man can.

Kate smiled. "Our future lies to the west, Moses, and nothing will stop us from getting there, especially Comanchero scum like those three."

Kate cracked her whip and the pair of oxen lurched into motion. Behind her, Shannon quietly sobbed, her child's sixth sense inherited from her Irish mother telling her that something was amiss. The adults were tense, slightly fearful, and the little girl felt it in her very soul.

Trace stuck his head around the canvas of the converted farm wagon and glanced behind him. "They haven't moved, Ma."

"Any Comanche with them?" Kate asked.

"No, only those three."

She nodded. "They're biding their time."

An hour later, flat scrubland gradually gave way to gently rolling country covered with pecan and mesquite. Here and there Apache plume, yucca, and thickets of white honeysuckle added a splash of color. Almost hidden from sight among a few wild oaks was a burned-out cabin with three walls and part of the roof still standing.

"There might be water there," Kate Kerrigan said to Trace. "If there is, we can fill our barrel."

"Ma, the Comancheros are following us," Trace said. "Jesus, Ma, they're close."

"I know they are. And please don't take the Savior's name in vain, Trace. I thought I'd taught you better than that."

Kate stuck her head into the wagon. "Now you children be quiet as church mice. In a little while you might hear guns going off, but I want you to stay right where you are."

"Mama, I'm scared of those bad men," Shannon said.

"Don't be scared, little one, I'll let no harm come to you." Kate smiled and put her forefinger to her lips. "Now remember, quiet as a mouse."

She rummaged through a small trunk behind the driver's seat and brought out an emerald-green silk scarf with the famous war cry of the Fighting 69th, the Irish Brigade, *Faugh a Ballagh*, printed along its four sides. Translated from the Gaelic, the cry meant Clear the Way, and that's what Kate intended to do . . . clear the way for her young family.

Trace had seen his mother use the scarf to tie back her glorious, flaming mane of red hair only once before, when a band of marauding Apaches attacked their cabin on the Brazos. Now she did it again. A lump in his throat and fear spiking at his belly, he knew what it meant . . .

Kate Kerrigan was going to war.

CHAPTER TWO

After telling Trace and Quinn to stay behind guarding the wagon, Kate advanced on the three Comancheros. Since he would not consider leaving her alone, Moses was at her side. She held the Henry close to her, hidden in the folds of her dress, the hammer back.

The three men watched her, grinning as they made comments about her walk, her breasts, her hair, and her ultimate fate.

The Crate brothers, Sam, Jake and Andy, had lived with the Comanche for five years and were content to pick up whatever scraps fell from the bowls of the Lords of the Texas Plains. In their time, they'd murdered, raped, and thieved whatever took their fancy, and Jake, the fastest with the iron, had killed seventeen men, not one of them near his equal with the iron.

Living in a warrior-dominated society for so long, they had no regard for women and considered them things to be used for their pleasure and amusement. But in Kate Kerrigan, they knew they'd hit the jackpot. They'd take their pleasure with her and then sell her in

Old Mexico, where white women with red hair brought a premium price.

Many years later when belted men talked of Kate Kerrigan, they wondered if the Crate brothers would have underestimated her so badly had they known that she'd killed three bad men in a revolver fight and had fought Apaches. The answer was, probably not. They were vicious, the Crates, but they were also quite incredibly stupid.

Before she stopped walking, Kate estimated her distance carefully. The fact that the three men had not touched the booted rifles under their knees told her much. The Crates were draw fighters, a new breed of gunmen Texas had produced in large numbers after the war. Had she been a gun-toting man, they would have closed the distance, but she was only a woman and didn't merit such caution.

Kate had a fine voice for talking or singing, and it carried. Ten yards from the Crate brothers, she spoke. "Why are you following us? If you need coffee or food, you can have it and welcome."

"We want you, little lady," Sam said. "Tonight, once you have a taste of the Crate brothers, you'll throw your arms around our legs and beg us for more. Jake, Andy, ain't that so?"

"Damn right." Andy was a scar-faced savage with a thick-lipped wide mouth. "Lady, this is your lucky day. Sam, take a squeeze of them bobbers. Make sure they're real. And kill the Negro while you're at it. He's in the way."

Kate had an Irish temper that some compared to an erupting volcano, and she unleashed it. "You foul-mouthed white trash. I'll kill the first man who tries to put a hand on me."

That last brought gales of laughter from the Crates, and Sam was still bellowing as he began his climb out of the saddle. But he needn't have bothered. Kate blew him out of it.

Suddenly, Jake and Andy realized they had a she-wolf by the tail. The violent surprise stunned them for just a moment, giving Kate all the time she needed. She levered another round and shot from the hip, putting a bullet into Andy's throat. The man's eyes went big. Gagging blood, he fired wild, then slumped over in the saddle. Jake drew and for a split second, her life hung in the balance.

Moses two-handed his .44 cannon to eye level and cut loose. Maybe because he knew what a disaster a miss would be, the old man's aim was true. The .44 ball tore a great hole in Jake's chest. Moses, to his own surprise, managed to score another hit before the man fell out of the saddle.

In those unreal moments that follow a gunfight when ears clang and what has just occurred in the space of a few seconds has not as yet reached the combatants' full consciousness, Kate and Moses stared at the dead men on the ground as through a tunnel.

Kate was snapped back to reality by a shriek behind her. It came from the wagon! She turned and saw Trace beckoning to her.

"Ma! Ma!" he yelled. "Niall's been shot."

Panic surging through her, she dropped her rifle and ran, unaware that Moses had fired again, shooting the dying, bent-over Andy Crate out of the saddle. Then, as Kate had done, the old black man ran to the wagon.

Niall had died instantly. Andy Crate's wild bullet had hit him in the center of the chest and the boy's small body could not survive such a wound. The young girls huddled around him, crying. Trace and Quinn, trying hard to be men, stood in stunned silence, shocked by the time and manner of their brother's death.

Kate Kerrigan was inconsolable. It was a time for grief, for lament, a time for rebellion against God's will. Moses, more sure of his manhood than the teenage boys, let his tears flow, cutting channels through his dusty cheeks.

Moses watched Kate throw herself on her dead child and said nothing. Born a slave and the son and grandson of a slave, he'd witnessed grief many times before. Since he could neither cure nor help, he waited stoically and silently until the time Miz Kerrigan would need him.

That time came at midnight when she left the wagon and stepped into firelit shadow. Trace and Quinn had dragged away the bodies of the Comancheros, and their horses grazed nearby. The guns and saddles of the dead men were valuable and had been piled up near the campfire.

If she noticed, she did not say. She called Moses to her side. "We will take my son with us to his new home. I will not bury him in foreign soil."

Moses bowed his head, then said, "That is not the way, Miz Kerrigan. Old Moses is feeling the daytime heat and the farther west we travel, the hotter it will become." He gave a great, shuddering sigh. "Master Niall would not wish to travel in such heat, no."

"Ma, Moses is right," Trace said. "We could be weeks on the trail and high summer is coming down on us."

"You would bury your brother in this vile wilderness?" Kate asked, a storm gathering in her eyes.

As he had done many times before, Moses jumped in to shield one of the children from their mother's wrath. "Miz Kate, Master Niall's soul has moved on from this place. Now he has a shiny, heavenly body and he sits at the right hand of God. We will bury his poor little bones, grieve for a while longer, and remember his life. Then we will all smile again."

"It's a hard thing for a mother to bury her child," Kate said.

"I know, and I seen it too many times in my life," Moses said. "You ever wonder why black women always ask merchants for empty Arbuckle coffee crates? 'Cause they make good coffins for their dead children. Black women bury their little ones and grieve just as white women do. Miz Kerrigan, we can't take Niall with us, no."

A horned moon rode high in the sky and night birds pecked at the first stars. Coyotes yipped close to camp and a rising wind rustled in the tree branches. Kate Kerrigan walked to the fire and gazed into the flames. Without turning she said, "Come first light we will bury my son."

CHAPTER THREE

A week after Niall's death, the Kerrigan wagon pushed along the south fork of the Llano River into Lipan Apache country. Hereditary enemies of the Comanche, the Lipan were disposed to be friendly with whites, but like all Indians they could be notional. When Kate drove into the settlement of Menardville she had seen no sign of them.

Menardville claimed to be a town, but consisted of a general store, saloon, and blacksmith shop only. However, the community served as a trading post and a welcome stop on the north and west cattle trails.

When the Kerrigan wagon creaked to a halt outside the general store, it caused a stir among the loungers sitting on the saloon porch. As usual, Kate, a beautiful woman at any time, attracted her share of attention even after hard weeks on the trail, but it was the three blood horses tied to the back of the wagon, standing with the milk cow and the buckskin, that started tongues wagging. Since the war ended, fine horses were few and far between in Reconstruction Texas.

Kate and Moses stepped into the store with the girls while Trace and Quinn guarded the wagon. Most of their grub had been shot on the trail, but they lacked necessities like bacon, flour, salt, coffee, and sugar. Shannon and Ivy soon made it clear that candy canes and mint humbugs should be included in that list.

Moses was window-shopping with the girls when a tall man approached Kate as she stood at the counter. He touched his hat. "Howdy, ma'am. Are those your horses out there?"

Kate said they were.

"Are they for sale?" The man wore a frayed frock coat and collarless shirt, very dirty along the band. A Colt Navy in a cross-draw holster hung on his hips and he had the flat black eyes of a carrion eater.

"The horses are not for sale," Kate said. "We paid dearly for them."

The man smiled. "You got real purty hair, ma'am." His grin was not pleasant. "And you got real purty everything else."

"If you'll excuse me, I'm quite busy here," Kate said.

"Too busy for the likes o' me, is that it?" the man said.

The storeowner, a gray-haired man with mild brown eyes, spoke up. "Let the lady finish her shopping in peace, Jansen."

"You shut your trap"—Jansen's hand went to the butt of his gun—"or I'll shut it permanent."

"And I'll see you hang," Kate gritted out.

The outlaw took a short step back. "Whoa! Uppity, ain't we? You know how I tame a woman like you, little lady?"

"We don't want to know," Moses said. He had the

dragoon in his hand. "If I was you, mister, I wouldn't draw that hogleg, no."

Jansen was caught flatfooted and he knew it. The old black man had the drop and no doubt would kill him.

"Get out of here while you still can," Kate said. "One more thing, a lowlife like you couldn't tame me on your best day."

Malachi Jansen was six feet tall when he walked into the store. He felt half that height as he walked out. But he was a man given to grudges and primed to plot his revenge.

"You take care, ma'am," the storekeeper said. "Jansen has only been in town for a month and he's already killed two men."

"I'll bear that in mind," Kate said as she and Moses lifted their packages from the counter.

Menardville boasted a two-story hotel, but Kate, mindful of her diminishing dollars, considered it an unneeded luxury. The family camped next to a creek five miles south of town within sight of the Blue Mountains, the peaks that marked the northern limit of the Edwards Plateau.

The tall grass country around the campsite supported stands of oak, mesquite, and juniper. A single cottonwood grew on the creek bank. The Kerrigans ate a supper of fried bacon and pan bread, then settled down for the night. Massive ramparts of black thunderheads loomed above the mountains. In West Texas, more often than not, clouds did not always mean rain. Often, thunder banged and lightning flashed, but not a single drop hit the ground. For that reason, Kate did not think it necessary to bed the girls down in the wagon.

Exhausted from the trail, the Kerrigans slept soundly. Midnight came and went and the moon dropped lower in the sky. A gray fox approached the camp on silent feet, her eyes filled with firelight. She stopped and sniffed the air. Alarmed, she slunk into the night like a gray ghost.

And out among the mesquite, Malachi Jansen made his move.

CHAPTER FOUR

As always, Moses was first awake and he rolled out of his blankets ready to get the coffee started. He saw immediately that the three Comanchero horses were gone. The rawboned buckskin still grazed, but he and the milk cow were alone.

Moses woke up Kate Kerrigan. "Miz Kate, the horses are gone. Stole."

Kate was awake instantly. She rose in her shift in the morning chill and held her blanket around her. "Coffee, Mose. And heat up last night's bacon grease. I'll dip some bread in it."

Trace and Quinn got out of their blankets and stood in their long johns, lanky youngsters as yet lacking a man's height and weight.

"The horses have been stolen," she said. "I'm going after them on the buckskin."

"And I'm going with you, Ma," Trace said.

"No you're not."

"Ma, I'm almost man-grown. I'm going with you."

"Riding double on the buckskin will slow me down," Kate said.

"Then I'll run alongside. And I'll still be running when the buckskin quits."

Moses, a big old man with a good face, said, "Boy's right, Miz Kate. Let him grow up and become a man."

Expecting argument, Moses was surprised when Kate said, "You can run alongside, Trace. But I warn you, when you can't go any farther, I'll leave you."

"I'll stick, Ma." Trace looked at his brother. "And no, Quinn, you can't go. This is Indian country. You stay behind and guard our sisters."

"I can't run those long distances like you can anyway," Quinn said. "I'll stay behind."

Kate and Trace drank a quick cup of coffee and ate pan bread while Moses saddled the buckskin. "One man, Miz Kate, took off due north. And I got me a good idea who he was."

"The man at the store in Menardville?" Kate asked.

"He wanted them horses real bad," Moses said.

Kate nodded. "And we made him look small."

"Ma, he wouldn't drive the horses back to the settlement, would he?" Trace asked. "Is he that arrogant?"

"He might be," Kate said. "But there's one way to find out."

Moses helped her mount, then handed her the Henry.

At that time in her life, she always rode sidesaddle and settled her dress over her legs "Well, Trace, are you ready to run?"

"Sure I'm ready, Ma."

"Then let's get it done."

Moses stood with the girls and Quinn and watched

them leave. His heart was heavy as he hoped for the best and feared the worst. "Your folks gonna be jus' fine," he said to Shannon and Ivy. "Old Moses, he knows these t'ings. Speaks to God all the time, him."

He didn't know if the girls believed him or not.

Kate Kerrigan drew rein. "What do the tracks tell you, Trace?"

"Same story, Ma. They're headed right for Menardville."

"He's not even trying to lose us." Kate shook her head in amazement.

"Maybe he has friends at the settlement. Do you still reckon it's that Jansen ranny?"

Kate looked at the country ahead, her beautiful face thoughtful. "It's him all right, and he's not afraid of being followed to Menardville. I wonder why?"

"Like I said, he has friends there." Trace held his rifle and wore a Colt Navy holstered in a gun rig he'd taken from one of the dead Comancheros. He'd owned such a fine revolver before, but that one was a bad luck pistol and he'd gotten rid of it. He'd never owned one since.

"How are you holding up, Trace?" Kate asked.

"I'm just fine, Ma."

"When we get to the settlement, stay close, son. Let me do the talking and if it comes to it, I'll do the shooting."

"I can take care of myself, Ma. And you."

Kate looked him in the eyes. "I know you can, but I don't want to lose another son."

CHAPTER FIVE

The thunderstorm that had threatened the evening before decided that rain was a viable option after all. As Kate rode into Menardville, Trace walking head-down at her stirrup, a downpour driven by a stiff north wind lashed across the open ground in front of the buildings.

As she'd expected, her horses were confined in a small pole corral between the blacksmith's shop and the saloon. A shaggy old yellow dog lingered near the corral but slunk away as Kate rode to the grocery store and dismounted. She left Trace outside on the porch and stepped into the store, momentarily enjoying the familiar down-homey smells of molasses, dried apples, and freshly ground coffee.

She didn't need to ask.

Right away, the storekeeper said, "He's in the saloon, ma'am. Got Brick Larkhall and Dan Poteet with him. Ma'am, you don't want to go in there. Jansen is with some mighty hard company."

"No need for that," Kate said. "I'll just collect my horses and move on."

"Ma'am . . ." The storekeeper's face was alarmed.

"I intend to recover my stolen property."

She stepped out of the store and stopped at the edge of the porch where rain fell from the roof like a waterfall. The street was already muddy. She'd need to lift her dress and petticoats to reach the corral and at the same time balance the Henry. It was well nigh impossible. "We'll wait until this passes, Trace."

The boy smiled. "I'll get them, Ma. I'm wearing boots."

"No. It won't rain this heavily for long, then we'll both go."

The saloon door opened and a tall, heavy man with a spade-shaped beard stepped outside, a glass in his hand. "Still comin' down," he said to someone inside. Then he saw Kate. "Hey, pretty lady, come inside out of the rain and have a drink."

"No, thank you."

A voice came from the saloon and the bearded man answered. "I'm talking to a lady who don't want to drink with me, Mal. Purty little thing with red hair, too."

Malachi Jansen stepped through the door almost immediately and stopped when he saw Kate. "What the hell do you want?"

"I'm taking back my horses," Kate said. "Just as soon as the rain stops."

"I got a bill of sale for them nags," Jansen said. "Ain't that right, Dan?"

"Sure is," Poteet said. "I give you that bill of sale my ownself." He glared at Kate. "Go home now, girly. Mr. Jansen has his affydavey all signed, sealed, and delivered. Now git out of here afore I put you over my knee."

"Don't you talk to my mother like that, trash." Trace was mad clean to the bone.

"Well, well, well, the hoss thief has a brat." Poteet fancied himself a draw fighter and reckoned he could get two bullets into the skinny youth before he could get his rifle into play. The man would have shucked the iron, but a voice from the street stopped him.

"Hold up there, feller. Don't draw that gun." A man wearing a slicker, rain cascading off the brim of his hat, led a big palouse horse closer and then stopped, his eyes on Poteet.

"Who the hell are you?" Poteet glared.

"Name's Luke Trent, B Company Texas Rangers. Who the hell are you?"

"Dan Poteet. I was about to arrest these hoss thieves."

Trent's eyes shifted from Trace to Kate where they lingered for a moment. "Yup. They sure look like a couple desperate characters." Long hair fell over his shoulders and he sported a great, sweeping cavalry mustache, the sort that made ladies' hearts flutter. He was the kind of man who could cut a dash but seldom did.

To Kate he said, "Ma'am, did you try to steal horses from these men?"

Jansen said, "Yeah, she did and—"

"I wasn't speaking to you," Trent said. "Ma'am?" His eyes flickered for an instant as Brick Larkhall stepped onto the porch.

"Those horses in the corral are my property." Kate

pointed to Jansen. "He stole them last night or in the early hours of this morning."

"Do you have a bill of sale for the animals, ma'am? Those are thousand-dollar horses, first I've seen in Texas since I was a younker."

"My bill of sale was written in lead, Ranger," Kate said. "My bill of sale is the three dead Comancheros who attacked our camp and murdered my son, a nine-year-old boy. The horses they rode that day are mine by right and I'm taking them back."

"I got a bill of sale," Jansen said. "And I'm willing to show it."

Trent glanced at the gunmetal sky. "I'll come over there and read that." He looped his horse to the hitching rail and stepped onto the porch of the saloon. A distant thunder rolled and lightning glittered.

"There you are, Ranger," Jansen said. "As legal a document as was ever signed by an honest man like myself."

"Is that so?" Trent glanced at the bill of sale and his eyes lifted, "You Poteet?"

Poteet nodded. "As ever was, Ranger. And a straight dealer through and through."

"Where did you acquire three Thoroughbred horses, Poteet?" Trent asked.

"Huh?" Poteet frowned.

"It says here in the bill of sale that you sold three horses to one Malachi Jansen for fifty dollars. Where did you get them?"

Poteet hesitated, and his shifty eyes telegraphed his unease.

"Well?" Trent said impatiently. "Where did you get them?"

"My pa bred them horses and he give them to me." Poteet said, proud he'd thought up the lie so quickly.

Trent nodded. "Your pa was Lucifer Poteet out of the Nueces River country, right? There ain't two men in Texas with that name."

"Yeah, that was my pa. His pa gave him that name on account of how he wanted a girl child and reckoned his new son was the seed of the devil."

"The three horses in the corral are no more than four years old," Trent pointed out. "Lucifer Poteet was hung in El Paso for rape and murder ten years ago. I know because it was my pa who hung him."

"Ranger, I'm shocked," Jansen said. "I had no idea the horses might have been stolen."

Trent smiled at that, then said to Kate, "Ma'am, you can pick up your horses any time you want."

"The hell she can! This is fer my pa!" Dan Poteet went for his gun.

Luke Trent shucked iron from inside his open slicker and shot Poteet before he cleared leather. In the moment of his death, Poteet learned he wasn't even close to being a draw fighter.

Jansen thought he had a chance to get the drop and went for his gun. He died on the muddy porch floor, puking up scarlet blood. Brick Larkhall had his gun ready but decided he wanted no part of Ranger Trent. He shrieked and dropped his Colt as though it was suddenly red hot.

"You thought about it, mister, didn't you?" Trent said. Then yelled, *"Didn't you?"*

"Yeah, I did, but I reckoned you were too fast for me."

Trent shot Larkhall and watched him drop. "Then you're just as guilty as the other two."

Raised in New York's Five Corners hellhole, Kate was used to violence in all its forms, and she'd killed with a gun herself, but the shooting of Larkhall troubled her. "That man had surrendered."

"Not in his mind, he hadn't," Trent said, reloading a charged cylinder into his 1860 Army Model Colt. "Where I'm going, I can't take a prisoner. He would have dogged my back trail until he got a chance to shoot me in the back." The Ranger glanced at Larkhall's body. "He had the option of staying inside the saloon but didn't take it."

Horrified as she was, Kate Kerrigan still realized the value of a real Texas fighting man like Luke Trent. The death and destruction he could inflict in the space of a few seconds was devastating. She made a vow then and there that when she established her ranch, she would hire only riders who could use a gun. Hard men like Luke Trent would be the pillars of her empire.

Trace had also seen what fast hands meant in a gunfight and he knew he could never come close to matching a man like Luke Trent. He also made a vow. Never again would he wear a belt gun. Even in dangerous times, his weapon of choice would be the repeating rifle.

Ranger Trent arranged for the bodies to be removed and paid in scrip for their burials. From the saloon, he brought a whiskey back out to the porch. The rain had lessened and Kate was at the corral. He followed her there. "Where are you headed, ma'am?"

"My name is Kate Kerrigan." Her voice was cool.

Although she admired the Ranger as a fighting man, she felt as a person he left much to be desired. "As for where I'm headed, my destination is west. I want to start out again on my own and not be beholden to other folks, no matter how well-meaning they may be."

"About a month ago, I rode through the Llano Estacado down into the Pecos River country and camped at a place called Live Oak Creek," Trent said. "To the east of there is some mighty fine grazing country that hasn't already been took."

"Are there Indians?" Trace asked.

"Plenty, young feller. Comanche mostly but some Apache."

He frowned. "Are they friendly?"

"Nope. They ain't the most amiable folks you'll ever meet. But it's good cow country."

"Thank you for your advice, Ranger Trent. I'll take it under consideration," Kate said.

"If I'm ever passing that way again, I'll look you up," Trent said.

"It's big country. I may be hard to find," Kate said.

"No ma'am, you won't be hard to find at all. All I'll have to say is, 'Where's Kate Kerrigan?' and a hundred male fingers will point in your direction."

CHAPTER SIX

Kate Kerrigan's direction was due west, but fate stepped in to do everything in its power to delay her journey.

After another week on the trail, the wagon's rear axle broke, and it took Moses and the boys three whole days to replace it. A day later, Kate drove into a mud hole and the wagon had to be dug out, a full day of backbreaking toil. A band of Lipan Apaches trailed the wagon for a while until Kate bought them off with coffee, sugar, and a slab of bacon.

But as they drew closer to the Pecos, the graze got better. It had been a dry year in those parts, but the springs held water and the cottonwoods seem to be prospering.

Kate took Shannon and Ivy by the hands and showed them the first wild longhorn cattle they'd seen, a couple mature bulls with horn spreads of six feet tip to tip and a much older bull that Kate later swore had horns eight feet wide. It was rough, broken country, and the long-horns were holed up in mesquite thickets mixed with dense growths of prickly pear, through which some of the old mossy horns moved with the grace and quiet of deer.

Trace and Quinn were mounted and wanted to go into the thickets after the cattle and see if they could roust out a steer, but Kate would not hear of it. "You need good cutting horses for that, not Thoroughbreds. I don't want to see a thousand-dollar stud gored chasing a steer he has no idea how to catch."

"What's a stud, Ma?" Shannon asked.

"A daddy horse," Kate answered. "And no more questions. We have to move on."

To Kate Kerrigan's untutored eye, the Texas Ranger had not steered them wrong. As far as the eye could see, the land to the east of the Pecos promised graze for hundreds, if not thousands, of cattle. Where the banks of Live Oak Creek narrowed was a spot about a hundred yards between bluffs. On the west bank stood a row of eight ancient cottonwoods, along with a few pecans and willows.

To her joy, the remains of a burned-out fieldstone cabin still stood in the center of a stand of wild oaks. Most of its timber roof was intact and the door, though hanging by one hinge, was of polished mahogany. It had a tarnished brass knocker, handle, and letterbox with the number twenty-seven still intact.

Though the land itself was breathtaking, the door was such a wonder that Kate, Moses, and the children gathered around it. Used to rough-sawn timber doors with rawhide hinges, they'd never seen such a beautiful thing.

Trace said, "How did it get here, Ma? In the middle of nowhere."

Kate looked at her son. "This is not the middle of nowhere, Trace. Not any longer. The land you're standing on is the Kerrigan Ranch and here it will prosper and grow. As to how the door got here, I have no idea."

"I've seen doors like that, me," Moses said. "Seen them in Louisiana when I was a boy. The big houses always had doors like that, all shiny brass an' the like. But that's not from a plantation house, no. It's from a street where rich white folks lived at Number twenty-seven."

"Then whoever built this cabin brought their front door with them," Kate said. "All the way from . . . well, wherever . . . to remind them of better times."

Moses looked around him at the ruined cabin. "Who done this, Miz Kate? Indians, probably so." His eyes grew to the size of silver dollars. "I t'ink their spirits is still around, watching us, Miz Kate. I sure feel dead eyes on me."

The girls huddled close to one another and little Shannon stuck her thumb into her mouth and shivered.

"Mose, don't talk that kind of nonsense in front of the children. The dead are dead and they don't come back." Kate smiled. "Well, except for the banshee, but she isn't really dead, is she?"

"What's a banshee, Ma?" Ivy asked.

"Nothing for you to worry about, child. The banshee stay in Ireland and don't travel. Mose, you and the boys hunt around and see if there's anything left that we can use. I'll take a look inside."

"May be snakes in there, Miz Kerrigan," Moses warned.

"Mose, I am not in the least afraid of snakes after St. Patrick chased them out of Ireland. But I'd better take my rifle just in case."

The cabin was empty but for the remains of a table and some chairs. The walls were scorched and blackened and smelled of smoke, an acrid odor that lingered long after the fire was out. Since there was nothing more to be seen, Kate stepped back outside.

"Miss Kate, you better come see this." Moses stood at the corner of the cabin. "Best Quinn keep the girls away."

Trace stood staring down at scattered bones in the grass. "Five skulls here, Ma. Looks like maybe two grown people and three children. It's hard to tell if there were more."

"Animals do that. Scatter unburied folks' bones around," Moses said knowingly.

Kate nodded in agreement. "Somebody took the time to lay out the bodies, but didn't have time to bury them. That's how it looks to me."

"Maybe there was another Indian attack and he had to run," Moses said.

"Well, we'll bury them now. I'm sure they were decent Christian folks and deserve to lie in the ground." She looked around the site.

Moses pointed. "Up on the bluff there, Miz Kate. It's a good place to bury folks. Peaceful up there among them trees."

"Yes, good. We'll start a cemetery up there where one day my bones . . . and yours, too, Mose . . . will rest."

"But not too soon, no," Mose argued. "First we got a ranch to build."

Kate smiled. "I know, and we already have the door for the house."

"Number twenty-seven, Pecos River Street," Trace said. They all laughed.

CHAPTER SEVEN

Cornelius Hagan had helped Kate Kerrigan and her family escape a life of poverty in Nashville and took them to Texas. He was a rich man, kinfolk and good-hearted, but Kate had had no wish to impose on his charity any longer than necessary. When she'd proposed moving west to settle her own land, he had resisted. But seeing how determined was her decision, he'd insisted on giving her a stake to get started.

Although proud as only the Irish can be, Kate was a practical woman. She knew she could not establish a ranch without funds. "It's a loan, Cornelius, only a loan," she'd said the day she left. "I'll pay you back with interest, I promise."

"Then pay me when you sell your first herd," Hagan had said.

More than anything else that was Kate's goal, but she was a long way from selling a herd. As she cleaned out the stone cabin and rehung the door, she didn't even have a herd.

But the cattle were there, out in the thicket country

where some of the mossy horns hadn't seen a human being in years. Brush popping was hard, dangerous work, and it required suitable horses and experience that Trace and Quinn lacked.

Kate needed grown men of courage. She found one such man in Steve Keller, a lean, mean, slow-talking man with sky blue eyes whose stare seemed to bore right into a person and come out the other side.

He explained. "Ma'am, the Texas brush popper is a feller who knows he'll never catch a cow by looking for a soft entrance into the brush, so he hits the thicket, hits it flat, hits it on the run and tears a hole in it. Like his rider, a good brush horse is game and tough as they come. Between rides, a man gets a chance to rest up and let the thorns work out and his wounds to heal. But no matter how stove up he becomes, he's ready to hit the brush thickets every chance he gets."

"Where can I find such horses and such men?" Kate asked.

"You can find them through me, ma'am. I can supply men for the gather, and they'll work for seventy-five cents a day. They're vaqueros, ma'am, Mexican riders. You got any objection to hiring Mexicans?"

"Not in the least if they do their work," Kate answered

"They'll work, ma'am. They're good hands, every last one of them." Keller's eyes moved beyond her to the cabin where Trace and Quinn worked on the roof. "Your boys are almost man-grown, ma'am. Do you want the vaqueros should teach them? Mind you, ma'am, they cuss and sin like any other men."

Kate ignored the question and asked, "Can you supply the horses?"

"I sure can, ma'am. Them big English studs of your'n ain't cut out for brush work."

At five dollars a day, Steve Keller didn't come cheap, but he was as good as his word. Eight vaqueros gathered fifty head the first day, mostly heifers and young stuff. The big bulls were wary as antelope, fought like tigers, and were hard to catch. Trace took to brush popping like he was born to it, but Quinn held back. He was not as good a rider as his brother and had no real understanding of cows and where they might brush up. On the fourth day, Keller pulled him out of the thickets and set him to riding herd on the increasing number of cattle that had been driven to graze east of the Pecos.

A week passed and then another. The days grew hotter and the big steers became fewer and harder to find in the thickets. One of the vaqueros holed up with a broken leg after a roped mossy horns rolled on him and another just quit, saying he was heading back home to his wife in Mexico.

Then came a day of trial and tribulation for Kate Kerrigan, a terrible event she was destined to remember for the rest of her long, eventful life.

CHAPTER EIGHT

A vaquero named Vasquez and another rider, Pablo Morales, were hunting the draws for strays, but without much success, when they stumbled onto a camp set among the mesquite. Two white men broiled meat over a fire and close by was the butchered carcass of a young heifer.

When the men saw the vaqueros ride in, the older of the two made a grab for his rifle. Vasquez was quick with the iron and a bullet just two inches in front of the man's reaching hand convinced him that he should leave the rifle alone."

They were ragged men, possibly father and son, dirty, slovenly and overgrown with hair. They wore old Confederate greatcoats and lace-up infantry boots and both looked tired, beaten, part of the tens of thousands aimless, wandering flotsam and jetsam washed up by the late war.

Morales swung out of the saddle and inspected the heifer. He straightened up and asked, "Which one of you shot this animal?"

The older man rose to his feet. "I did. We were hungry."

The pair still under his gun, Vasquez said, "This is the land of the Kerrigan Ranch. The cow was not yours to shoot."

"Like I said, we were hungry." The older man's pale blue eyes were defiant.

Vasquez left Morales to guard the rustlers and returned to give his report to Kate. "You must hang them, I think."

Kate disagreed. "I won't hang a hungry man for shooting a cow."

Steve Keller's face looked like it had been carved out of a granite block. "Then pack up your wagon and move out now, ma'am. When the word gets around that Kerrigan cattle can be shot or rustled with impunity, you soon won't have a ranch."

"But . . . but it wasn't even my cow," Kate said.

"It was on your land, was it not?" Keller said.

"Yes. I aim to claim the land as far as the thickets and even farther east."

"Then it was your cow," Keller said.

"Hang two men for stealing a cow?" Kate said. "That's . . . that's barbaric."

"This is a hard, unforgiving land, ma'am. We saddle our own broncs and fight our own battles. The strong survive in this country. The weak go to the wall and then they leave and nobody ever hears of them again. If you think that's barbaric, then don't stick around, ma'am. If you're not strong enough to fight for what's yours, even one cow, then this country doesn't need you. Texas doesn't need you." Keller touched his hat. "Ma'am." And then he walked away.

"Wait!" Kate said, her temper flaring. "I will fight for what's mine. I'll let no man take from me or my family."

"The cow was yours, ma'am," Keller said. "A man shot it and now two men are eating it. Let this go and they'll be back . . . and they'll bring others with them. A no-good, shiftless bunch too lazy to work, but who know how to steal. If they'd shot a hundred of your cows, would you ignore it?"

"You're talking nonsense, Mr. Keller," Kate said.

"No, ma'am. I'm talking numbers. How many cows can a man shoot on the Kerrigan ranch without consequences? A hundred? Five hundred? A thousand? In case you're stuck, ma'am, the answer is, not one. There is no law here. On Kerrigan range, *you* are the law. You are judge and jury. There is no one else."

Kate, despairing, turned to Moses Rice. "Moses, tell me. Must it be so?"

"I don't want to talk out of turn, Miz Kate, get above my station, no," Moses said.

"Tell me. I order you to tell me."

Moses bowed his head and talked to his feet. "My granddaddy tole me this one time. He said that in Africa where he came from a man's wealth is measured in cows. If you steal a man's cow you take mealy bread out of the mouths of his children. That is why, in Africa, when they catch a cow thief they kill him."

"Black man talks sense, ma'am," Keller said.

Since Trace and Quinn were out with the cattle, Kate said, "Mose, take care of the children." Her throat tight, she added, "I may be gone for quite some time."

CHAPTER NINE

The two rustlers were still under Pablo Morales's gun when Kate arrived at the scene of the cow killing. She dismounted and Steve Keller and Vasquez flanked her, their Colts drawn.

The day was hot, the air still. A tiny lizard did pushups on a rock and insects made their small sounds in the grass.

Keller, more used to the breed of men he faced, talked first. "This land belongs to the Kerrigan Ranch. And you're on it."

"We didn't know that," the older man said. "How could we know that? One wilderness looks much the same as any other."

"Well, you should have known. Who shot the cow?"

"I did. I was hungry."

"Plenty of folks around here willing to feed a hungry man," Keller said. "But you'd rather thieve than ask. Ain't that right?"

"The war made many a thief, mister, and Reconstruction made me a pauper. Before the war, I taught school."

The man smiled, revealing bad teeth. "It's kinda funny when you think about it."

"Nothing here is funny." Keller motioned to the younger man. "Is this your son?"

"Nope. We just met up on the trail. If you look in his shirt pocket, you'll find the medal he won at Kennesaw Mountain."

Keller nodded. "I'll do him honor by burying him in it. Now, if you got prayers to say do it now. Your time is short."

The older man was defiant, the younger frightened.

"What's your age, son?" Kate asked.

"I don't rightly know, ma'am, but the cavalry told me when I enlisted that judging by my teeth I was sixteen. "

"You're about a hundred and sixteen now, judging by what I can see. What's your name?"

"Toby Tyrell, ma'am."

"Then you bear the name of great Irish lords," Kate said. "That is to your credit."

Keller said, "Vasquez, Morales, throw loops over a bough of one of the wild oaks. Make sure it's strong enough to bear the weight of two skinny fellows. When you've done that, put them up on your horses."

"Sí, patrón." Vasquez's face was stiff, unreadable.

Kate knew that the older man's fate was sealed. There was no stepping away from it. Any sign of weakness in the wild country would be seized on and the result would be that she'd lose what she had and all she would ever have.

But she could save the boy.

"Just one loop," she said to Keller. "Let Toby Tyrell go free. I think he can make something of himself and I will help him."

That last was overheard by Pablo Morales, who stepped up to Kate and said, "I spoke with him while you were gone, señora. His real name is Max Harley. He has no medal in his pocket and he was not in a great battle. He said he was conscripted into the army but deserted three days later." The vaquero reached into his pocket and produced a pocketknife. "He said he killed a man for this up Fort Concho way. If you look at the handle—right there, señora—you see the initials L.S. They must be those of the murdered man."

Kate looked confused. "But he told me—"

"That he had an Irish name. That's because I told him an Irish lady owned the ranch. He's a murderer and liar who tried to get into your good graces, señora."

"Why didn't you tell me that earlier?" Kate said.

"Because if he was to be hanged anyway, there was no point in burdening you with his real story, señora."

"The damned greaser is lying," Max Harley yelled. "He knows I was just funnin' with him. Are you going to take his word over a white man's? Answer me, you gal!"

Keller grinned and said to Kate, "As the nice old ladies say at a hanging tea party, ma'am, one loop or two?"

Kate swallowed hard. "Hang them both. Then put a sign around their necks and make it say, 'I shot a Kerrigan cow.'"

* * *

For the next couple weeks, Kate was withdrawn and irritable. She had a fine singing voice and used it often, but it fell silent until Moses told her he missed the old Irish songs, and him a black man who'd never been in Ireland.

She began to sing again and by the end of the gather was almost back to her former self.

The cabin had been cleaned and made habitable. Moses used the carpenter trade he'd learned as a slave to build furniture and beds for Kate and the children. Trace and Quinn bedded down wherever they could but mostly spread their blankets outdoors near the cattle.

Nearly a thousand head grazed on Kerrigan land and one of the nearby ranchers, a man named Colonel Jason Hunt, stopped by with his segundo, a taciturn man named Kyle Wright, to offer Kate a proposition. "I'm pushing two thousand head north to Abilene on the Chisholm Trail, Mrs. Kerrigan. Mix your cows in with mine and I'll get the best price for them I can, I promise."

Every inch a former soldier and Southern gentleman, Hunt was forthright and courteous and nothing about him rang false. What you saw was what you got, a tall, raw-boned man in his mid-fifties with iron gray hair and blue eyes that had seen much. He'd been wounded at Chancellorsville and again at Spotsylvania. Just a twelve-month before, Comanches had put a strap iron arrowhead into his left thigh and he still walked with a pronounced limp.

"That is most kind of you," Kate said. She was serving tea outside the cabin under the shade of an oak and both men seemed to enjoy her sponge cake, a favorite of

Queen Vic, which was vanishing at a rapid rate. "Do I bring my herd to you, Colonel?"

"No ma'am. I know how shorthanded you are. My riders will pick up your herd on the way to the Chisholm."

"You are most gracious, sir."

"No trouble at all, Mrs. Kerrigan. If you feed us cake like this, I'll drive your herd with mine every time." Hunt looked at Wright. "Isn't that so, Kyle?"

Wright, his mouth full, could only nod.

"I would be honored, Colonel," Kate said, her eyelashes fluttering. "You may stop by for tea and cake anytime you wish. Ah, Mose, more tea for Colonel Hunt, please."

Moses poured the tea and when his eyes met Kate's he saw a twinkle. Kate Kerrigan could play a man like a fish and then land him on her side of the riverbank.

"A beautiful service, Mrs. Kerrigan," the colonel said, holding up his cup. It looked as fragile as eggshell in his big work-worn hand. "Is it Chinese?"

"It's English actually. Staffordshire I believe. A parting gift from a relative before we headed west."

Hunt gently laid his tiny cup in the equally tiny saucer. "I had an ulterior motive in coming to visit you today, Mrs. Kerrigan."

"Ah, that's very mysterious, Colonel." Kate's sun-dappled hair rippled to her bare shoulders and shone like burnished copper.

"Mrs. Kerrigan, I came to see the woman who hanged two men for shooting one of her cows. You're not what I expected."

Her eyes were very green. "And what did you expect, Colonel?"

Men who are not often around woman don't know when to tread lightly, and the colonel smiled and barged on. "Oh, I don't know. Mannish maybe, with cropped hair and a bigger mustache than mine."

"And you were disappointed, Colonel Hunt?" Kate said.

"Oh dear no, Mrs. Kerrigan. Just surprised. Why, you are a beautiful woman, and right now you look as though you're ready to attend a ball in Richmond. Hanging is work for mighty rough men."

Wright swallowed a drink of tea. "I heard tell those two died hard."

Kate nodded. "Yes they did. It took a long time."

"Well, they deserved it," Wright said. "I've got no time for rustlers and their ilk."

"I'll never hang a man again," Kate said.

"You're probably right about that, ma'am. Shooting is better, less messy."

Colonel Hunt said, "You have our complete admiration, Mrs. Kerrigan. You stood up to a testing time very well. Thugs, vagabonds, and no-accounts must be taught a lesson and in that you did not fail."

The colonel moved in his chair. "And now, dear lady, I must leave you. We will collect your herd in three days and hope that beef prices are better in Abilene than they were a few months ago." He bowed and kissed Kate's hand. "By all that's holy, ma'am, under all that gingham and lace you are a woman to be reckoned with. You will go far and cut a wide path or I've never seen a rancher before."

Wright rose. "Mrs. Kerrigan, don't you concern yourself none about them two you hung. They were men who needed killing, and that's the beginning and the end of it." He touched his hat. "Good day to you, ma'am."

Only when the two men had gone did Kate Kerrigan allow herself a tear.

CHAPTER TEN

"Let him go, Mrs. Kerrigan," Steve Keller said. "I guarantee Trace will leave a boy and come back a man."

"He's too young to go up the trail," Kate said. "He's only fifteen."

"Around these parts that's man-grown, ma'am." Keller turned to Trace. "Don't think that a thousand miles of Chisholm Trail is like a ride in the park. A cattle drive is hard work, making do and doing without, expecting the best and getting the worst. It's riding wet, riding hungry, riding hurt. It's laying your duds out over an anthill to get rid of the vermin and being told to do things that shouldn't be asked of any human being. And if you do what you're asked to do, you should have your head examined because you're crazy. A lot of men don't make it, some die, some turn back, but those who go all the way are forged in steel by the fires of hell itself and it shows in a man's bearing and how he thinks of himself and treats others. And now I've done enough talking to last me the rest of the year."

He pushed his plate away from him and got to his feet. "Thanks for the bacon and biscuits. The best breakfast I've had in a coon's age, ma'am. Now I got to be moving on."

"Where are you headed, Mr. Keller?" Kate asked.

"Fall's almost here and winter will come down right after it, so I figure I'll head for Old Mexico and see what's shaking the sagebrush. I never was a man for snow and brushing ice off my mustache."

"You are happy with what I paid you?"

"You kept up your end of the bargain, ma'am. I got no complaints."

Standing tall and lean in the small cabin, Keller gave Trace his hand. "Colonel Hunt is a fine man and he knows cattle. You'll learn a lot from him." And to Quinn, whose eyes glowed with hero worship, "You're a good rider, boy, one of the best I've ever known. Keep up with them studies of yours, but don't let books hurt your eyes." To the girls, "You're growing into right pretty young ladies. Mind your ma now." He shook hands with Moses. "Take care of them, all of them."

Then Steve Keller was gone. A man of the West, he was part of it and the West was part of him. One could not exist without the other.

"Ma, I want to join the drive," Trace said the next day. "I won't stay safe and home and see our cattle leave and no Kerrigan with them."

"Trace, you heard what Mr. Keller said. It's just too dangerous for a boy your age."

"Ma, you were younger than me when you lived in the Four Corners in New York. You told me once that every day was a struggle just to exist. It was that experience that helped you become the strong woman you are today. Ma, I no longer want to be referred to as a boy. I want to become a man. So, please don't coddle me."

Quinn grinned. "Let Trace go up the trail and you can coddle me, Ma. I don't mind."

Kate looked to Moses. "What do you think?" Kate said.

The old man smiled. "You asked me that because you've already made up your mind, Miz Kate. I say let Trace go with the cattle and that's just what you are thinking."

"It's three months to Abilene and back, Trace. I'll be worried out of my mind the whole time you're gone," Kate said.

Trace smiled. "Thanks, Ma. And don't worry. I've got a good rifle and a good horse and I can take care of myself."

It was with a heavy heart that Kate watched Trace ride away with the herd. She felt like a mother seeing her son go off to war, and indeed that's what it was. He would fight a war with cattle, a war with weather, a war with the dust, drought, fire, and flood . . . and above all a war with himself.

CHAPTER ELEVEN

Kate Kerrigan loved dappled places. A week after Trace left, she rode east into hill country and stopped at a favorite spot she'd discovered, a shallow bluff crested with wild oaks, its bountiful grass bright with yellow damianita and evening primrose. The day was hot, the sky blue except for a few white clouds that drifted like lilies on a pond, and a mild-mannered south wind stirred the tree branches.

She sat at the base of an oak and as was her habit in recent days took a rosary from her riding dress and prayed for her son, the pink beads clicking through her fingers.

Gunshots, very close, interrupted her devotions.

Her first thought was that Apaches had waylaid a poor traveler, but then she heard hoarse shouts, the yells and curses of white men.

She rose, put away the rosary, and slid her Henry out of the saddle boot. Moving slowly and carefully, she stepped to the edge of the bluff. Down below among the mesquite, a man lay behind his dead horse, a revolver in each hand. Less than a hundred yards away three mounted men sat their horses, presumably pondering their next move.

It came soon enough.

The three riders put spurs to their horses and charged, dust ribboning away from pounding hooves.

Kate wanted to cry out, end it. But the men below would not hear her and even if they did, they would not care. She levered her rifle and fired a shot into the air, but the charging horsemen did not slow their pace or even look in her direction. They were firing with Colts, their arms extended in the old guerrilla fighting style.

The man behind the dead horse stumbled to his feet. The entire left side of his gray shirt was scarlet with blood, but it looked like he was cut from the same cloth as Texas Ranger Luke Trent.

The wounded man worked his guns steadily and Kate saw a puff of dust rise from his pants as he took another hit. The range was finally close and he came into his element. Thumbing his Navy Colts with amazing rapidity, he emptied two saddles and then the horse of his remaining assailant stumbled and fell.

The horse went down hard, kicking up a tremendous cloud of dust. She watched its rider roll free until the man's back fetched up hard against a rock. She heard him yell in pain. Big, bearded, and determined, he scrambled quickly to his feet and fired the same time as the wounded man. The man in the gray shirt took another hit, but the big man dropped his gun and clapped both hands to his eyes. Even at a distance, Kate saw blood seep through his fingers and pour down the back of his hands in red rivulets.

The big man stood swaying for a few moments and then one of his scarlet hands left his eyes and he pointed at the man in the gray shirt. "That's fer Will!" he yelled before pitching forward on his face. He lay still, spread-eagled in the dust.

Kate watched the man in the gray shirt sway on his feet, trying to remain upright, but the effort proved too much for him. The Colts dropped from his hands and he fell on his back.

Gun smoke drifted among the mesquite and dust kicked up by the battle drifted in the breeze and began to settle. The two surviving horses, one with the saddle hanging under its belly, grazed without concern as though the violent deeds of men had nothing to do with them.

Kate mounted and took the gradual talus slope that led from the bluff to the flat. The sunny land was silent but scarred by the roar of guns. She rode with her rifle booted, considering that the dead posed no risk to her.

She dismounted and one by one checked the bodies. All three of the men who'd taken part in the charge, big, fine-looking fellows, were dead, but the man in the gray shirt still lived, though barely.

Kate found three bullet wounds. One was a grazing wound to the left side of his chest that for certain had broken some ribs. The man had taken another bullet in his thigh and a third, probably the last shot fired by the bearded man, had hit low on the right side of his waist about an inch above the gun belt. As gently as she could, Kate rolled the man onto his left side. The shot had passed through the man's waist and exited through the thick muscles of his lower back. The ball had traveled in a straight line and come out clean, but the exit wound was large, ragged, and bloody.

She nodded to herself. It was a death wound all right, unless this man had enough fortitude to bite back the pain and battle for his life. Few did.

The man's eyes flew open and she recoiled in shock.

"What are you doing to me, woman?" he whispered. "Go away and let me die in peace."

Once over her surprise, Kate was not intimidated. "I may do just that, mister, depending on how you answer my questions."

The man laughed and then winced as pain jolted through him. "I'm dying here, shot through and through, and she wants to ask me questions. Only a female would say that."

"Who are those men you killed?" She removed her shawl, folded it, and gently placed it under the man's head.

"I killed all three of them?"

"Yes, you did. Are you an outlaw? Wait there a minute." She stood.

"I'm not going anywhere, lady."

Kate brought the canteen from her saddle and held it to the wounded man's mouth. After he drank, then drank again, she said, "Who are those three men? I hope they're not policemen."

"Policemen? Lady, this isn't the big city."

"Who are they? Come now, answer me."

Blood stained the man's lips and his breathing was labored. "If I answer you will you leave me alone?"

She brushed a fly away from his face. "We'll see."

"Those three called themselves the White Oak gang.

There was four of them at one time, but I hung one of them. Will Stevens was his name. The two lying over there are Sid Collins and Danny Sadler. I'd say Danny was the worst of the bunch, made a hobby out of rape, if you'll forgive the word. The one that done for me in the end was Will's huggin' cousin, Joe McDermott. Joe was a bad one, but true blue in the way he stuck by his kinfolk.

"There, I've told you. Go away and let me make my peace with the Man Upstairs. Him and me haven't exactly been on speaking terms. And don't blubber. I can't abide blubbering women."

"You need have no fear of that . . . Mister?"

"My name's Frank Cobb." He saw the question in Kate's eyes and said, "Oh God, you ain't ever going away, are you?"

Kate made no answer.

He sighed. "Joe and them have been dogging my back trail for the past six weeks. I was sheriff of a small town on the Brazos by the name of Last Chance when I hung Will Stevens for murder and attempted bank robbery. Well, Joe made it known that the White Oak Gang was coming into town to kill me and then burn Last Chance to cinders. When the word got around, the nice townsfolk got together and run me out, said they didn't want to take a chance on Joe McDermott. Well, Joe caught up with me here and you know the rest. Now you're a right pretty lady, but leave me the hell alone."

"Think you can ride?"

"Lady, I'm all shot to pieces. Hell no, I can't ride. All I can do is die with as little fuss and bother to folks as possible." Cobb grimaced as another wave of pain hit him. "Hell, I'm surprised I ain't dead already. You've done near talked me to death."

Kate rose to her feet. "You lay still and drink plenty of water. I'll send my son and hired man with our wagon to pick you up. Later, they'll come back and bury your hurting dead."

"Good. I'll be dead as a doornail by the time they get here," Cobb said.

Determined, she looked squarely at him. "No, you won't die, Mr. Cobb. You won't die because I do not wish you to die. And when I don't wish a thing, it does not happen."

CHAPTER TWELVE

Kate Kerrigan removed the ball from Frank Cobb's thigh and patched up his other wounds as best she could. "Now it's in God's hands."

The three dead men were buried in the bluff above the cabin and the little cemetery grew. Moses made wooden crosses with their names on them and Kate said the words. The Kerrigan family allowed that outlaws though they were, the men were laid to rest in a decent Christian manner as befitted white men.

The cabin was small and cramped, but a bed was made up for Cobb in what Kate optimistically called the parlor, a space to the right of the door that was furnished with a chair, table, and usually a bunch of wildflowers in a canning jar vase.

To everyone's surprise, he was sitting up in bed after a week and could step outside for fresh air and sunlight after three.

Kate admired the man's grit and one morning as they sat outside she told him so. "You're a strong-willed man,

Mr. Cobb. And I'm gratified that my efforts on your behalf were not in vain."

"I'm beholden to you, ma'am. And I do not say that lightly." The sun had restored color to his face and Kate's cooking was adding weight to his lanky frame. "I owe you my life."

"First of all, you may call me Kate. And secondly, you owe me nothing. I would have done the same for any poor soul in distress."

"Will you call me Frank?"

"When I decide that you've earned that privilege, Mr. Cobb."

The man grinned and shook his head. "I've never met a woman like you . . . Kate."

"There are many like me. Unfortunately, they're all in Ireland. Do you wish to cultivate that scraggly beard, Mr. Cobb?"

"No, ma'am . . . Kate. But I'll keep the mustache. It's my only vanity."

"Then you may borrow my late husband's razor. And you will bathe in the creek with plenty of soap. And you will leave off your clothes so they can be washed. I will not have a scraggly bearded man who needs a bath and wears dirty clothes around the Kerrigan Ranch."

Another week went by and Frank Cobb's appearance passed Kate's critical eyes, but only after she personally trimmed his mustache, telling him that a cavalry mustache was one thing, but a dead rat hanging under his nose was quite another.

Although he still hadn't fully recovered, Cobb did

some chores around the cabin and helped Quinn and Moses with the horses. Despite his wounds, he moved easily, gracefully, with never a wasted movement. By nature, he was not a talking man, but when Kate or one of the others, including the girls, engaged him in conversation he gave them his full attention and looked straight into their eyes like a man should.

All in all, Kate was well pleased with Cobb, not as a potential lover, but as a steady, hardworking man on whom she could depend. He'd already revealed his skill with a gun and before the month was out he would demonstrate it again.

Hack Rivette was scum, an illiterate, brutish thug who had sunk to the bottom of the frontier pond and was happy to exist there amid the slime and filth. He made a living by theft, robbery, and murder and had a deep hatred for all humanity—man, woman or child. His only care was the fulfillment of his own twisted desires. Barely above an animal, he was vicious, deadly, and without pity.

That such a man would happen upon the Kerrigan cabin was unfortunate but not surprising. West Texas was a haven for the lawless element—outlaws of every stripe, gunmen, con men. Led by the carpetbaggers and Yankees on the make, they were happy to feast on the carcass of the South. Hack Rivette fit right in. He'd found his happy hunting ground.

He rode up to the cabin and sat his horse, looking the place over—fine horses in the corral, a milk cow and chickens in the yard, and a good wagon next to the house. Rivette smiled to himself. It seemed like a cozy berth to winter and with a bit of luck, he'd also find a woman there.

In greasy buckskins and a battered Union kepi, he yelled, "Hello the cabin!" He packed two Army Colts, and a Henry rifle was nestled under his right knee.

The door opened immediately and Kate stepped outside, a child clinging to her dress. Normally, she would have asked a traveler to light and set, but the look of the man gave her pause and she wished she hadn't left her rifle behind. "What can I do for you?"

The rider grinned.

Kate watched his eyes undress her.

"I'm a simple man, lady. Bacon and eggs is what I need. Just keep your brats away from me, especially when I'm drinking whiskey. Now come here and put my hoss in the corral, then me and you will get acquainted, like." Rivette swung out of the saddle, and then his voice suddenly turned harsh. "Do what I say, woman. Git over here and take care of my hoss. Throw that damned brat off your skirts before I do it."

Kate was suddenly frightened. Quinn and Moses were out hunting and Frank Cobb . . . well, she didn't know where he was. He often just wandered off to be by himself.

"Ma . . ." Shannon said.

Kate's fear turned to anger. "Get back on that horse, mister, and ride out of here. I have nothing for you."

"Sure, sure. I'll ride on come next spring and maybe I'll take you with me if you've been nice, and I mean real nice, to me." Rivette held out the reins. "Now take my hoss if you don't want to feel the back of my hand."

"The lady told you to move on, mister."

Frank Cobb's voice cracked like a whip in the silence of the afternoon. He stood at the corner of the cabin, his lean, ready frame and the guns on his hips telling the world that there stood *somebody*.

Rivette jutted his slab of a chin in Kate's direction. "Is that yours?"

"The lady's name is Mrs. Kate Kerrigan and she owns the ranch you're trespassing on. Now get back up in the saddle and ride on out."

"If that's yours, I want it," Rivette said to Cobb. "And everything that goes with it. Now you get the hell out of here and don't come back. I see your ugly face around here one more time I'll put a bullet in it."

Rivette had intimidated many weak and timid men and had killed a few of them, but he quickly realized that Frank Cobb didn't intimidate worth a damn. That meant a gunfight. The tall, lean man with the quiet eyes, steady hands, and twin Colts looked as though he'd been in shooting scrapes before.

"I won't tell you again, mister," Rivette said, but a coward and bully at heart, he knew he'd lost the gunfight without a shot being fired.

Cobb stepped away from the cabin, the ivory handles of his revolvers yellow as old bone. "You got a clear choice, mister. Pull those pistols or shuck the gun belt. But know that I'm not a patient man."

His heart thumping, Rivette considered his next move. Damn, he was in a bind. Draw fighter. The tall man was a draw fighter, had to be. He didn't want any truck with them Texas fast guns. He saw something that made him sick to his stomach.

Kate had stepped inside the door and come back with a Henry rifle. The child was no longer with her. She pointed the rifle at him. "Mister, if he doesn't shoot you, I will."

"I'll ride out and be damned to both of ye," Rivette said.

"Shuck the guns first," Cobb said. "I don't want a lowlife like you coming back here armed."

"Damn you!" Rivette squealed as a bullet from Kate's rifle clipped a neat half-moon out of the top of his left ear. He put his hand to his head and it came away bloody.

His reactions were remarkably swift and Kate decided later that he might have been sudden enough on the draw and shoot. But the man's hands didn't go for his guns. They went to the buckles of his gun belts and he dropped both of them as though they were poisonous snakes.

"Step away from the iron," Cobb said. "Yes, that's it. There's a good fellow." He stepped to the man's horse and slid the Henry out of the boot and tossed it onto the gun belts. "Now we're all perfect friends again."

"What's your name, mister?" Kate said. "Next time the Rangers pass this way, I'll be sure to let them know."

"Name's Hack Rivette."

"How very unfortunate for you."

"Mrs. Kerrigan, may we have coffee? I'm sure dear Mr. Rivette would like a cup."

"You go to hell," Rivette said.

"And bear sign would be nice if there's any left," Cobb said.

Kate was puzzled. She lowered her rifle and stared at him.

He winked. "It's good to be hospitable to folks." At gunpoint, he forced Rivette to sit under a cottonwood tree.

Kate brought out the coffee and doughnuts.

After Rivette had drunk coffee and eaten, Cobb thumbed back the hammer of his Colt and shoved it into the other man's belly. "Comfy?"

"Go to hell," Rivette said, seething with impotent rage.

"Now I'm going to tell you my life story, Hack," Cobb said. "If I find that you've dropped off, I'll take it as a personal affront and shoot you in the guts. Is that clear?"

"Go to hell," Rivette said.

"Good, then we understand each other. Right, here we go. My life began when I was very young . . ."

The long day shaded into night and the moon rose and silvered the sleeping land. The only sound was the steady drone of one man's voice and the whimper of another.

Kate looked out the window several times. Cobb and Rivette remained under the tree. She suggested to Moses that she go outside with supper, but the old man grinned and shook his gray head.

"Mr. Cobb, he's had plenty of rest this last month and feels like staying awake and talking. The other man though, he don't seem like he cares to listen. I stepped outside and heard Mr. Cobb talking and the other man was groaning something terrible."

"It's a terrible torture, Ma. Like something the Inquisition would dream up." Quinn shook his head. "I even feel sorry for the bad man out there."

At one in the morning before she went to bed, Kate opened the door and listened to what Frank Cobb was saying.

She heard him solemnly intone, ". . . but my ma was having none of that. She'd asked for calico cloth and by golly she would accept no substitute. Mr. Brown the storekeeper offered her gingham and he said he'd throw in a dozen sewing needles for her trouble. But my Aunt Agatha, remember she's the one who grew them giant plants on her porch, the ones with the caterpillars in 'em, well she said that the cloth was for a dress for her and she was too old and set in her ways for gingham. Well, sir, finally Ma decided that silk might work for a dress, but Mr. Brown had no silk cloth so Aunt Agatha said . . ."

Kate quietly closed the door. Like Quinn, she almost felt sorry for poor Rivette. Almost.

Dawn came and Cobb was still talking on and on. Hack Rivette still listened, his glazed eyes staring into space.

Kate came out of the cabin with coffee and heard Cobb say, ". . . but then I had a decision to make up there in El Paso. Should I order the beans and bacon or try the steak and eggs? Mind you, flapjacks sounded pretty good to me then and so did—"

Rivette had reached his breaking point. He jumped to his feet, spread his arms, and yelled, "Kill me! Get it over with! I can't take any more of your damned life story."

Cobb pretended hurt. "You don't like my story, Hack? But I'm only getting started. Wait until you hear about Aunt Agatha and the aspidistra and Ma and—"

"Frank, he's had enough," Kate said. "Let him go."

"You called me Frank," Cobb said.

"Yes, well, you earned it yesterday."

Cobb got to his feet. His joshing tone gone, he said to Rivette, "Ride on out. Next time I see you around here again, I'll kill you."

"My guns—"

"Stay where they are. I'm sure you'll steal others."

Rivette saddled his horse and mounted. "I won't forget this, Cobb."

"Nor will I." Kate watched the man ride away.

CHAPTER THIRTEEN

The badlands to the east of the Kerrigan Ranch had been pretty much picked clean of wild cattle, but over the next month Frank Cobb and Quinn managed to bring in another forty head of longhorns, most of them young stuff.

There was no news of Trace Kerrigan or the herd, but a passing drover said he'd not heard of bad weather on the Chisholm, though the Apaches were out and several small farms and ranches had been raided. "I ain't no hand to be causing you worry, ma'am," he said to Kate, but it ain't like the Apaches to be raiding this late in the fall."

"You think it's something to do with the cattle drives?" Kate asked, pouring the puncher more coffee.

"Might be, ma'am, but then Apaches are notional folks and it's mighty hard for a white man to take a stab at what they're thinking."

Cobb said, "Trace is riding with some good well-armed and mounted men, Kate. I reckon the Apaches will give them a wide berth. They're notional all right, but not stupid."

She set the coffeepot back on the stove. "I'll say a rosary for Trace tonight and ask the Virgin to keep him safe."

The puncher rose to his feet and touched his hat. "I got to be riding, ma'am. I reckon them prayers will get the job done."

Cobb was unshaved and dust lay thick on his range clothes. He touched the back of Kate's hand with the tips of his fingers. "He'll be all right, Kate. I know he will."

A week later, he was proved wrong.

Trace Kerrigan was brought home in the chuck wagon. His left leg was heavily bandaged and under his trail tan his face was ashen.

Kate had him carried into the cabin and laid on her own bed. "What happened? Was it Apaches?"

Grimacing from pain after a bumpy carry into the cabin, Trace didn't seem much inclined to answer, so the rancher Jason Hunt did it for him. "Not Apaches, ma'am. It was a white man."

"How did it happen?" Cobb asked.

Hunt looked uncomfortable and his words dried up.

His segundo Kyle Wright stepped into the silence. "It was over a woman, Mrs. Kerrigan."

Kate had been attending to her son and looked like she'd been slapped. "Trace . . . a woman . . . I don't understand."

Wright said, "Ma'am, she was a lady of ill-repute,

sometimes referred to as a fancy woman. I have no wish to offend, ma'am."

"Mr. Wright, I know what such a woman is," Kate said. "In my time, I've known many. How did it happen?"

"Well, ma'am, Trace had never . . . ah . . . been with a woman before and the boys thought it would be fun if they put money into the hat to buy him one."

"Fun? And was that also your idea of fun, Mr. Wright?" Her eyebrows met in a frown.

"No ma'am. I was not aware of such coarse behavior." Wright's eyes met Hunt's, and he quickly looked away.

From the bed, Trace said, "I was set up, Ma. I was sitting at a table with the girl when a man stepped over and said she was his wife. He demanded my money, horse, and rifle to satisfy his honor."

"Or what?" Cobb asked.

"Or he'd kill me," Trace said.

Wright said, "It's an old trick, ma'am. The crook and the woman work as a team and usually they pick on a married man. But there's a shortage of such men in Abilene."

Kate took Trace's hand. "What happened?"

Hunt cleared his throat. "I can tell you that, Mrs. Kerrigan. There was a shooting scrape. Trace refused to pay the man, his name was Curtis though some said it was Collins, and when words failed, the crook went for his hideout gun and put a ball into your son. Trace's rifle was on the table and he fought back. Ma'am, he worked that Henry so fast, he shot that feller all to pieces. It was a fair fight and all agreed that Curtis had drawn first."

"Trace stood his ground and let no man bully him, Mrs. Kerrigan," Wright said. "He didn't dodge the fight, and I reckon he proved himself a man."

"Where is the ball that hit my son? Is it still in there?"

"No, ma'am. It was removed by a mule doctor, and last I looked, it was healing well. No smell of the gas gangrene or anything like that."

"I'll be the judge of that," Kate said.

"Of course you will, ma'am," Wright said.

Shannon and Ivy had climbed onto the bed and were consoling their wounded hero with hugs. For his part, Trace looked as though all he wanted was sleep after his weeks of jolting misery in the back of the wagon.

"I know it's hardly the time to talk business, Mrs. Kerrigan, but it has to be done." The rancher looked thin and worn, but everyone who went up the trail and back bore the traces of their hardship. "The count in Abilene was nine hundred unbranded Kerrigan cows. Beef prices are still low, but after shipping costs and agent's fees, I managed thirty dollars a head. I knew you'd prefer cash to a bank draft so"—Hunt took a paper sack from his coat pocket—"this here is twenty-seven thousand dollars in Yankee greenbacks and gold coin."

Kate took the sack, her face thoughtful. "I've never had this much money before in my life."

"I'm sure you'll put it to good use, Mrs. Kerrigan. It's the last money you'll see until after the gather next spring." Hunt touched his hat brim. "I'll be going now, Mrs. Kerrigan." With a small smile, he added, "You can be proud of your son. He played the man's part on the drive and proved his worth in Abilene. Trace will make his mark one day."

CHAPTER FOURTEEN

September brought cooler temperatures and high winds. Trace healed with the season, but Kate saw a difference in him. He was quieter, more reserved, and less inclined to roughhouse with Quinn or play ring-around-the-rosy with the girls. He was still willing to do anything Kate or Cobb, recently made segundo of the Kerrigan Ranch, asked of him, but he kept to himself much of the time, his nose buried in a volume of the recently acquired *Complete Works of Charles Dickens* or Gibbon's *History of the Decline and Fall of the Roman Empire*.

One afternoon when a raging east wind rattled the new glass windows of the cabin and made the stove chimney gust smoke into the living area, Kate took Cobb aside and asked if he could explain her son's change in behavior.

Cobb smiled. "Kate, he's grown from a boy to a man, that's all. It's nothing to worry about."

"Is this how it was with you, Frank? Can you remember?"

"Sure I can remember. I was about Trace's age when I had my first woman and not much older when I killed my first man. Certain things happen in a boy's life that change him, mostly for the better, sometimes for the worse. Trace is one of the better ones, but he knows he still has to prove himself, prove that he's worthy of the manhood we've bestowed on him and he knows his greatest challenges are yet to come."

Kate frowned. "You mean making our ranch a success, building a Kerrigan dynasty that will last for a hundred years and maybe two?"

"That's part of it, Kate. I can't read Trace's mind, so I don't know what else he thinks. Maybe just being expected to live the rest of his life as a man and not a boy scares him. This is a hard land, Kate. It tests a man . . . and a woman . . . constantly and never lets up."

"What do I do to help him?"

"Nothing. Just let him be. Only Trace can work it out."

Trace caught a drift of wood smoke borne on the wind that stirred the grass on top of the ridge. In the lonely hill country it could be a puncher riding the grub line who'd decided to make camp early or it could be trouble.

It smelled like trouble.

Trace swung out of the saddle and, crouching as low as his still hurting leg would permit, he stepped carefully to the edge of the windswept rise and looked down on the vast sweep of the land below. It was rolling hill country thick with scattered mesquite, piñón, and a few red oak. Coming in hard off the Gulf of Mexico, the south wind was strong enough to lift veils of dust from the dry ground and toss the branches of the mesquite and piñón into a frenzied dance. The smoke was rising briefly from behind a hill where the red oak grew before it was shredded by the wind.

He remounted and searched for a way off the ridge but everywhere he looked the rock face toward the smoke was thirty feet straight down. He decided to go back the way he'd come and loop around the base of the rise, a twenty-minute detour in a wind that tore at him and his horse. The big Thoroughbred weathered the storm and once among the mesquite, Trace slid the Henry out from under his knee and rode toward the smoke.

Squatters were a possibility and outlaws were another. He discounted the possibility of Lipan Apaches. They were unlikely to have a fire that smoked so much it gave away their presence. Only white men did that.

A few yards of the hill, Trace swung out of the saddle and went forward on foot. Not Indians or white men. Blanket-wrapped Mexicans—a man, woman, and three children—huddled around a mesquite fire that smoked better than it burned.

"Howdy." Trace held his rifle across his thighs, a sight that made the woman afraid. "This is Kerrigan land."

In truth, Kate claimed any land she could ride a horse over.

Trace didn't move. "What are you doing here?"

The man rose to his feet. He wore the shapeless white cotton garb of a peasant and the wind tugged at the sombrero he pulled low down on his head. "We're not here to steal, señor." He spoke hesitant missionary-taught English. "We are lost. No food for the *niños* or ourselves."

"Where are you from?" Trace asked.

"Chihuahua, señor. But there is no work at home and my wife and I seek employment."

Trace shook his head. "It's a wonder you're alive to seek anything. The Apaches are out. Didn't you know that?"

The man shook his head. "No, señor. We did not know." One of the children started to cry, and he said, "She is hungry."

"Damn it. I took a ride for my health's sake, but I didn't count on meeting pilgrims."

"I am sorry, señor. We will move off your land."

"Wait. I have grub, probably enough for three hungry men." Trace backed away to his horse and untied the sack his mother had tied to the saddle. She would not let him leave the cabin without his lunch.

He returned to the Mexicans with the sack. "What did I tell you? Beef sandwiches and a piece of dried apple pie. Maybe dried apple pie doesn't sound good, but it is."

"To a hungry man, all food sounds good," the Mexican said.

Trace passed the sack to the man. "I guess there's enough to feed all of you."

"But you must eat, señor," the man said.

Although he was hungry, Trace saw a need greater than his own. "I'll get something later. I ate a big breakfast."

The adults fed the hungry children first—and this met with Trace's approval—before they shared what was left. The food seemed to help. The button-eyed children smiled shyly at Trace and their parents, though still thin and gaunt, were more animated.

"We will leave your land now, señor," the man said. "Thank you for what you have done for us."

"Where will you go?"

The man shrugged. "Wherever a good blacksmith is needed." He smiled. "And a Mexican woman who can cook."

"The fall is here. And next thing you know, winter will be cracking down hard. Your children could die in this country."

"They will most certainly die in my own country if I can't feed them," the man said.

"You better come with me," Trace said, making up his mind. The Kerrigan Ranch could use a blacksmith and a good cook. A thought struck him, and he stared into the Mexican's eyes. "Any man can call himself a blacksmith who is not."

"That is so, señor." The little man reached into the sack his wife had carried and produced a foot-long bowie knife. He passed it to Trace.

He examined the blade closely and tested the edge. "It's a beautiful knife. The best bowie I've ever seen."

The Mexican nodded. "Any man who can forge a steel blade from a piece of raw iron is a blacksmith. You may keep it, señor. It is my gift."

Trace shook his head. "It is a fine gift, but it's too much. Perhaps one day you can make me one just like it." He returned the knife. "Your wife and the little ones can ride my horse. The Kerrigan Ranch is not far."

"He's a blacksmith, Ma," Trace said. "Every ranch needs a good blacksmith."

Kate glanced out the cabin window. "He looks a bit tiny to be a blacksmith." She smiled. "'Under the spreading chestnut tree the village smithy stands; The smith, a mighty man is he with large and sinewy hands; And the muscles of his brawny arms are strong as iron bands.'" Kate turned and frowned at Trace. "Mr. Longfellow tells us how a real blacksmith should look."

She turned to the window again. "His wife is quite pretty. What can she do?"

Trace deadpanned, "She's a cook."

"A cook?" Suddenly, Kate was interested. She could bake a mean sponge cake, but that was about the limit of her culinary skills. It was not for nothing that she so often praised the Good Lord for creating bacon and beans. "Can she cook for white folks?"

"I'm sure she can. Why don't you ask her, Ma?"

"I will. What's her name?"

"I don't know."

Kate frowned. "You didn't ask?"

"No. It didn't seem important at the time."

"Well, if she can cook, it's important now, isn't it?"

The Mexican woman's name was Jazmin Salas and her husband's name was Marco. Yes, she could cook for white folks and any other color of folks, come to that, and yes, Marco was a fine blacksmith and very good with horses.

"Can you bake Queen Victoria's favorite sponge cake?" Kate asked.

Jazmin was hesitant, then she said, "I have never heard of it, señora."

Kate was pleased. "Good. Because that I will make myself."

Since there was no accommodation for Kate's extra staff, Marco Salas said they could sleep outside under the shelter of a tree or some such.

Kate wouldn't hear of it. "Until a suitable house for you and your family can be built, you must live in the cabin."

Trace pointed out that the cabin was already over-crowded.

Kate said, "Then we must make do, mustn't we?"

Trace wondered what Quinn and Frank would think of that, but they were out on the range . . . with troubles of their own.

CHAPTER FIFTEEN

After finding a half-devoured carcass of a yearling longhorn, Cobb and Quinn rode with rifles across their saddlebows and sat high in the saddle, their searching eyes constantly scanning the vast terrain around them.

In the worst of times, the terrain west of the Pecos was a wilderness of thorn, rock, and dust. But following the wet spring and summer, it was the best of times and the flats were grassy and covered with mesquite, acacia, and whitebrush. Small trees like walnut, oak, and Mexican ash were confined to the arroyos and creek terraces where a black bear with a taste for grass-fed beef would hole up to sleep off a meal.

"Tracks head south toward the canyon country," Cobb said. "Old Ephraim is no fool. But he'll be back, count on it."

"Judging by the tracks, he's a big bear," Quinn said.

Cobb nodded. "He's a big male all right, and he'll go six hundred pounds and more." His horse tossed its head and the bit jingled in the quiet. "A black bear ain't much inclined to attack humans, but if he does, watch out. A grizzly now, he may beat you up some and let you go, but not a black bear. He'll kill you every time."

Quinn smiled. "Nice feller, huh?"

Cobb shrugged. "It's just his way. As a rule, Ol' Ephraim minds his own business, but this one may be old and can't hunt his usual prey. He's decided Kerrigan yearlings are easy to kill and he'll come back every time he's hungry."

"So what do we do, Frank?" Quinn asked.

"The yearling's innards were still warm and the tracks are fresh, so he's still close. We find him and kill him and take his skin home to your ma." Cobb gave the boy a searching look. "You up for it?"

"I don't know. I've never chased a bear before."

Cobb smiled. "Well, that's honest. I reckon you'll do just fine."

The day was warm with no hint of the coming fall. A soft south wind walked across the long grass and bore the scent of late summer wildflowers. Of the bear there was no sign, only its tracks.

The rolling country was cut through by dry watercourses, and here and there grew patches of wild oak. A few cottonwoods stood by the streambeds and seemed to have prospered during the summer. A few fat cattle grazed, but they were a ways off the range Kate had claimed for herself and probably bore Colonel Jason Hunt's H bar H brand.

Quinn, with his sharp young eyes, saw the arroyo

first, its entrance almost hidden by mesquite. "There, Frank! Over there by the trees."

Cobb drew rein and studied the arroyo and its surrounding ridge. To the right of the entrance dropped a talus slope overgrown by bunch grass, and to the left was a sheer rock face about thirty feet high.

He swung out of the saddle and walked in the direction of the arroyo, casting around for tracks. After a while, he waved at Quinn to come on. The boy gathered up the reins of Cobb's horse and rode forward.

"He headed for the arroyo all right," Cobb said. "Mesquite usually means there's water close. Seems like he has himself all the comforts of home." He stepped into the saddle. "Let's roust him out. Ephraim, I reckon your cow-killing days are over."

Cobb and Quinn dismounted at the entrance to the arroyo, a narrow fissure in the rock face about fifteen feet wide. For long moments, Cobb listened into the afternoon. The only sounds were the small music of crickets in the grass and the rustle of the wind. His eyes lifted to the top of the ridge.

Quinn understood his thinking. "Can we get a shot from up there?"

After a moment, Cobb shook his head. "The arroyo narrows toward the crest and will limit our field of fire. The only way is to go in after him." His eyes met Quinn's. "I can't say I'm looking forward to it."

Quinn grinned. "Real glad to hear you say that, Frank, because neither am I." He bowed. "After you."

Cobb took a single step into the canyon . . . and was instantly hit by a runaway locomotive in the shape of three hundred pounds of snarling fury. The bear flattened him, slamming all the breath out of him. His rifle spun out of his hands and clattered against the wall of the arroyo. In a split second, the animal slashed its claws across Cobb's chest and then it was past him.

Startled, Quinn fired his Henry from the hip, missed, and fired again. He hit the bear just behind the left shoulder blade and scored a lung shot. Coughing up frothy blood, the bear staggered on for about fifty yards and collapsed.

Cobb was shooting!

Quinn ran to the entrance of the arroyo where the man was up on one knee, firing his revolver. Quinn stepped into the canyon, his rifle ready. About thirty yards away, almost lost in gloom, he caught a fleeting glimpse of a huge, black, shambling shape. Quinn tried a snap shot, but his bullet hit off a wall and chipped rock. S*paaang!*

From somewhere in the distance, the black bear roared its defiance.

A man doesn't track a game animal cross-country without learning something about him, and there was nothing about this bear Quinn liked. The roar had an unusual quality, as though the big boar had yelled, "Here I am. Come get me or I'll come get you."

He was a bear to be reckoned with.

Cobb got to his feet. The front of his faded blue shirt was ripped to shreds and scarlet with blood. He fed paper cartridges into his Colt, then looked at Quinn, no blame in his eyes. "You shot the wrong bear, kid. You killed Ephraim's mate."

"It's early fall and mating season is well over," Quinn pointed out. "They shouldn't have still been together."

"No, they shouldn't. This is a mighty unusual bear." Cobb holstered his revolver then picked up his rifle. "I think I got a bullet into him. Let's finish it."

The shadowed arroyo was dank. At the base of its walls olive green ferns grew, the like that Quinn had never seen before. Ahead of him the canyon narrowed and then stopped at a wall of rock before making a sharp turn to the right. Fed by an underground stream, a thin trickle of water ran down the rock face and splashed into a natural rock tank that was green with algae.

Feeling the effects of his mauling, Cobb slowed his step as he turned to his right and followed the course of the arroyo. Each breath he took was shallow—as though it pained him—and every now and then, he leaned a hand on the wall for support. Quinn grew anxious. He knew the segundo was almost out on his feet and needed medical help that he could not give.

Gradually the arroyo grew wider and then opened up into a circular area about half an acre in extent. A gnarled mesquite grew to the right of an undercut in the rock that was about eight feet high, the same wide and seemed to be several feet deep.

"Bones," Quinn said. "It looks like a graveyard."

Bones—some white, most yellowed—carpeted the area in front of the cut. A few still had streaks of red meat and shredded tendon clinging to them. Quinn identified deer, pronghorn antelope, jackrabbit, birds, cattle and . . . a human skull and partial rib cage.

Cobb took a knee next to the human remains. "A fairly recent kill, but some of the animal bones are years old. We're looking for a mighty elderly bear."

"Is that why he killed a human?" Quinn swallowed hard. "And ate him."

"Yeah. Seems like Ephraim is growing too old to hunt his regular prey. Young cows and humans are easy to kill." Cobb studied the skull. "It's a woman in this case. She was probably Mexican or Lipan."

Cobb slowly . . . very slowly . . . lifted his head . . . then his eyes . . . "Oh my God," he whispered.

Quinn followed the man's gaze to the top of the arroyo rim. The bear's head was in plain sight. Its emotionless black eyes stared hard at Quinn as though marking him, remembering every aspect of his features.

"Damn you!" Cobb yelled. He dropped his rifle, drew, and hammered five shots at the rim. But the bear was already gone.

All Cobb managed to do was shoot holes in the wind.

Quinn quickly made his way to the entrance of the arroyo and ran outside, his Henry at the ready. His eyes searched the top of the ridge, but he saw nothing except a broad swath of blue sky. The ancient talus slope was close and he tried to climb it, but the incline was too steep and he managed to only scrabble a few feet before sliding back to the flat, shingle showering around him.

"He's gone," Cobb yelled, making his way out of the arroyo. "We'll find him another day."

It was only then that Quinn saw how ashen was the man's face and the pain in his eyes. The front of Cobb's shirt was a bloody mess.

"I'd better get you home, You look all used up."

"An angry bear can do that to a man." Cobb collapsed and Quinn had to help him into the saddle.

CHAPTER SIXTEEN

For a week, Frank Cobb hovered between life and death, Kate at his side constantly. Jazmin Salas, whose father had been a respected village healer, prepared various potions and salves from herbs, trees, and cactus that seemed to help Cobb's pain.

On the eighth day after the bear attack, his fever broke and that night Kate was able to feed him a little beef broth.

As Quinn's worry about Frank faded, he and Trace had other concerns. They had discovered bear tracks and scat their side of the Brazos—once not a hundred yards from the cabin—and an abandoned bed in a clump of wild oak that the bear had made comfortable with a mattress of leaves and tree bark. They found no sign that the animal had eaten recently, even ignoring some rotten tree trunks it would normally have torn apart to feast on carpenter ants.

"Chances are that it's not the same bear," Trace said.

"It's the same bear," Quinn said. "He's got Frank's bullet in him and he followed us here."

Trace looked into his brother's eyes and saw a glint of fear that couldn't be explained away as just the teenager's vivid imagination.

"All right. We hunt him," Trace said. "If he's been shot already, he'll want to hole up and he's got a comfortable bed right here."

"Don't tell Ma, Trace," Quinn said. "She's already worried enough about Frank."

Trace nodded. "We won't tell her until we kill your bear."

"Frank calls him Ephraim."

"That was the name the old mountain men gave to a big male grizzly."

Quinn pulled a face. "This bear is a lot more dangerous than any grizzly."

Because of the overcrowding in the cabin, Trace and Quinn spread their blankets outside. The nights were not yet too cold and made for comfortable sleeping weather.

An hour before dawn, Trace shook Quinn awake and held a forefinger to his lips.

Quinn rolled out of his blankets and grabbed his rifle. When they were out of earshot of the house, he said, "If he's in bed, we can shoot him while he's asleep."

Trace smiled and his teeth gleamed white in the waning moonlight. "Not very sporting, is it?"

"This isn't sport," Quinn said. "This is kill or be killed."

"This bear really has you spooked, young brother," Trace said, still smiling.

"You'll see, Trace. You'll see."

* * *

The bed was empty, but the feral, musky smell of the bear hung in the air. Trace kneeled and placed his hand on the leafy mattress. "It's still warm. Damn bruin heard us coming and lit a shuck."

Quinn's hands were white knuckled on his Henry. "He's close. I can sense him."

"Look." Trace held out his hand palm up, showing a smear of blood from the base of his thumb to his middle finger. "Frank shot him all right. He's still bleeding."

From somewhere among the shadowed trees, came a growl, low, menacing . . . and close.

Trace lifted his rifle into a firing position. "Where the hell is he?"

"I don't know. His growl is coming from everywhere," Quinn said.

The two young men stood together, their rifles at the ready. A thin dawn light filtered through the trees, but shadows still lay like inkblots on the land—dark, mysterious, and hinting of unseen dangers.

"Back out of here, Quinn," Trace said. "Slowly . . . and I'll cover you."

"No, I'm staying right here with you, Trace."

The bear's growl prowled through the morning quiet and reached out for the Kerrigan brothers like a grasping hand. Trace looked wildly around him. Where was the damned animal? "Quinn!" he yelled. "It's you he wants. Back away like I told you."

The roar of Quinn's rifle was an emphatic *no!*

"Where is he?" Trace yelled. "Did you get him?"

"Up there, beside the fallen tree!"

"I don't see him!"

Quinn fired again. "I saw him! I saw him!" he yelled. "Look! He's there by the tree, standing on his hind legs!"

Trace looked and saw nothing but shadow. He stepped to his brother, grabbed him by the arm, and yelled, "We're getting out of here!"

"Did I hit him? Did you see him?"

"No. You were shooting at a shadow." Trace pulled Quinn by the arm. "Let's go."

The bear seemed to come out of nowhere.

Trace turned at the last second and took the full brunt of the animal's charge. The bear slammed into him with the force of a runaway brewery horse and Trace fell on his back, all the wind knocked out of him. Turning on a dime, the bear changed direction and went for Quinn, its slavering, fanged mouth wide open.

Boom!

The sound of a large-caliber weapon hammered across the aborning day. Startled, but not hit, the bear broke off the attack and vanished into the trees.

Moses Rice, his smoking dragoon in his hand, raised the big revolver for another shot, but lowered it again. "That bear is in the next county by now." His ebony face concerned, he looked at each boy carefully. "Either of you boys hurt?"

"Only our pride, Mose," Trace said, picking himself up off the ground.

Quinn's face was ashen, his Henry clutched tightly in his hands. "For a minute there, I thought I was dead."

"Don't play around with bears, no," Moses said.

"Look what happened to Mr. Cobb, lying all tore up an' hurtin' in Miz Kerrigan's best bed."

"Mose, it was the same bear," Quinn said. "He followed us home."

"Lot of black bears in West Texas," Moses said.

Quinn shook his head. "Not like this one."

"Did you tell your Ma?" Moses asked.

"No. I didn't want to worry her," Quinn said.

"Don't worry Miz Kerrigan, no," Moses said. "She's got enough worries right now. You boys wait here."

Moses followed the path the bear had taken and was soon lost among the trees. He was gone for thirty minutes and when he returned his face was solemn. "We leave the bear alone."

Trace agreed. "Hell, that's fine by me."

"No," Quinn said. "He took us by surprise this time, but we'll kill him next time."

"Let the bear be!"

It was the first time Trace and Quinn had ever heard Moses raise his voice.

The Kerrigan boys walked back the cabin in silence, but Moses's lips moved as though in prayer. When Trace listened closely, he realized the old black man was speaking in a tongue he did not understand. His was a prayer in the old language, a slave benediction that had its beginning hundreds of years before in the darkest reaches of Africa.

CHAPTER SEVENTEEN

September came and went, and the bear sign became less evident. Trace and Quinn figured the animal had given up and was probably holed up in a hollow log somewhere to sleep away the winter.

Frank Cobb, as tough a man as the West had ever produced, was up and about and showed little lasting effects from his close brush with death. Moses was strangely withdrawn, and took to walking the surrounding hills and forests with his Colt's Dragoon stuck in his waistband. If he saw anything on his rambles, he never mentioned it.

One Indian summer day in early October, following two weeks of cold, Kate decided it was high time to leave the cabin and check on her cattle and the state of the range. Her sons had already done it many times, but she insisted she wanted to see for herself. "I need to get out for a while. The cabin walls are closing in on me." She stepped outside.

The boys followed her.

"Ma, we didn't want to tell you this, but we've seen bear tracks out there," Trace finally told her. "We think it's the same one that tore up Frank."

"And I've never seen a bear before?"

"This one is dangerous," Quinn said. "Maybe it's stalking us."

"When did you last see its tracks?" she asked.

Quinn shrugged. "A month ago, I guess."

Kate sighed. "Then it's long gone. I'll take along the Henry and my derringer. I assure you I'll be quite safe."

"I'll ride along with you, Ma," Trace offered. "Just to be safe."

"No, I want to be alone for a little while. I need to get some fresh air and clear my head."

Trace protested. "Ma—"

"Don't you boys have chores to do? Frank and Mose need help with the addition to the cabin they're building." She stepped into the sidesaddle and arranged her dress over her legs. She was about to leave when Frank Cobb put a halting hand on the bridle.

"The boys are right, Kate. You should stay close to home for a while."

"Frank, I'm a grown woman and I can take care of myself. Now give me the road."

"Then take Trace with you," Frank said.

As always when Kate Kerrigan got mad, her Irish accent grew stronger. "Let go of my horse this minute, Frank Cobb, or do I have to take my riding crop to you?"

"You're a strong-willed woman, Kate Kerrigan," Cobb said, shaking his head.

"And you don't know the half of it. Will you give me the road?"

Frank smiled, stepped back, and bowed as he swept off his hat. "By all means, dear lady."

After Kate rode away Trace said, "We should have stopped her."

Frank said, "You can't stop a force of nature, and that's what Kate Kerrigan is . . . a beautiful force of nature."

Trace smiled. "You love my Ma, don't you Frank?"

"Madly. And she's a woman, so she's well aware of that."

"Then ask her to marry you," Quinn said.

"And grab a handful of stars while I'm at it," Cobb said. "One is quite as impossible as the other. Kate has a much more desirable suitor . . . it's the fair land we're standing on and her plans for its future."

Ah, but it was wonderful to be young and strong and feel the power of the fine horse under her and the wind tangled in her hair. Kate galloped for a couple miles, then held her horse to a canter and finally a trot.

It was good cow country with plenty of grass and water and it was hers. In her mind, that added greatly to its value. The cattle she saw still held their summer fat and looked healthy and content and she anticipated that come spring there would be plenty of calves on the ground.

She drew rein and watched a big grulla steer that must have gone almost two thousand pounds come up out of a draw followed by several lanky youngsters. The grulla was agitated and he tossed his head and snorted, the great sweep of his horns catching the morning sunlight. He stopped, turned, and looked back at the draw, then swung his massive head in Kate's direction, glaring red-eyed and mean at her. The points of his horns were needle-sharp and as dangerous as cavalry lances and he didn't seem to be in the mood to be sociable.

If the huge steer charged, she knew she'd be in a world of trouble, but to her relief, after a couple of feints in her direction, the longhorn thought better of it and trotted away. The others followed.

Kate swallowed hard. That had been close, and to her surprise her hands on the reins trembled. Something or someone in the draw had spooked the steer—an animal that feared nothing on earth, animal or human—and it had to be investigated. She slid the Henry from the boot, heeled her horse into a walk, and headed toward the draw, the sun warm on her shoulders. Kate told herself that she was being foolish going it alone and that she should turn around and go for help. But whatever hidden danger lay in the draw would probably be gone by the time she got back.

She sensed a threat to the Kerrigan Ranch and she could not let it go.

She eased into the draw, the Henry across her thighs, and wound her way around a few trees, her pert nose high, testing the breeze. She smelled only cattle and sun-warmed grass. For a few moments, she sat her horse, studying the way ahead. She thought she saw a tawny patch of color in the brush, readied the Henry, and moved slowly toward it. She suspected a cougar, and that would explain the odd behavior of the grulla steer. Whatever it was, her horse wanted no part of it. He acted up, reared, and tried to turn, alarm showing white in his eyes. Kate fought her mount for a few moments then let him swing around and trot out of the draw.

A scared, restless horse did not make for a steady rifle platform.

Kate stepped out of the saddle and the horse trotted away. After about fifty yards, he figured he'd put enough distance between him and the draw and lowered his head to graze.

By nature, Kate was not a profane woman, but she had a few choice words to say about the equine species as she walked back toward the draw. Once among the trees, she readied her rifle and stepped warily toward the brush where she'd seen the patch of color.

A moment later, her instinct for danger clamored and she stopped. Slowly, a little at a time, she turned her head to the left. The big grulla steer stood glaring at her, his head lowered, his glossy hide the color of a gun barrel. Tension between the animal and the woman stretched taut as a fiddle string. Finally, Kate managed a tight smile and said, "I've got no quarrel with you."

The steer jerked up his head in surprise as sunlight rippled on his horns, scaring her out of her wits.

Nonetheless, Kate straightened her back and walked on. If she had to, she'd use the rifle, but she knew that was a losing proposition. Even with a bullet in him, the longhorn would keep on coming and he wouldn't stop until he killed her. Half expecting the pound of hooves behind her, she shortened her step, her head slightly tilted toward the danger.

But the grulla steer stayed where he was.

One danger down, another to go . . . Kate Kerrigan still had a cougar to contend with.

But there was no cougar in the brush . . . just a dead old range cow.

The cow's neck had been broken by what looked like a powerful blow and her belly had been ripped open by sharp claws. Her intestines spilled over the ground, and it looked to Kate that the liver and heart had been eaten. It was not the work of a cougar or even a mountain lion. A bigger, stronger predator had done it.

Kate swallowed hard. The black bear Trace and Quinn had warned her about had not left the Kerrigan range. . . .

It was in the draw and it was close.

CHAPTER EIGHTEEN

Gradually, Kate became aware of two sounds. One was a distant thunder coming up from the Gulf, the other a different kind of thunder and much closer . . . the spine-chilling growl of a bear from hell.

She backed away from the carcass of the cow, her rifle swinging this way and that as she frantically tried to cover all the points of the compass. She needn't have bothered. The bear's roaring frontal attack came right for her.

Time and space shattered into fragments just split seconds long.

She fired once. Almost on top of her, she saw the bear's open, fanged mouth, smelled the rotten meat stench of its breath. Hit by a clawed paw, the Henry spun out of her hand, then razor-sharp claws the size of sickles slashed at her head. The bear roared.

Kate Kerrigan's life was saved by cow dung.

The heel of her riding boot came down on a ball of dung that had hardened in the sun into the consistency of knotted oak. The ball rolled under her foot, and she lost her balance and stumbled awkwardly to her left. She was spared the full savage power of the bear's slashing claws that would have killed her, but they raked across the top of her right breast, ripping apart the fabric of her dress and slashing open the skin underneath.

In pain, Kate tumbled onto her back. Her hand dropped to the pocket of her riding dress and fumbled for the derringer she kept there. It was gone, lost in her fall. The furious bear loomed over her, poised for the kill. Saliva from its open mouth dripped onto her bare right shoulder and mingled with her blood.

"Dear God, forgive my sins . . ." she whispered.

The bear roared, ready to attack, and then came the sound of another thunder.

Moving at the speed of a galloping racehorse, the grulla longhorn's lowered head, driven by a ton of bone and muscle, slammed into the bear's exposed side. Its ribs caved in and the bear was thrown to the ground. The steer was relentless. Its huge anvil-shaped head swung back and forth, plunging his horns deep into the bear's body.

The bear rose unsteadily and stood tall. It snarled and raised its paws, shuffling forward to mount an attack. But weakened by the pounding it had taken from the steer's head and horns, the bear was vulnerable. The big steer lowered its head again for another charge and crashed into the bear's belly, its horns doing terrible damage. Done, the bear fell on his back and the steer went in for the kill. Its horns plunged again and again into the bear's body, tearing apart flesh, spilling ropes of entrails into the dust. The grulla steer kept up the attack long after the bear was dead and it did not quit until only a tangled mass of blood, hair, and shattered bone lay on the ground.

Finally satisfied, the longhorn trotted backward a few feet, then swung around to face Kate. The longhorn's steaming head was covered in gore, and its horns dripped blood.

To her, the animal was an apparition from the lowest mazes of hell.

She looked around and saw with a sinking heart that the Henry was out of reach. Of her derringer there was no sign. She lifted her eyes to the raging steer and knew she must soon face the same fate as the bear.

But to her relief, the steer tossed its head in a defiant, triumphal gesture and turned and trotted away. Its fight had been with the bear, not the frail human.

Kate rose slowly to her feet. She didn't even glance at the mangled body of the black bear. That danger was over. She retrieved her Henry and then looked around for the derringer. Suddenly, to her surprise, she found herself on her knees. The front of her dress was scarlet with blood and her head felt strangely light. . . .

The ground came rushing up to meet her and Kate knew no more.

CHAPTER NINETEEN

Kate Kerrigan woke to candlelight. She tried to rise, but a strong, female hand pushed her back.

"You must rest and gather your strength," the woman said.

Kate took stock of her surroundings. The single candle did little to banish the smoky gloom that surrounded her and she smelled an odd odor, something like the incense that burned in churches. "Where am I?"

The woman drew closer. "You are safe here. Close to the Brazos and far from harm."

Kate saw her features for the first time and realized that the woman was stunningly beautiful. The luxuriant hair that cascaded over her shoulders was raven black, but her eyes, even in darkness, were a startling blue, and her full mouth was wide and expressive. She wore a buckskin dress, elaborately beaded, and a narrow headband with the same blue and white pattern.

"There was a bear," Kate said. "It attacked me."

The woman nodded. "I have treated your wounds, but

you will always remember the bear. Even when you are an old woman, you will still have the scars."

"You brought me here?" Kate asked.

"Yes. And your horse and Henry rifle."

"My name is Kate Kerrigan. I have a ranch hereabouts."

"I know. It is said you are a fine woman and a brave one."

Kate smiled. "Who told you that?"

"Jason Hunt the rancher and others." The woman laid her hand on Kate's forehead. "There is no fever. That is good." Her smile was slight, almost sad. "My name is Mary Fullerton. I'm a doctor."

"A real doctor?" Kate said, surprised.

"A real one. According to the Women's Medical College of Pennsylvania I can put MD after my name."

"Then why are you all the way out here in cow country?"

"Because like you, people find it hard to believe that a woman can be a real doctor. Back east, I hung out my shingle in several cities, but no patients came. I headed west and hung the same shingle with similar results, so five years ago, I came here to practice medicine among the Indians. At first, the Comanche were suspicious and only allowed me to treat their women and children, but after I patched up a few wounded warriors, they slowly came to accept me." The woman shrugged. "The Comanche are gone now, but occasionally Apaches come by."

Kate was apologetic and a little embarrassed. "I didn't mean—"

"There's no harm done," Mary said.

"Yes, there is. I said a very foolish thing and I whole-heartedly take it back . . . Doctor."

Mary smiled. "Practicing medicine among the Indians has its own rewards. A Comanche woman made this dress and the Apache built this hogan for me, though it's twice the size of their own."

Kate's eyes had become accustomed to the gloom and smoke and she could make out a single room with animal skins on the walls, the floor covered in cushions of various kinds and blankets. A fire burned in the middle of the floor. "It's very . . . cozy."

"The Apache build male and female hogans. The male is round, the female has six sides like this one." Mary rose, a tall, elegant woman who moved easily, and stepped to the fire. She ladled steaming broth into a bowl and brought it to Kate. "Now you must eat. I lack silverware so a horn spoon will have to do."

Kate pushed herself to a sitting position. "When did you bring me here?"

"Yesterday, after dark."

"I must get home. My family will be worried."

"It's night," Mary said. "Rest until first light and then leave. You lost a lot of blood and you'll feel weak for a while. Now open your mouth. Eat this beef broth while it's hot."

"I want to thank you for bringing me here," Kate said.

"That's what doctors are for."

* * *

In the dead of night, Dr. Mary Fullerton's voice woke Kate. "The only thing of value I have inside is a sick patient. Now be off with you before you wake her."

Kate was wide awake and listening.

"You got a five-hunnerd-dollar hoss there, lady," a man said. "What else do you have inside that hovel?"

"Nothing that would interest you," Mary answered.

"You interest me. That might be enough."

Kate sat up, waited until her head stopped swimming, then got unsteadily to her feet. The poultice Mary had put on her chest dropped off, and Kate saw parallel red slashes across the top of her breasts. She had no time to grieve about that. The man, whoever he might be, was speaking again.

"I'm a plain-speaking man, blunt you might say, so I'll keep this simple. I want you and I want your hoss. Do we do this sociable, like, or do I get rough? Of course, you might want me rough, huh?"

The door to an Apache dwelling always faces east. Kate stepped outside into moonlight, the Henry ready in her hands, knowing Mary and the unknown man were on the opposite side of the hogan.

As she rounded the structure, she heard the doctor say, "Mister, touch me and I'll kill you."

Kate stepped forward. "Let me say that a different way. Touch her and I'll kill you."

The man was big, bearded, and dressed in bits and pieces of an army uniform. Kate pegged him as a deserter and a murderer, rapist, and robber. If she had to, she'd shoot him.

It looked like that would be the case.

"So what's this? A little sick lady with a big rifle. You ain't gonna pull the trigger on that there Henry, now are you?" He had mean little eyes, but they were crafty and showed neither fear nor apprehension, only what could have been lust and the certainty of getting his own way by force.

"See, I need a hoss and a woman, and now I've got one of the first an' two of t'other. My name is Bill Hobson, by the way. So now we're acquainted, ain't you gonna invite me inside for tea and cake?"

The man who called himself Hobson wore a Colt butt forward in a flapped holster for a cavalry draw. He would be slow, and both he and Kate knew it.

"You back away and go elsewhere." Kate pulled her tattered dress together. "You're not welcome here." She swayed a little as a wave of weakness washed over her. "Go . . . go away." The rifle muzzle dropped, the Henry suddenly too heavy for her.

A born predator, Hobson saw vulnerability and took command.

Three fast steps brought him to Kate, and he wrenched the rifle from her grasp, tossed it aside, and followed up with a backhanded slap. The blow had little behind it, but it was enough to drop Kate to her knees.

Hobson grabbed her by the upper arm, pulled her roughly to her feet, and pushed her toward the hogan. "Get inside and wait for me there."

He turned his attention to Mary Fullerton just as a cloud scudded across the face of the moon. In the momentary gloom, he saw the flare of the derringer even as the .41 bullet thudded into his chest. That stopped him in his tracks, but the second shot Mary fired from Kate's gun missed and the big man moved toward her again, his right hand fumbling with the flap of his holster.

Despite her weakness, Kate saw the man's killing intent and dived for the Henry, landing on her right side. Pain jolted through her body, but she had the rifle. She fired, shoving the rifle out in front of her like a pistol. It was a shot she had to make. She knew she'd have no time to rack the lever for a second.

Her bullet hit Hobson between the top of his ear and the rim of his kepi. The man didn't cry out. He hit the ground in a heap like a puppet that just had its strings cut. The rifle's roar echoed through the moonlit darkness and flocks of alarmed birds exploded out of the oaks and mesquite.

Mary kneeled beside Hobson and after a few moments, she said, "He's dead."

"He doesn't need a woman now, does he?" Kate smirked.

"You handled yourself well, Kate."

"And so did you."

"I'd never shot a gun before."

"In this country, there's a first time for everything." After a few moments, Kate said, "Mary, I won't be handled and I won't be abused."

The doctor rose to her feet. "I think you made that perfectly clear. Now let me get you inside before you get really sick on me."

"Come morning, I'll loop a rope on my horse and drag this sorry piece of trash into the trees."

"You're not a forgiving woman, are you, Kate?"

"There are some things I can forgive readily. There are others I can't."

"You're a strong woman, Kate. If Texas is ever to prosper again, it needs women like you."

Kate smiled. "And like you, Mary Fullerton MD. That's why you're going to stop playing Indian and come with me to the Kerrigan Ranch. Hang out your shingle and I'll guarantee the patients."

CHAPTER TWENTY

Kate Kerrigan slept fitfully, her sleep haunted by dreams of dying men, but come morning she felt stronger and the scars of the bear claws across her chest looked less angry and were not as painful. When she rose from her blankets, coffee simmered on the fire, but there was no sign of Mary Fullerton.

Kate stepped outside and heard a man's voice. Her heart sank. Surely it was not another rootless, violent renegade seeking to steal what he was unable to buy. She was about to go back into the hogan for her rifle, but then she heard Mary's laugh and decided that all was well. A woman does not laugh so lightly if she is frightened.

The man talking with Mary was a peddler of some kind. He stood in front of a small, crammed wagon drawn by a fierce-looking mule. When he saw Kate, he swept off his hat and made a low bow. Straightening, he said, "My name is Count Ivan Boleslav Andropov, late financial adviser to His Imperial Majesty Alexander the Second, Czar of all the Russias." He bowed again. "At your service, dear lady."

"How do you do. My name is Kate Kerrigan."

"Ah yes, Karina in my native tongue," the count said. "In Russian or English, it is still a pretty name."

Andropov was a small, potbellied man with dark hair and intense brown eyes. He wore a black frock coat, striped pants, and a colorful waistcoat of Chinese silk adorned with a massive watch and chain. "I am sorry we meet at such a sad time," he said, nodding in the direction of the dead man. "Alas, death comes like a thief in the night."

"He was the thief who came in the night," Kate said dryly. "That's why I shot him."

Count Andropov seemed at a loss for words, but Mary filled in the silence when she said, "Did you bring the medicines I ordered, Count?"

"Indeed I did, Doctor," the little man said, relieved to change the subject. "Including the laudanum. It's becoming hard to come by since so many wounded soldiers returned from the war."

Mary nodded in understanding. "So many amputees in pain."

Andropov agreed. "War is a terrible thing. Now I'll get the medicines and the precious book." He glanced at the dead man. "On second thought, perhaps we should do something with the deceased first, even though my most singular illnesses are of the greatest moment."

"I'll put a rope on him and drag him away from the hogan," Kate said. "My sons may soon be here searching for me and we can bury him then."

It seemed that Count Andropov was a great one for bowing. After bending low again, he said, "I'll do it, dear lady. As one who suffers from constant ill health, I readily recognize miseries in others. You are very pale and your fair bosom is quite bloodstained."

Deciding to have a little fun with the Russian, who could be quite pompous, Kate said, "I fought a bear a couple days ago. He laid one on me with a left hook."

Andropov took a step back in amazement and bumped into his irritable mule. He'd obviously been in a similar situation before because he stepped aside with alacrity and the mule's long yellow teeth snapped like a mousetrap on thin air. "Karina, you are a remarkable woman. You wrestle a bear one day, kill an outlaw the next. Should you ever think about leaving this country, Mother Russia could use a woman like you." His patriotism asserting itself, he added. "Of course, we already have many fine, strong women in the homeland."

"Why did you leave Russia, Count?" Kate asked.

"Ah, Karina, to hear my tragic story would curdle your young blood. Let me just say, in short . . . an indiscretion with a chambermaid . . . a missing royal jewel . . . discovery . . . and a mad sled dash across the snowy steppes to safety in Prussia." In a paroxysm of grief, the count threw up his arms, dropped to the ground and wailed, "Mercy! Mercy for poor Count Andropov the peddler! Let him return to Moscow!" Then he launched into a torrent of Russian interspersed with agonized moans and howls.

Dr. Fullerton turned to Kate. "I believe no other language communicates the melancholy spirit like Russian. Don't you think?"

"Will he be all right?" Kate asked, frowning her concern.

"Oh, yes. The count will be just fine in a little while."

And indeed that was the case.

The wailing stopped and Andropov jumped to his feet, yelled something in Russian, and did a few kicking steps of a wild Cossack dance. "Now, I must remove the deceased," he said, breathing hard. "I think you ladies should retire to the *dacha* while the deed is done. Drink coffee. It restores the troubled soul." He shrugged. "Or vodka."

Thirty minutes later, Count Andropov returned to the hogan. He didn't mention the dead man. He passed Mary Fullerton a package of medicines wrapped in brown paper tied with string. "And now we will consult the book, Dr. Fullerton."

"Only five ailments, Count," Mary said.

"I will honor our agreement, dear lady. Five of my afflictions in return for the medicines. Or was it six?"

"It was five."

"Very well. I have marked the relevant pages in"—he spoke in a tone of deep reverence—"the book."

The front cover of the massively thick tome under the count's arm read *1,000 Maladies That Plague Mankind*, written by someone who called himself *Dr. Ebenezer Snoad, late of Mannheim University.*

Kate decided that the thousand miseries in the book must be very important indeed to merit such a prodigious volume. She suffered through two of the count's diseases and his list of symptoms, but when he got to *Adenosine monophosphate deaminase deficiency* and complained of breathlessness and a lack of energy, she threw in the towel and stepped outside . . . just in time to see Trace and Frank ride out of the trees and wave to her.

CHAPTER TWENTY-ONE

"His name was Hobson, and he was of the same breed as Hack Rivette," Kate said. "He was just a wild animal who wanted nothing better than to rape and pillage."

"He ran into the wrong ladies." Cobb acknowledged.

Kate nodded. "He was notified, but he didn't heed the warning."

"He underestimated you, Kate," Mary said.

Kate smiled. "And you most of all."

"Well, we buried him deep where the sun don't shine." Cobb stared hard at Kate as though gauging how much more stress she could take. "The Apaches are out. We need to get back to the ranch in a hurry."

Trace answered the question on his mother's face. "We met a patrol of Yankee soldiers just north of here who told us the Apaches had been raiding into Chihuahua and were headed for Texas. They already attacked an isolated homestead down on the Nueces and the word is that the Rangers buried what was left of eight people, five of them children."

Cobb said, "Of course, they probably won't come this way."

Kate smiled. "Thank you for trying to spare me, Frank." She turned to Mary. "You better come with us."

"I've had no trouble with Apaches in the past."

Cobb said, "The Apache buck is the most notional creature on God's green earth. He can be your friend on Saturday and try to cut your throat on Sunday. In other words, Dr. Fullerton, it's a mistake to put your faith in an Apache's good nature."

"Come with us, Mary," Kate said. "I'll feel a lot better if you do. And you too, Count."

"Damned Cossacks," Andropov said. "It seems that every country has them. Yes, dear lady, I'll join you. As we say in Russia, there's safety in numbers."

Cobb's gaze moved to the wagon and its clanking, clattering load of pots and pans, cheap crockery and samples of just about every item a prairie wife might need, from needles to nightdresses. "The wagon will slow us, Andropov."

"Then I will bring up the rear guard," the count said. "I have a fine Berdan army rifle that served me well on the Russian steppes and it will do the same against Apaches."

Small, dark and portly though the count was, Cobb pegged him for a fighting man and he acknowledged that fact by a nod. "Keep a good watch, Count. If the Apaches come at us, they'll come a-running."

"You can depend on me, Mr. Cobb," the little man said.

"I aim to do just that."

* * *

Despite her wounds, Kate refused to ride in the wagon. She and Frank took the point and Trace rode drag. Dr. Mary Fullerton rode with Count Andropov in the wagon, which pleased the Russian greatly. Not only was the woman quite beautiful, he had plenty of time to reel off his symptoms and then listen intently to her suggested treatments, especially surgery, for which he had a morbid fascination.

Riding across the grass and mesquite country east of the Brazos meant that the Apaches had little chance to surprise them . . . but a band of three belligerent teenagers decided to cause trouble.

One of the young warriors had a brass telescope and he used it to scan the party of whites. He wanted the horses, guns, the goods in the wagon, and the two women. The three riflemen gave him pause. An Apache would fight only when the odds were in his favor, and evens didn't signify as *favorable*.

The Apaches talked among themselves for a while and then took a few ineffective pots with their rifles. The one with the glass got off his pony, bent over, waggled his bare butt, and mounted again. Yipping in derision, the three rode away and were soon lost from sight.

Kate and Cobb rode back to the wagon.

Andropov said, "That was a Cossack trick. Those barbarians show contempt for their enemies by baring their rears."

"I guess that Apache studied in Russia, huh?" Kate said, tongue in cheek.

"Do you think so?" Andropov frowned.

"No, Count, I don't."

"Then you made a joke?"

Kate nodded. "Yes, something like that."

The Russian smiled. "It was a good joke."

Cobb swung his horse away from the wagon. "Let's go. Those Apache kids might come back with their big brothers."

Another mile across the range, the three Apaches returned. They dismounted on a shallow ridge and resumed their long-range sniping. Cobb and Trace returned fire, but at a distance of a hundred yards, their shooting was wildly inaccurate.

"I think they're trying to pin us down here while they wait for the rest of the raiding party to show up," Cobb said. "We may have to make a run for it."

Kate frowned. "Maybe that's what they want. If we run, we'll be spread out, and they can pick us off."

"Count, if you have any ideas, this would be a good time to air them." A bullet spit the air a scant yard over Cobb's head.

"Take away their horses and they're finished. That's how it works with Cossacks." Revealing surprising alacrity for a plump man, the Russian jumped from the wagon and shouldered the .42 caliber Berdan. He took careful aim and fired. On the rise, a paint pony dropped and lay kicking on the ground. Andropov fed another round into the Berdan's chamber, worked the bolt, and fired again. A second horse fell.

A moment later, the Apache youths were gone, vanished like puffs of smoke. All that was left on the ridge were two dead war ponies.

Trace Kerrigan whistled between his teeth. "That was good shooting."

The count accepted the compliment with a little bow. "When I was a young man not much older than you, I won a gold medal for marksmanship at the Imperial Military Academy in Rostov."

"You could have killed the Apaches just as easily as the horses," Cobb said.

"Yes I could, but I don't make war on boys, even Cossack boys," Andropov said. "Now, shall we proceed, this time in an orderly fashion?"

Cobb nodded. "That sets fine with me, Count. I don't make war on boys, either."

BOOK TWO
Kate Rides the Terror Range

CHAPTER TWENTY-TWO

Two years after her brush with the black bear, Kate Kerrigan wrote a letter to Cornelius Hagan, the man who helped her escape a life of poverty in Nashville and brought her and her family to Texas. He had loaned Kate money to start the ranch, a favor she never forgot. With the letter, she enclosed a bank draft.

My Dear Cornelius,

I hope this short missive finds you and yours well and prosperous.

You will be happy to know that I have made a full recovery from the bear attack, though my upper chest is somewhat scarred. I rather fancy that my poor body will suffer more and perhaps deeper scars ere this wild land of mine is tamed.

Thanks to two years of mild fall and winter weather, my herd increased apace with plenty of calves on the ground and I introduced a small number of Herefords, a gift from Mr. Charles

Goodnight, that, despite all my doubts, seem to be thriving. Trace, who is growing into a fine young man, once more ramrodded—La! What a Texan I am becoming—my herds up the Chisholm Trail to Kansas, and my neighboring rancher Jason Hunt obtained top dollar for my cattle. Thus, happily, I am able to pay you some of what I owe, though my entire debt to you can never be paid in full, as I am well aware.

The Apaches have left us alone, no doubt because the army is leading them a merry chase, and Frank Cobb my foreman gives rustlers and other thieves short shrift with his gun and a rope, the only language they seem to understand. Those who would steal from the Kerrigan Ranch must know I will fight tooth and nail for this blessed land, no matter the cost.

Our cabin has been greatly expanded and it now begins to look like a real home. Ivy and Shannon each have their own rooms, but Quinn, grown as tall as a young oak, bunks with Trace, Frank, and the rest of my seasonal hands. A regular little settlement is growing up around the ranch house.

Dr. Mary Fullerton built a home and surgery and sick people come from miles around to be treated by her. She is indeed a fine doctor. My Mexican couple, Marco Salas and his wife Jazmin, set up their own blacksmith's forge and are doing well. The Russian émigré Count Ivan

*Boleslav Andropov I told you about also decided
to settle here and has opened his own general
store, though he longs to one day return to his
native land. Frank says that if any more people
arrive, I'll have to change the name of my ranch
to Kerrigantown! Not such a bad idea.*

*On a sad note, I just heard last week that
Steve Keller, the brush popper who helped me so
much when I first arrived, was killed in a saloon
fight somewhere west of here. I have no more
details.*

*Once again, dear Cornelius, thank you for all
your help and if God wills it, may we meet again
soon.*

> *With all my best wishes,*
> *Kate*

Three days after Kate wrote that letter, Jason Hunt
and his segundo Kyle Wright brought more details of
Steve Keller's death.

There was no sponge cake that day, but Jazmin's
cherry pie was deemed to be an excellent substitute.

After he'd eaten and Kate poured his third cup of tea,
Hunt said that Keller was shot by a man named Hickam at
a saloon in the Panhandle, close to the New Mexico border.

When he heard this, Frank sat up and took notice.
"Would that be Jack Hickam out of Yuma County in the
Arizona Territory?"

"Could be," Hunt said. "You know him?"

"If it's Jack Hickam, yeah, I know him. He's bad news."

"He a gun?" Wright asked.

"Draw fighter. He's fast, very fast, and he's a scalp hunter. Killed eighteen men, or so I heard."

"Mr. Hunt, why did this Hickam person choose to murder Steve?" Kate asked.

"I don't know how it come up, Mrs. Kerrigan," the rancher said. "But I was told that Hickam was holding a herd of ten thousand cattle fifty miles west of the Pecos. Maybe that had something to do with it."

Cobb shook his head. "I can't see Jack Hickam in the cattle business. That sounds way too much like hard work. He must be selling his gun to whoever owns the herd. Mr. Hunt. Ten thousand head need a lot of graze. I'd hate to think they're headed this way."

"I don't know where they're headed, but I plan to send a rider to find out," Hunt said.

"All the land west of the Pecos is already taken," Wright said. "My guess is those cattle are headed for Old Mexico."

"We have a claim on the land, but it is open range." Kate said. "That's enough to make me uneasy."

"What you say is true, Mrs. Kerrigan," Hunt said. "I aim to find out the right of the thing. I'll send a rider out today."

"Lowery is a good man, boss," Wright pointed out. "He's a youngster, but he's smart and fast with the iron when he needs to be."

Hunt nodded. "Then that's who we'll send." He rose to his feet. "Don't worry. I'll get to the bottom of this, Mrs. Kerrigan."

"I'll say one more thing. Jack Hickam never made an honest dollar in his life and only somebody as crooked as he is would hire him. Don't ask me how, but I got a feeling big trouble is coming down." Cobb pointed west. "Just over the horizon."

"Jesus, Mary, and Joseph, and all the saints in Heaven protect us." Kate shivered. "I have that feeling myself, like a goose just flew over my grave."

CHAPTER TWENTY-THREE

At twenty-two, Lowery was a top hand who'd been up the trail three times, the first riding drag. Everybody agreed he had sand. Although the Chisholm took the measure of a man and he'd stood the test, he'd never fired a gun in anger and had never shot at anything more dangerous than cactus pads and empty bean cans.

To sum it up, he was not a match for Jack Hickam in any way, shape, or form.

Nobody knew that better than Lowery himself.

He was young with steady hands and a fire in his belly, and he feared no man. He was off on the scout to set Mrs. Kate Kerrigan's mind at rest and that pleased him greatly. He'd seen her only from a distance, but it had been close enough to realize that she was a fine-looking woman with a mane of red hair any Irish princess would envy. Young Lowery figured if he earned just one smile from beautiful Kate Kerrigan it would be payment enough.

Lowery rode across the plateau country of the Staked

Plains, mile after mile of rolling grassland cut through by deep canyons that some called upside-down mountains, since they suddenly plunged steeply from the flat. The summer grass was sown with wildflowers, mostly honeysuckle and fragrant sumac, and here and there in splendid isolation stood plains cottonwood, bur oak, and red cedar.

As he rode west, a few miles south of the New Mexico border, Lowery drew rein and his gaze reached out across the distance. His sturdy paint pony was a mean bucker, biter, and snorter that the other hands had dubbed Rat's Ass. He liked the little horse and shortened the name to just Rat, figuring that was plenty enough to describe his steed's personality.

"Rat, what do we have here? It looks like a settlement where there might be grub for me and oats fer you."

The pony hung its ugly hammerhead and lost itself in evil thoughts.

"Well, we'll go take a look." Lowery was no trail cook and for the last three days had eaten nothing but stale soda bread and beef jerky. Like all cowboys, he wouldn't pass up the chance of a hot meal, not knowing when he'd get another.

It was a settlement of sorts, served by a wagon track. He rode past a general store with sleeping rooms on the floor above and fifty yards away an adobe cantina with a blue coyote painted on the wall to the left of the door along with the words *El Coyote Azul*. The charred ruins of a stage station lay at a distance, a relic of some forgotten Comanche raid, and a fat hog wallowed in the mud of what had once been the corral.

Lowery looped the reins to the hitching rail outside the cantina. His paint looked stunted beside the pair of big American studs that already stood there. He walked to the door, a massive portal of iron-studded oak scarred by arrow and bullet holes, and stepped inside a large pleasant room, the walls whitewashed and hung with Navajo blankets. A small bar stood to his right and behind that a curtain partitioned off what Lowery guessed was the kitchen and sleeping quarters. Tables and chairs covered the rest of the floor space. Two men sat at one of the tables sharing a bottle of mescal. Both were tall, angular, dressed in gambler's broadcloth finery, and carried a pair of holstered Colts in crossed cartridge belts such as Lowery had never seen before. His eyes clashed with theirs, cold as his stepmother's breath.

"What can I do for you, young feller?" A short, bearded man wearing a stained white apron stepped from behind the curtain and ushered Lowery to a table. When he was seated, the man said, "Sharp set, are ye?"

"I could use some grub." Lowery smiled. "I'm missing my last six meals."

One of the gamblers snickered, a nasty, unfriendly, belligerent sound.

Lowery didn't look at him. He wasn't scared, but he knew that two men with four Colts was probably a tad more than he could handle.

"I got fried beef and tortillas," the cantina owner said. "You like beef fried with peppers?"

"I recollect a trail cook fed me that one time," Lowery said.

"And?"

"I liked it just fine, once I got over the first bite."

"Drink?"

"Just coffee. I'm partial to sugar and milk in it, if you got them."

"Honey and goat."

Lowery nodded. "All right. That sounds good."

"Comin' right up." The proprietor disappeared behind the curtain.

One of the gamblers said, "Where you headed, cowboy?"

Lowery was prepared to be sociable. "Headed west of here, looking for a herd. Figure I'd sign on."

"What herd?" the man asked.

"I don't know who owns it. I only know it's supposed to be ten thousand head. You need a lot of punchers to drive that many cattle."

"You here to sign on or are you hunting trouble?" the other gambler asked pointedly. He opened his coat and showed the lawman's shield pinned to his vest. His companion did likewise.

"I don't plan to cause any trouble," Lowery said. "I told you, I aim to sign on." He tried a smile again. "I reckon the herd is headed for Old Mexico. Am I right about that?"

"And what if it isn't?"

"No matter. I'm just curious is all," Lowery said. "Are you fellers lawmen?"

"You could say that." The man had strange eyes, almost yellow in color. "We're range detectives."

"Never met one of them before."

"Well, you've met them now," Yellow Eyes said. "What was the last outfit you worked for?"

"The H bar H on the Pecos southeast of here. Mr. Jason Hunt's spread."

"And he sent you to find out where the big herd is headed, huh?"

"No. I got paid off with the other seasonal hands." Lowery looked around him. "I could sure use that grub I ordered. What's taking him so long?"

Lowery didn't recognize the danger, even when both men rose to their feet and stepped toward him. "You boys leaving?"

"No," Yellow Eyes said. "You are."

The man was tall and big as a blacksmith in the chest and arms. The powerful right hook he slammed into the side of Lowery's face knocked the young puncher out of his chair and sent him sprawling onto the floor. His head ringing, Lowery tried to get up and collided with another roundhouse right that smashed into his face and put him down again.

Then the boots went in.

Lowery felt kick after kick thud into his ribs and head. He was aware of pain, razor sharp and unrelenting, the taste of green bile in his mouth, and the salty tang of blood. Then a man's voice, muffled, as though he talked underwater.

"Leave that cowboy be. You'll kill him."

Lowery was hauled roughly to his feet and slammed into a chair. "Put the honey and milk into the coffee," a man said. A few moments later, the rim of a cup rammed into his mouth and scalding hot coffee was poured into his mouth and ran down his chin. The young man choked and gagged and the cup was taken away. But his torment wasn't over. Greasy beef wrapped in a tortilla was rammed into his mouth and a strong hand forced it deeper into Lowery's throat, the palm twisting back and forth to push the food deeper. For a moment, he thought he'd choke to death, but then mercifully it was over. He was left alone to retch uncontrollably and then throw up all over himself.

Yellow Eyes dragged the young puncher to his feet and slammed him against the wall. "Now that you've had your grub, listen up, boy. You go back to your boss and tell him the big herd is coming to the Brazos. You tell him to get off the range or he'll think he fell asleep and woke up in hell."

The man pounded Lowery against the wall. "Did you hear that, boy?" The young cowboy said nothing, and Yellow Eyes yelled, *"Did you hear that?"*

Lowery's answer was to throw an enraged punch, but it was a feeble effort.

The man slapped away the puncher's fist, then delivered a vicious backhand to Lowery's bloody, broken mouth. "Speak to me, boy, or by God I'll beat you to death."

"I . . . heard . . . you." Lowery was barely holding on to consciousness.

"Another thing, boy. Tell your boss that any man standing in the way of the big herd will be shot. No excuses, no apologies. He'll be gunned on sight. Are you listening?"

Lowery knew he was hurt bad and couldn't take more punishment. "I'm listening," he whispered. "I heard you."

Yellow Eyes and the other man dragged Lowery outside and threw him onto his horse. Without another word, they pointed Rat south and slapped the pony into an ungainly trot.

Lowery, facedown over the horse's neck, slipped in and out of consciousness. Moving between darkness and pain, he didn't think he was going to make it.

CHAPTER TWENTY-FOUR

"He made it, Mrs. Kerrigan," Jason Hunt said. "Beaten to the threshold of death's door, but he got through. Damn it all, if you'll forgive my language, ma'am, but Lowery has sand."

"Where is the young man now, Mr. Hunt?" Kate Kerrigan asked as she poured more coffee into the rancher's cup.

"Lying in my own bed being attended to by the ranch cook. Lowery's almighty sick, ma'am, coughing up blood and hurtin' every time he moves."

"Has he eaten or drunk anything?" Dr. Fullerton asked.

"My cook got a little water down him and urged him to make a trial of some salt pork and beans. But he refused to eat."

"And no wonder," Mary glanced out the cabin window. "The surrey is for me, Mr. Hunt?"

"I surely hate to impose, ma'am, I mean Doctor."

"Attending to the sick is no imposition. It's my job. I'll leave right away."

"Young feller by the name of Henry Brown is at the reins, Doc," Hunt said. "He's a good man and being afeard doesn't enter into his thinking. Henry will see you safe to the H bar H."

"Then I'm most reassured, Mr. Hunt," Mary said.

"Doc, one more thing," Hunt said, his craggy face lined with worry. "I don't care what it costs or how long it takes, but get that boy well."

"I'll do my very best." Dr. Fullerton laid her slender hand on the rancher's gnarled paw. "He sounds like a fine young man."

Kate and Hunt watched as she climbed into the surrey and left in a cloud of dust.

"Mrs. Kerrigan, an attack on one of my hands is an attack on the H bar H, and I will not let it stand. I'll be calling on young Trace and Frank Cobb to ride with us." Hunt saw the confusion in Kate's face. "The big herd is headed this way and we've been ordered to get off the land. Lowery told me that much . . . maybe with his dying breath."

"It's open range," Kate said. "We have every right to graze our cattle here."

"Indeed we do, ma'am, but the owner of the herd wants his cows on it, not ours. The only way we can claim open range is to fence it, and we don't have time for that."

"Then what are we to do, Mr. Hunt?" Kate asked.

"I plan to ride against the owner, whoever he is, and

force him to turn his herd around. There's plenty of grass in Old Mexico."

"And if he doesn't turn around?"

"Then we'll have a range war on our hands," Hunt said. "I won't be pushed off ground I fought for against Comanches, rustlers, Yankee raiders, and the land itself. West Texas did its best to break me, Mrs. Kerrigan. Sure, it made me old and gray before my time, but I never raised the white flag and by God, I won't do it now. The H bar H is mine and I'll surrender it to no man."

"Nor will I, Mr. Hunt," Kate said strongly. "I'll fight to the death for what is mine."

"Mrs. Kerrigan, you got young'uns to think about, two little girls to raise. If it comes, you leave the fighting to the menfolk."

"That I will not do," Kate said, her pretty chin stubborn. "I can ride and shoot as well as any man and I will not stay home when mine go off to war. I am not a wilting magnolia of a Southern belle weeping in the big house while her menfolk ride away. The land is mine and I will defend it to my last breath."

Hunt smiled. "I believe you will. Let's hope it will not come to that. The herd might yet turn south."

"But you don't believe it will," Kate pointed out.

Hunt's big shoulders sagged as he glanced out the window, the waning afternoon light gray on his face. Without turning he said, "Last night in a dream, I walked across a prairie that was all afire. But when I looked at the flames, it wasn't fire at all. Each blade of grass was scarlet with blood. As far as the eye could see there was blood shining on the grass . . . like a sea of rubies." He turned and started at Kate with haunted eyes. "It was a terrible dream."

From the time before time, the Irish have set store by dreams. Kate reached into the pocket of her day dress and clutched her rosary in her hand. "May God in his mercy protect us all."

Hunt bowed his head. "Amen."

Dusk shadowed the land and the sky looked like a sheet of tarnished copper as Dr. Mary Fullerton returned to the Kerrigan cabin. Her driver refused to wait for coffee, citing chores that needed to be done, and Mary lingered outside the door for several minutes after he left. Finally she took a deep breath, steeling herself for was to come, and stepped inside. She was greeted with smiles and the good smells of coffee, fresh-baked bread, and beef stew simmering in the pot.

Kate laid down the book she was reading. Frank and Quinn looked up from their checkerboard and Trace ran an oily cloth up and down the barrel of his Henry. The girls made too much noise in their bedroom, and Count Andropov glared at their door in disapproving silence.

Kate rose to her feet and smiled. "How is your patient, Mary?"

Her lovely face like stone, the doctor said, "Lowery died two hours ago."

Kate talked into the silence that fell on the room. "Oh, Mary, I'm so sorry."

"His internal injuries were too extensive. I couldn't save him. I couldn't do anything for him but ease his pain." Mary let her medical bag drop to the floor. "Maybe a better doctor, a male doctor, could have saved the young man. I could not."

Count Andropov jumped to his feet. "*Manya*"—he used the Russian form of *Mary*—"I will not allow you to say that. You are a fine doctor, but when a man is torn up inside, nothing can be done for him. I remember in Russia a young prince of the blood was gored by a wild ox in the Khimki Forest outside of Moscow. The czar ordered the best physicians in the empire to tend him, but his internal injuries were too great and he soon died. The doctors could not do the impossible and neither can you, Manya." Andropov smiled slightly. "And they were all men."

Moses was perched on a stool opposite Kate, an open Bible in his lap. He could neither read nor write, but the Book spoke to him in a language only he could understand. He got to his feet, carefully laid the open Bible on the stool, and stepped to Mary. "Doctor, you don't blame yourself for that boy's death, no. The ones who kicked him until his ribs and chest caved in are to blame."

"Mose is right, Mary." Kate rose and then motioned to her chair. "Sit here by the fire and I'll make you a nice cup of tea."

Mary managed a smile. "'There is no trouble so great or grave that cannot be much diminished by a nice cup of tea.' I read that somewhere."

"And truer words were never spoken," Kate said.

Mary seemed glad to sit by the fire, a cup of tea in

her hand. But for the rest of the evening, she gazed into the flames and said nothing.

Kate wanted to say a hundred things that might console the woman, but she could not come up with even one.

CHAPTER TWENTY-FIVE

Kyle Wright laid down his steaming coffee cup and said, "How do we play this, boss?"

The six hands gathered in Colonel Jason Hunt's parlor looked at the old rancher, waiting for his answer. The faces of the young punchers were grim. Lowery had been a well-liked man.

"We ride out to that hell and damnation herd and I tell the owner I want him to hand over the two men who murdered Lowery. Then I'll hang them." The stern old rancher lit a cigar. "Two men dressed like gamblers, toting lawman's badges shouldn't be hard to find. We ride out at first light." He looked around at the punchers who stood holding up the walls. "Sanchez, you and Brown are the fastest with the iron. If it comes to a fight, make sure you get your work in."

"Ain't nobody gonna get the drop on me, boss," Esteban Sanchez said. "And Brown won't let it happen, either."

"Damn right," Henry Brown said.

Kyle Wright looked around the room. "Any man who

wants to step away from this can, and I won't blame him. You boys ain't making gun wages."

After a moment's silence, a tall, lanky puncher spoke for the rest of them. "I reckon we'll stick."

"I expected nothing less." Hunt rose to his feet in a blue cloud of cigar smoke. "Get a good night's sleep, all of you. An hour before dawn, we'll meet in the cook-house for breakfast."

After the hands left, Wright said, "What do you expect, boss?"

"I expect a range war," Hunt said. "That's what I expect."

"Nothing good ever came out of one of them."

"Dead men, widows, grieving mothers, and burned-out ranch houses." Hunt looked at his segundo with weary eyes. "Nothing good at all."

A puncher named Ben Clark rode into camp at a gallop because a fast-riding man made a difficult target. He swung out the saddle and hit the ground before his horse had halted.

"Well?" Jason Hunt said, his face showing his worry.

"The herd is three miles thataway," Clark said, pointing west with a bladed hand. "It's a big herd, boss, at least ten thousand head, but them cattle are in bad shape, like they'd been held on the caprock. There's water up on the escarpment but little graze for a herd that size."

Rain drizzled and spat into the fire under the coffee-pot. The sky was iron gray and the air unseasonably cool that deep into summer.

"I reckon the herd came up from the south," Wright said. "No cause for them to keep their cattle on the caprock. If the cows don't look good, it's for some other reason."

Hunt frowned. "Ben, were any of those cows down when you saw them?"

"Yeah, boss, quite a few."

"They should've been grazing this early in the morning," Hunt said.

Wright stared hard at the rancher. "Boss, you got something sticking in your craw?"

"Maybe," Hunt said. "Throw the coffee on the fire and get the boys mounted, Kyle. We got things to do, people to annoy."

The drizzle turned to rain and the clouds lowered. A gusting wind rippled the long grass as Jason Hunt and his punchers caught their first glimpse of the big herd.

Wright's experienced eye swept the landscape ahead of him. "Ten thousand all right, all of them longhorns." He studied the cattle. "Those cows are mighty thin, and they don't seem inclined to move much."

"Maybe they've been driven far," Hunt said. "Now that they're on good grass, whoever owns them probably plans to hold them here until they put on beef."

"Speak of the devil," Wright said. "This might be him coming."

Jason Hunt was not a trusting man. He ordered his hands spread out on either side of him, the fastest guns—Wright, Carlos Sanchez, and Henry Brown—in the center.

A dozen horsemen came on at a canter, led by a big, yellow-haired man on a fine gray horse.

As they drew closer, Wright sized them up. "Those boys ain't punchers."

Hunt nodded. "Looks that way, don't it." He scanned the riders but none matched the description of the two who had kicked Lowery to death.

The man on the gray drew rein, savagely jerking the bit. As his men shook themselves into a skirmish line, he said, "You boys are trespassing and that means you suddenly got a choice. Ride away or be carried away."

"Mister, this is open range and we don't intend to leave until we get what we came for," Hunt said.

The big, blond man's handsome face showed surprise, as though he was not used to defiance or to Western men who didn't scare worth a damn. He backed down, but only a little. Kyle Wright's steady stare unsettled him. He recognized that Wright was the gun of the outfit and would be sudden.

"My name is Rube St. James and my sister Savannah has claimed all the land from here to a hundred miles east of the Pecos and south to the Rio Grande," the big handsome man said, but his small, sensuous mouth hinted at cruelty and thick eyebrows shadowed his deep-set blue eyes as though they kept terrible secrets.

"That's a fair piece of range your sister is claiming," Wright said. "Pity the land is already taken."

"That is no concern of mine," St. James said. "We're driving the herd west and we'll trample underfoot anyone who stands in our way." He smiled, showing the white incisors of a predator. "That's a polite way of saying that any man who tries to stop us will die."

Wright's smile was less threatening, but just as effective. "We'll stop you, mister. Depend on it. And I have a guarantee for you. If you open the ball right here and now, you'll be the first to die."

If St. James was intimidated, he didn't let it show. "This is not the time nor the place. A reckoning will come soon, but not now."

"Then I'll look forward to us meeting again," Wright said.

"Kyle, let it go. I have pressing business here." Hunt stared at St. James, his eyes like chips of flint. "Two men in your employ murdered one of my hands. I want you to hand them over. It is my intention to hang them."

"I have no such men," St. James said. "My riders don't brawl with cowboys."

"The men I want dress like gamblers and wear a lawman's badge." Hunt saw a few of the men in the line glance at each other.

St. James blinked as though he feared his eyes would betray him. "I have no such men." He waved a hand. "These are my riders, my friends, my compadres."

"And not a puncher among them," Wright said. "How do you plan to drive ten thousand head east with a dozen hired guns who've never nursed a cow in their lives?"

"If a twenty-a-month puncher can figure it out, then these men will do it even better," St. James said. "I will not argue the point with you. Now clear out of my range."

Kyle Wright, a man with a notoriously short fuse, was primed for a fight. "Suppose you try and make us."

"Kyle, no!" Jason Hunt said. "Not today. There will be other days."

Without another word the rancher swung his horse around and the crestfallen H bar H riders followed.

Laughter and derisive cheers rang out behind them and Wright's face burned.

CHAPTER TWENTY-SIX

The devil was in Kyle Wright. As the day shaded into night and the dejected, head-bowed men of the H bar H headed for home, it was an easy matter to turn his horse around and lose himself in the gloom.

Wright's big American stud walked with his head high and his ears pricked forward. He was unused to night sounds since he'd never been used as a cowpony, but he stepped out well and kept to the trail, and Wright rode him on a loose rein.

Heat lightning flashed in the sky to the west and Wright was pleased. The shimmering sky could make the herd uneasy and more inclined to run. He kept to the shallow hollows between the hills, using every inch of cover he could find. His success depended on surprise, and he didn't want some sharp-eyed night herder to spot his silhouette in the darkness and raise the alarm.

He patted the stud's neck and smiled. Rube St. James was big on threats and bluster, but how would he handle his first taste of war in a land of hard men living rough lives?

Ten minutes later, Wright came upon the herd, a black sea of cattle that stretched into darkness. Lightning flashes lit the sky and here and there bobbing horns glowed with the eerie green incandescence of St. Elmo's fire. Wright slid his rifle out of the boot and carried it upright, the butt on his right thigh. He swung away from the herd, not wishing to stampede it . . . at least not yet.

In the distance, a campfire twinkled like a sentinel star in a dark sky. He kneed his horse forward, the only sound the lowing of the stock, the creak of saddle leather, and the soft footfalls of his mount. The air smelled of ten thousand cattle, an odor that overpowered all else. As he rode close to a lone wild oak, an irritated owl demanded his identity. "Just me, that's whooo," he whispered, and rode on.

Anxiety twisting in his gut like a knife blade, he kept to the shadows as he rode closer to the camp. A holdover from his Comanche-fighting days, nothing on his horse or person was shiny. He'd allowed even the brass buckle of his cartridge belt to tarnish so that it didn't gleam in moonlight or the bright Texas sun.

As Wright rode along the outer fringe of the herd, an odd realization struck him . . . no one was riding night herd. A herd that size needed four or five nighthawks, maybe more since the cattle were skittish, way off their home range, and ready to run. His face was grim. Did this bunch have anybody with a lick of cow sense? Obviously they didn't, and that's why they were about to tie into a heap of trouble.

He rode as close to the camp as he dared and studied the layout with farseeing eyes. It was difficult to count heads as men came and went between tents in flickering firelight, but he figured they were all there—Rube St. James and a dozen gunmen drinking too deep and laughing too loud and not a soul with the herd.

Wright's cowman's soul was outraged. He nodded to himself. All right. Those boys deserved everything that was coming to them.

He turned and retraced his steps to the very eastern edge of the herd. Under a flaring sky, the restless long-horns kept bunching, then separating and then they'd bunch again and drift. A seasoned nighthawk would not have allowed them to drift. He would have ridden among them, his tuneless renditions of "Goodbye Old Paint" or "Far and Away" keeping them calm and separated.

Of course, Kyle Wright didn't want the cattle calm. He wanted them running due west, into and through the St. James camp and leaving carnage in their wake.

It was time.

Wright racked his Winchester and fired.

All hell broke loose.

For perhaps several seconds the herd stood, then they were off and running, stampeding westward away from the noise of the gun. Wright fired again and again, and the stampede gathered steam, the cattle's pounding hooves making a sound like thunder. The herd charged through the shallow valley like water from a broken dam, a dangerous, unstoppable force of nature. In the distance, rifles banged as the hired guns tried to shoot the leaders and turn the herd. But it was a hopeless task, like using a peashooter to stop a charging buffalo. A thick cloud of rising dust mingled with the darkness and visibility dropped to a few yards.

His devil prompting him, Wright grinned and decided to add to the misery of Rube St. James and his gunmen.

Riding across churned-up ground in the wake of the thundering herd, he pulled his bandana over his mouth and nose. Lost in ramparts of rising dust, he was hidden from sight. He rode for several minutes, his horse picking its way around dead cattle, and then in the near distance he heard men yell. Swinging hard to his right, he rode out of the dust cloud into clear air. His rifle still at the ready, he headed toward the camp but ahead of him he saw only darkness and heard the back and forth shouts of frightened men. Somewhere amid the chaos, a man screamed incessantly, piercing shrieks that suggested serious and painful injuries.

Dipping down into a draw among mesquite, Wright drew rein and again studied the night. He saw nothing. His plan had been to take a few pots and shake up St. James and his cohorts, but he had no clear targets, only screams and voices in the gloom.

Wright had won a victory of sorts, but it was just the opening skirmish of what could be a long war. The herd was scattered to hell and gone and without experienced drovers it would take days, maybe weeks to round them up. Rube St. James would not push the herd west any time soon and for the moment, Wright was content to leave it at that.

Used up, he booted his rifle and rode out of the draw, looking forward to coffee and his bunk. He saw lightning flash, heard a roar of thunder, and felt something hard slam into his right shoulder. . . .

Then blackness took him and he felt nothing at all.

CHAPTER TWENTY-SEVEN

"We thought he might have come this way, beggin' your pardon, ma'am," the young puncher said.

"No, I haven't seen him," Kate said. "How long has Kyle been gone?"

"Since last night, ma'am. Mr. Hunt had a powwow with the owner of the big herd, well his sister is the owner—"

"A woman owns the herd?" Kate asked, surprised.

"Yes, ma'am. But we didn't talk to her."

"And it was after the powwow that Kyle disappeared?" Kate confirmed.

"That's the way of it, Mrs. Kerrigan."

"Did you hear gunshots, anything like that?"

"One of the boys thought he heard a couple shots, but he couldn't be sure. Anyway, we though Kyle was still with us. The trail was real dark, you know."

Kate was coping with noises of her own. Jazmin Salas's baby cried and fussed in her cradle, demanding to be fed. Up on the rise, Moses, expecting trouble, discharged the old loads in his Dragoon, taking his own sweet time about it. Marco Salas hammered iron at his forge and Count Andropov bellowed instructions at Trace and Quinn on how to erect what he called his general store, but did no work himself. The girls had discovered an indigo snake and shrieked in unison as it wound toward them. Only Frank Cobb was quiet, attentively listening to the exchange between Kate and the H bar H puncher.

She frowned. Raising her voice above the din, she asked, "What is this person's name?"

"His name is Rube—"

"His sister's name."

"Savannah St. James, ma'am. You ever hear of her, Mrs. Kerrigan?"

"No, I have not. With a ten-dollar name like that I would remember." Kate kept at it. "What did Rube say at the meeting?"

"Only that his herd is moving west of the Pecos and he's laying claim to all the range that's worth claiming. Says he'll gun anybody that gets in his way." The young puncher's eyes flicked to Frank Cobb. "He's a pistolero. Real bad news, I reckon." Then to Kate, "I got to get back on the scout, Mrs. Kerrigan. When we find Kyle, we'll let you know."

"Hold up. We're coming with you." Kate turned. "Trace, let Quinn work on the store. Get your rifle and saddle up."

Trace grinned and let go of the beam he held upright. Immediately, the rickety structure of the general store swayed and fell in a crashing heap. "Fix that, Quinn," he said as Count Andropov turned the air blue with a string of Slavic curses and Quinn added a few Anglo-Saxon ones of his own.

The puncher—his name was Loop Davis and he was sixteen years old that summer—retraced the route the H bar H men had taken to meet the St. James herd. "Mr. Hunt said he'd search to the south, then swing north again. We'll meet him along the trail."

As they rode, four sets of eyes scanned the land around them, a vast, rolling expanse of long grass where a man's body might lie hidden in a hollow and never be found. Yesterday's rain was just a memory and the day was hot, the burned-out sky cloudless.

After an hour, Loop's young eyes saw a rider emerge through the shimmering heat haze and canter toward them. "That's Monk Boone. They must have found Kyle." He turned to Kate. "Nobody knows what Monk's real given name is, Mrs. Kerrigan, but he was a monk for a spell when he was younger. He's kinda sad all the time, is ol' Monk."

And ol' Monk looked sad indeed. A tall, skinny drink of water with the face of a middle-aged saint, his voice sounded like it came from the depths of a sepulcher. "Howdy, Loop."

"Colonel Hunt find Kyle?" Loop asked.

"He found him."

After a moment, Loop said, "Well?"

"It ain't good, Loop."

"What happened?"

"Kyle is dead."

"Dead how?"

"Hung dead. That's how, Loop."

"Where is Mr. Hunt?" Kate asked.

"Up the trail a ways. I was sent out to find Loop."
Boone removed his hat, revealing sparse brown hair.
"You must be Mrs. Kerrigan. I'm right pleased to meet
you, ma'am, if that's in keeping with the sad occasion."

"Take us to Mr. Hunt, Monk," Kate said. "And I'm
pleased to meet you, too."

If Jason Hunt was surprised that Kate Kerrigan and
the others had joined in the search, he didn't let it show.
He merely touched his hat brim then said, "You see it,
Mrs. Kerrigan."

Kyle Wright hung from the bleached branch of a
dead cottonwood that stood next to a dry creek. His
purple tongue poked out of his mouth, his chest was
bare, and someone had used a knife to cut words into
the white skin. *Stampeder & Murderer.*

"For God's sake get him down," Kate said. Her face
was pale and her rosary was in her hand.

Hunt nodded. "I wanted all the boys to see this.
All right. Get Kyle down and we'll bury him at the
H bar H."

"And after that?" one of the hands asked.

"There's no after that," Hunt said. "Loop and Monk
will take Kyle back to the ranch. You boys wash his
body and then lay him out like a Christian and a white
man. When I get back, we'll bury him."

"What are your intentions, Mr. Hunt?" Kate asked.

"I aim to hunt down the men who did this," the
rancher said. "Now two of my boys are dead and there

must be a reckoning. Mrs. Kerrigan, you got no call to get involved in this, but I'd surely like your son and Frank Cobb at my side."

"I'll ride with you," Kate insisted. "I can handle a rifle."

That was met with stony silence.

At the dead cottonwood, Loop and a couple other men gently lowered Kyle Wright's body to the ground. Above them, a single buzzard quartered the sky.

Finally Trace said, "No, Ma. You're needed back at the house. You have too many people depending on you. The girls and Quinn need you there."

"Trace speaks the truth, ma'am," Hunt said. "I think the time will come soon when you'll need to fight to protect what's yours. But it will be on your own ground, not here."

Kate turned to look at Cobb. "Frank? Have you anything to say on my behalf?"

The segundo shook his head. "Trace and Mr. Hunt said it best, Kate. What's ahead of us is rough work for mighty rough men. Whether you wanted it or not we'd be always looking out for you. A man who gets distracted like that can get himself killed."

Kate sat her saddle frowning. Then she made up her mind. "I'll ride to the H bar H with Loop and Monk and help them lay out Kyle's body and then I'll pray over him." She glared at Cobb. "That's women's work."

CHAPTER TWENTY-EIGHT

Loop Davis, Monk Boone, and Kate Kerrigan left with Kyle Wright's body.

Trace and Cobb stood with Jason Hunt and four of his hands. They numbered seven, but all were good gun hands and had shown sand in the past.

After riding for thirty minutes, they saw the path of the stampeding herd stretching away from them like a dirt road, cutting a swath a hundred yards wide across the grassland. Carcasses of downed cattle mounded the flat all the way to the shimmering horizon. Trace counted fifty before he gave up the task. He reckoned there was probably three times that number.

Hunt drew rein and studied the stampede road for a couple minutes, then he swung out of the saddle. The rancher kneeled and studied one of the dead cows, then he moved to another, his face troubled. Finally, he waved a hand at Sanchez. "Carlos, come over here and take a look."

Sanchez had ridden for Charlie Goodnight and was

cow-savvy. He examined the carcass for several minutes until Hunt said, "Well, what do you think?"

"You know what it is, boss," Sanchez said.

Hunt frowned. "Charlie Goodnight taught you well, and I want to hear you say it."

"This cow had tick fever." Sanchez, a small, black-eyed man, waved a hand. "And probably all the others you see dead. They were the weakest of the bunch and they fell and were trampled."

"That could mean the whole herd may be sick," Hunt said.

"No, boss. It means the whole herd *is* sick," Sanchez said. "And it will infect any other cattle in its path."

"Damn it all," Hunt swore. "It could wipe out the whole range."

"Tick fever spreads like wildfire, boss. If the big herd comes east, all you can do is move your cattle out of the way."

"No, we'll turn them, by God." Hunt looked at Cobb. "You heard all this?"

"I sure did. Tick fever is not something to mess with."

"And?" Hunt said, slightly irritated.

"All we can do is turn the herd," Cobb said. "We can't shoot ten thousand cattle, even if we had all the ammunition in the world."

"Frank, you reckon this St. James gal knows her cattle are infected?" Hunt asked.

"Probably not. From what I've seen, nobody in that outfit knows the first thing about cattle."

"Then let's go educate her," Colonel Hunt said.

* * *

Trace, riding scout, discovered two bodies about fifty yards apart lying in the scar cut across the grassland by the stampeding herd. He recognized the pounded mass of jelly flattened into the earth as males, but that was about as far as he could go.

"Looks like they tried to turn the herd on foot." Hunt shook his head. "My God in heaven, how stupid can these people be?"

"Stupidity can make some people dangerous. They do bad things without considering the consequence." Cobb smiled. "Something to bear in mind, I guess."

"Well, there's nothing we can do for these two." Hunt stared ahead of him. "Let's see if we can find any more stupid dead people."

The young gunman lying in the wreckage of what had been the St. James camp was not dead . . . but he seemed close to it. When he saw Hunt and his riders move toward him, he picked up the Colt that lay beside him and yelled, "That's far enough!"

Hunt was not inclined to be sociable. "Touch off that hogleg and I'll hang you, boy." He rode to within a few feet of the man and swung out of the saddle. "Let the pistol drop."

After a moment's hesitation, the kid dropped the gun and said, "Both my legs are busted. Damned cow rolled over them."

Hunt received that information in silence. He drew his own revolver and said, "I'm going to ask you one question, boy. You give me the wrong answer and I'll scatter your brains. Understood?"

"Damn you, my legs are broke!" the young gunman cried.

"Do you want to hear the question?" Hunt asked.

The kid looked at the men who were still mounted, his stare lingering for a moment on Trace. But, like the others, he saw nothing in his stony expression that offered sympathy.

"Ask your damned question, old man," the gunman said.

"Did you have any hand in the hanging of my foreman?" Hunt asked.

"Hell, no," the kid said. "I didn't even know he'd been hung. After the stampede, Rube brought a man here who'd been shot. Rube beat him up some, then he and the others put the man on a horse and left. My legs was broke so they told me to stay here."

"Where is St. James now?" Cobb asked.

"He's with his sister, I guess. She come up from San Antone to join the drive but that was a few days ago."

"The herd is scattered to hell and gone," Cobb said. "Who's rounding them up?"

"A bunch of men like me who don't know nothin' about rounding up cows," the gunman said. "But I heard Rube say he could hire vaqueros down on the border. Maybe that's where he is."

"Where's your hoss, boy?" Hunt asked.

"Rube and them took it. We lost a bunch of horses in the stampede." The young man shook his head. "Your foreman sure played hob."

Hunt stared on the gunman. "Yeah, well, he ain't likely to do that ever again, is he?"

"I didn't kill him," the young gunman said, his face defiant.

"No, but you were a part of it," Hunt offered.

Henry Brown turned his cold blue eyes to the rancher. "Want me to gun him, boss?"

Hunt shook his head. "No, leave him be. It's Rube St. James I want and them that's with him."

"You can't leave me alone out here," the young gunman cried. "Rube ain't coming back for me. He don't give a damn."

"And frankly, neither do I. You should have thought about all this when you tied in with him." Hunt turned his back and stepped to his horse. He had seconds to live.

The young man retrieved the gun he'd dropped, thumbed back the hammer, and yelled, "Stop right there, damn you!"

Without turning, Hunt said, "Go to hell."

The gunman fired, one shot into the center of Hunt's back. Henry Brown's bullet slammed into the young man's forehead and killed him instantly, but he was too late.

His spine shattered, Jason Hunt also lay dead on the ground.

Trace Kerrigan and the other riders dismounted and gathered around Hunt's body.

Cobb kneeled beside the rancher, then looked up and shook his head. "He's gone."

"I left it too late," Henry Brown said, his young face pale.

"You did what you had to do." Cobb rose to his feet. "You were faster than any of us."

"Not fast enough." Brown said. "Why did that little son-of-a-bitch shoot Mr. Hunt? He must have known we'd kill him."

"Because the gun was all he knew," Cobb said. "That's how he'd been taught to settle a dispute and doing it any other way didn't even enter into his thinking. You know how many kids there are just like him in Texas? The gun removes all difficulties and solves all problems. Their fathers and brothers who fought in the war taught them that."

"High-sounding words, Cobb," Brown said. "But the next one of them St. James boys I see, I'll shoot first and save the fancy words for his funeral."

There were nods of approval from the other H bar H punchers.

Trace Kerrigan said, "That sets just fine with me."

They were angry, bitter men and the stage was set for a bloody war that in later years only the dead would not regret.

CHAPTER TWENTY-NINE

Kate Kerrigan stood in dappled moonlight under the ancient oak that stood in front of the H bar H ranch house. Coyotes yipped in the distance as though mourning the dead and inside the oil lamps were dimmed and cast little light.

Cobb stepped out of the house and saw Kate. Even in the gloom, her beauty burned like a candle flame. He stepped beside her. "Can you bear my company, Kate?"

She turned and smiled. "I'd appreciate it, Frank, especially tonight. I see hard times coming down."

"Predicting the future is like driving a galloping four-horse team down a country road in the dark. You just can't tell what's going to happen."

"I wish I could believe that. The Irish have the gift. I can see a fair piece down that dark country road."

"I won't let anything happen to you, Kate," he promised.

"I know, Frank. And I appreciate your concern." The moonlight touched her hair gently, like a shy lover. "I have so little, a cabin and a few cattle. Why would someone want to take it from me?"

"I don't know, Kate. I can't think like Rube St. James and his sister. I don't know what drives people like that. Greed, power, a need to hurt others? I just don't know."

Kate managed a smile. "Well, the danger is over for now. It will take them a while to gather the herd again."

"It's not over. Jason Hunt and Kyle Wright are dead. There's got to be a reckoning."

"No, Frank. I don't want that. What can punchers do against professional gunmen? All we'd do is to fritter away our strength. We must fight St. James, I agree, but on ground and at a time of our own choosing."

"They lost four men as a result of the stampede," Cobb said. "Henry Brown is good with a gun and so is Carlos Sanchez. If we hit St. James now while he's on the ropes, we can take him."

"How many men has he, Frank?"

"I don't know, maybe eight or so, nine including St. James himself. I don't know if he's any good with the iron."

Kate shook her head. "It's too thin, Frank. I won't let it happen that way. You could all be killed. We have time for me to talk with some of the other ranchers and enlist their help. We'll gather our strength and be ready."

Cobb, deeply aware of the moonlight that enhanced Kate's spectacular loveliness, didn't let his irritation show. "Kate, there are only two ranches that count, the H bar H and yours. Sure there are a few one-loop outfits to the north of us, but they'd be of little help. We need pistol fighters and all we'd get is a few used-up married men with kids and money worries."

"I hope I can prove you wrong, Frank. Now if you'll excuse me, I must go pray over the dead."

"Then I'll join you. But me and God ain't exactly on speaking terms."

Kate was serious when she said, "He'll listen though. Depend on it."

"They'll listen to me. I'll make them listen," Savannah St. James said.

"And if they don't?" Rube asked.

"Then I'll shoot and hang them all, man, woman, and child. I need that land and I'll take it." Savannah sipped bloodred wine from a crystal glass. "What of the herd?"

"The vaqueros I hired say we lost no more than three hundred head," Rube said. "But some of the others are sick."

The woman dismissed that with a wave of her elegant hand. "Cows are always sick. What news of the guns?"

"You'll recall I wired Jack Hickam from San Antone. I reckon he'll be here in a few days. He's coming down from Fort Concho and Pete Slicer is with him."

"Only those two?"

"Savannah, when you got Hickam and Slicer that's all you need."

"Reuben, when you *have* Hickam and Slicer . . . please don't lapse into the vernacular of the barbarians. It does not become you." She rose to her feet and her rust-colored silk dress made a soft sound. She glanced out the window and sighed. "A wilderness populated by savages. I must get back to Boston, Paris, London . . . anywhere but this howling wasteland."

As it so often did, Savannah's restless mind changed course. "Reuben, that man you hanged, did he suffer? I want him to have suffered."

"It took him a long time to die, sister mine."

"I asked you did he suffer?"

"Yes, he did. At the end, he didn't know where he was or who he was."

"Good. That makes me feel better." She dropped a little curtsy. "You are most gracious."

Rube smiled and gave a little bow. "Your obedient servant, Savannah."

Savannah St. James was a once ravishing beauty who'd been, in turns, the mistress of a German prince, a rich American industrialist, the English actor Drink-water Meadows, and more recently Maximilian, Emperor of Mexico. But as she approached her fortieth year, though still a beautiful woman, her loveliness was fading fast. The worm of age was in the rose and no one knew that better than Savannah St. James herself. Maximilian was dead by a Benito Juárez firing squad, Charlotte, the loyal wife who had tolerated Savannah's dazzling presence in her husband's life, had suffered a mental breakdown after his death and was confined to an insane asylum. Bereft of her lover and benefactor, Savannah had sold all her jewels to support a lifestyle she could no longer afford. All that stood between her and grinding poverty was a cattle herd. Her brother had assured her that, come spring, the cattle could bring forty dollars a head. Even after expenses and wastage, that amounted to close to four hundred thousand dollars, enough for Savannah and Rube to live in luxury back east or in Europe.

That was Savannah St. James's dream and she'd kill and kill again to make it a reality.

Marmaduke Tweng, who'd been silent, stirred in his chair, then laid his teacup aside. "Mr. St. James, how is the terrain to the west?"

"You mean for the safe passage of the *Emperor Maximilian*?"

"Indeed, sir," Tweng said. "That is my concern."

"Flat, rolling country," Rube said. "Ideal country for the *Emperor*."

"Then, sir, you have set my mind at rest. There is very little that can stop a steam-powered colossus like the *Emperor*, but—"

"It can't fly across a canyon," Savannah said.

Tweng nodded. "That is indeed the case. One day, steam engines will launch us into the sky, but, alas, the time has not yet arrived."

Tweng was a former London cabbie, a tiny man whose wizened, weather-beaten face resembled a withered yellow apple. He wore a brown felt derby hat adorned with driving goggles and an olive-colored tweed suit with elastic-sided boots. As was his habit, he carried an 1866 Remington derringer in a leather-lined back pocket and a brass compass hung around his neck from a cord chain. He had once driven Queen Vic's consort Prince Albert around Hyde Park one rainy Saturday afternoon in 1859 and had considered it the highlight of his career . . . until he met Savannah

St. James and she asked him to the take the driver's seat of the mighty land liner *Emperor Maximilian.*

Savannah sat again and shook the bell that stood on the arm of her chair. A door opened behind her and a slim black woman in a smart maid's uniform stepped into the room and gave a little curtsy.

"Ah, Leah, there you are," Savannah said. "Please prepare my bath." She looked at Marmaduke Tweng. "I presume we have plenty of hot water."

The little man got to his feet. "I'll check the valves right now, ma'am. But I can assure you that there's a plentiful supply."

"Make it good and hot, Leah. It's the only way to get rid of this prairie dust."

Leah bowed. "As you wish, my lady."

After Tweng and the maid left, Savannah looked at her brother. "Reuben, I want to begin the drive west as soon as possible."

"No more than a week, perhaps less."

"This is an affair of the greatest moment. Please instill a sense of urgency in yourself and the rest of our people."

Rube grinned. "Savannah, this time next year you'll be summering in London town."

"I do hope so. I must confess I'm all at sixes and sevens over this whole business." Savannah rose to her feet, the silk of her afternoon dress clinging to her shapely body like a second skin. "Tell the guns that they must kill without hesitation."

"They already know that, Savannah."

"Yes, yes of course they do. You think of everything, Reuben. Why do I doubt you?"

"Relax in your bath and all will be well." Rube gave a little bow. "Now, if I may be excused?"

"Of course. May I expect you for dinner? Cook assures me that we will have a chicken pie, a quantity of boiled ham served cold with mustard, and a steamed treacle pudding for dessert."

"I wouldn't miss it for the world."

CHAPTER THIRTY

Kate Kerrigan stepped out of the darkness and stood in the scarlet glare of Marco Salas's forge. Showers of sparks cascaded from the foot-long billet of iron he'd thrust into the charcoal. He stared intently at the flames that would change color when the iron began to absorb the carbon that would turn it into steel. The leather bellows huffed and puffed and the fire glowed like a pool of molten lava. Salas saw the flame he wanted, tonged the billet out of the forge, hammered it flat, and then plunged it hissing and steaming into the water. He shoved the iron back into the coals and said, "It will be a knife for Mr. Cobb."

Kate nodded. "I know. He told me. I'd never seen a blade made before."

"It takes time, much heating and hammering, to turn iron into steel, Mrs. Kerrigan. The flames will tell me when the miracle happens."

Kate smiled. "It's a miracle, Marco?"

His face lit by fire, the little Mexican said, "Yes it is,

and that's why I pray to holy St. Dunstan, the patron saint of blacksmiths, locksmiths, goldsmiths, and silver-smiths, to deliver the miracle on time." He nodded to the horseshoe that hung above the doorway of the forge. "Do you see that, Mrs. Kerrigan?"

Kate nodded. "A horseshoe is lucky."

"It is more than that. One time, as St. Dunstan was working at a monastery forge in Glastonbury, the devil came to him disguised as a beautiful young girl and tried to tempt him into sin. But St. Dunstan saw the devil's cloven hooves under the girl's dress and nailed a horseshoe to one of them. This caused the devil so much pain that he begged St. Dunstan to remove it. The saint said he would but only on the condition that the devil never again enter a blacksmith's shop." Salas stared at the flames. "To this day, as long as a horseshoe hangs above the door, the devil will not come near a forge because he is too afraid." Salas removed the white-hot billet from the fire.

Kate took a step closer. "May I try the hammer?"

"Of course. I want the metal flatter so I can form the blade."

He laid the billet on the anvil and gave Kate the hammer. She did what the Mexican had done and pounded the iron as hard as she could.

"No, Mrs. Kerrigan, you don't need to hit that hard. The hammer blow must be accurate, not powerful. The trick is to hit the metal where you want." He watched for a while then said, "Ah, now you're chasing the blade all over the anvil."

Kate stopped and grinned. "I think you'd better take over, Marco."

The iron went back into the fire and the blacksmith said, "Your mind must be one with the metal, Mrs. Kerrigan. If a smith has worries and concerns, it is better he turns off the forge, cleans the shop, and goes home. Tomorrow will be another and better day."

"I hope I didn't ruin Frank's knife," Kate said.

Salas shook his head. "There are no mistakes in blacksmithing. The iron is forgiving because it can always be reused and reshaped. There are always second chances, in metal and in men."

Kate nodded. "That's something to remember."

"A clear mind means good work, Mrs. Kerrigan, and tonight your mind is not clear, I think."

"Is it that obvious, Marco?"

"The iron told me, did it not?"

"The ranchers I've spoken to told me our fight with Savannah St. James is none of their concern. They say her herd won't come their way and the killings of Jason Hunt and Kyle Wright have them really shaken."

Salas nodded. "If the owner of one of the biggest ranches in West Texas can be killed, then so can they."

"That's how they see it," Kate said.

"Not one?"

Kate shook her head. "I really can't say I blame the small ranchers. Savannah St. James wants the H bar H and Kerrigan range. Why would they fight for us?"

"You've been good to me, Mrs. Kerrigan. Your ranch is now my home and I will fight."

Kate smiled. "I know you will, Marco. And I appreciate it."

A voice came from behind them. "The night is getting cool, Kate. Maybe you should get inside." Cobb stood half in shadow. He wore his gun, a thing he seldom did that close to the cabin.

Salas turned away from the forge. "Mrs. Kerrigan helped me with your knife."

"I didn't do much. I . . . what was it you said, Marco? Oh yes, I chased the iron all over the anvil."

"All it takes is practice," Salas said.

"And dedication." Kate stared at Cobb for a moment, then turned back to Salas. "Thank you for letting me try the hammer, Marco. I'll leave it to you from now on."

She took Cobb's arm and they walked together toward the cabin. "What has happened, Frank?"

"The H bar H punchers have pulled out, all but Henry Brown."

Kate was shocked into silence and Cobb took up the slack. "Brown says with their boss dead, the hands reckon they got no brand left to fight for. Sanchez, Monk Boone, and Loop Davis and the others talked among themselves and figured they'd be up against a stacked deck taking on a bunch of hired guns."

She found her voice. "But I thought they wanted revenge for the murder of Mr. Hunt. Frank, you know how angry they were."

"Kate, anger can carry a man only so far before common sense takes over. Four of St. James's men were killed in the stampede, and they shot to pieces the man who killed Jason Hunt. I reckon they figure they done enough."

"Did Jason Hunt have an heir, someone who could

take over his ranch and get the punchers back?" Kate asked.

"I once heard Hunt say he had a sister back east somewhere, but that she was ailing with a cancer."

"Do we know how to reach her?"

Cobb frowned. "Maybe her address is in Hunt's correspondence. We'd have to look. But if she was as poorly as he made out I reckon she's dead by now."

After a few moments, Kate lifted her chin. "Then there's only us."

"Seems like."

She stared at her segundo. "I'm afraid, Frank."

"No shame in that, Kate. I'm afraid, too."

CHAPTER THIRTY-ONE

Rube St. James drew rein and studied the ranch house that lay a mile or so to the east of Table Top Mountain. The limestone mesa itself, rising two hundred feet above the flat, was covered in a thick growth of juniper, oak, chaparral, and cactus, but the surrounding area was rolling grassland where a scattered herd of about two hundred longhorns grazed. To his envious eyes, it seemed like an excellent place for part of his own herd to fatten over the rest of the summer and into next spring. Savannah might disagree, preferring to drive the entire herd farther west, but the ranch was still worth acquiring.

Rube took a brass ship's telescope from his saddle-bags and scanned the ranch house more closely. It was a modest affair, small and cramped with a sod roof. A few shabby outbuildings, a pole corral, and a well with an iron pump were nearby. A woman who looked to be pregnant stepped out of the door, tossed away a pan of dirty water, and went back inside.

Then Rube saw what he needed to see. A man came round the side of the cabin leading a yearling colt. He wore no belt gun and looked exactly like what he was, a one-loop rancher living a hardscrabble existence at the ragged edge of nowhere.

Rube St. James smiled, put the glass a way, and kneed his horse forward. He anticipated no trouble. He'd tell the man to go and he'd go.

In an age corset-bound by the Victorian code of ethics, a visitor was expected to hail the dwelling and then sit his horse until given permission to light and set. That is what Rube St. James would have done for people he considered members of his own class, but a cockle-bur rancher, like the poor, blacks, Mexicans, and Indians, merited no such consideration.

Rube swung out of the saddle and fisted the rickety door so hard it rattled on its hinges. The door was opened almost immediately by a brown-eyed, brown-haired man of medium height and build, a striking contrast to the tall, blond, blue-eyed St. James.

The rancher was angry. "Why the hell do you hammer on a man's door like that?"

Rube smiled. "Howdy. I'll sum things up for you in two words. *Get out!* "

The man was taken aback. "Mister, are you crazy? I want you off my property now."

"I told you to get out," Rube said. "Take what you can carry and light a shuck."

The rancher turned his head. "Jane, I got a crazy man here. Bring me my rifle."

"No rifle!" Rube yelled. He drew and fired.

Hit dead center in his chest, the men staggered a few steps backward and then fell on his back. The impact of his body hitting the timber floor made the cabin shake. The woman screamed. She ran to her husband's side and threw herself on his body, sobbing uncontrollably.

In a conversational tone, Rube said, "Ma'am, I'll saddle the horse in the corral for you so you can be on your way. I thought it might rain earlier, but all I see now is blue sky. Real nice weather for riding."

The woman's tearstained face turned to Rube and she shrieked, "You fiend! You . . . murderer!" She scrambled to her feet and dashed into the cabin. A moment later, Rube heard the *click-clack* of a lever rifle and then the thud of heels on the floor. He shot the woman as she appeared at the door. The Henry dropped from her lifeless hands and she collapsed on top of her husband.

Rube lowered his head in thought. As Savannah often told him, the lower classes had no idea how to act in a civilized society and could always be depended on to do the wrong thing. "All you had to do was walk away," he said to the dead. "You fools, was that so damned difficult?"

His first thought was to burn down the cabin, but the summer grass was tinder dry and now that he'd acquired new graze, he didn't want it to burn away under his feet. He contented himself with kicking legs aside and closing the cabin door.

A few minutes later, he rode away with the Henry rifle, the paint cow pony from the corral, and the mustang colt. Those were the only items of worth the dead couple had possessed.

* * *

Marmaduke Tweng was indignant. "That, my dear sir, is the *Emperor Maximilian*, a triumph of modern steam engineering. Put wings on it and I could drive it to the moon."

"Damn thing looks like a railroad car cut in half," Jack Hickam said.

"The *Emperor* does not need rails," Tweng said. "It will go anywhere there is a road and it can ford rivers and climb hills if need be."

The land liner had six great drive wheels, each as tall as a man. The cabin was up front, the boiler, smoke box, and coal tender behind the driver and then the passenger compartment. The steel of the great coiled wheel springs were polished to a silver sheen and the tangle of brass steel pipes glowed like solid gold. The liner was painted dark green and boasted four windows to a side and an engraved brass plaque a yard long read, EMPEROR MAXIMILIAN, each letter picked out in red.

"The steam liner was a gift to Miss St. James from the Emperor Maximilian himself," Tweng said. "He brought engineers over from Germany to build the machine and they later declared it their masterpiece."

"You must be the men my brother is expecting." Savannah St. James stood in one of the *Emperor*'s three side doorways. Her black hair was undone and hung over the shoulders of a bright scarlet robe that revealed a great deal of her milk-white breasts and thighs.

His eyes popping out of his head, Hickam said, "We

sure are, ma'am. Jack Hickam at your service as ever was and my associate Pete Slicer."

Slicer bowed from the saddle. "Your servant, Miss St. James."

Hickam was a rough-hewn man with a broad, savage face and experienced eyes that slowly removed Savannah's robe. Pete Slicer was thin, almost frail, a small-boned man who was fast beyond belief, as the sixteen men he'd killed could attest. He was being eaten away by a stomach cancer, and it pained him.

"We were just admiring your . . . ah . . . wagon, Miss St. James." Hickam's eyes never left Savannah's body.

"Mr. Tweng," Savannah said, enjoying Hickam's heat, "fire up the *Emperor*. I'm sure Mr. Hickam will enjoy a ride."

"Perhaps some other time, Miss St. James," Hickam said quickly. He didn't trust the infernal thing not to blow up and take half of Texas with it.

"Very well," Savannah said. "Yes, then some other time." It pleased her that she'd put the crawl on the most feared gunman in the West. The barbarian would have to be kept in his place. "Put up your horses and come inside for a drink, gentlemen. My home on wheels is a humble one, therefore I trust Martell cognac is to your taste."

Tweng unbuckled his hooded leather coat and removed his goggles from around his neck and replaced them on his hat. He was relieved he had not needed to fire up the *Emperor Maximilian*. Raising sufficient steam was a long and labor-intensive process.

A movement in the distance attracted his attention and then a rider emerged through the heat haze leading two horses. The little man finally recognized the rider as Rube St. James. Tweng would not ask where the man got the horses. It was pretty obvious.

Mr. St. James was forever killing some poor soul.

CHAPTER THIRTY-TWO

"I've called you all together because I've reached an important decision and I wish to know if you concur," Kate said.

Cobb smiled. "Kate, since when did you need our approval for anything?"

"You're right, Frank. But I don't want your approval because my mind is already made up. What I wish is for you to agree or disagree as your conscience dictates."

"Ma, you plan to shoot that St. James woman," Quinn said.

"Not quite, Quinn. And please don't speak with your mouth full."

The boy laid his biscuit on his plate. "Sorry."

"You're being very mysterious, Karina," Count Andropov said. "Have you decided to take a husband and am I the lucky one?"

Kate smiled. "No, Count, that is not the case."

"Then I am devastated," the Russian said, spreading

his hands. "My heart is broken. I should have known that a peddler dare not aspire to a queen."

"Since you don't have marriage in mind, don't keep us in suspense, Kate," Cobb said.

"Very well then." She took a deep breath. "I've decided to take over the H bar H—the land, the cattle, horses, the ranch house, and outbuildings pertaining thereto. In other words—all of it."

Kate's words were met with silence, then Moses Rice asked, "Mr. Hunt didn't have kinfolk, no?"

"A sister maybe," Henry Brown said. "If she's still aboveground."

"And if she comes to claim the H bar H then I will surrender it to her willingly," Kate said. "But in the meantime, I will not have squatters moving onto Hunt range." She looked first to her segundo. "Frank?"

"Sets just fine with me, Kate. You'd surrender the Hunt spread willingly?"

"We'll see," Kate said, refusing to meet his smiling eyes. "Trace?"

"I have no objections, Ma."

"Mose?"

"You always do the right thing, Miz Kate."

"Marco, I'd like your opinion," Kate said.

"You are my patrón. That is all I have to say."

"Mister Brown, you worked for Jason Hunt," Kate said. "What do you say?"

"Ma'am, if you can take the land and hold it until spring, then go right ahead. The H bar H will make the Kerrigan spread the biggest ranch in West Texas."

Kate frowned. "Hold it, Mr. Brown?"

"You got a diseased herd and some mighty hard people headed this way, ma'am," Brown said. "It ain't happened yet, but in a week or two, maybe less, a war will come right to your doorstep."

"Will you stand with us, Mr. Brown?" Kate asked.

"Sure. Now Mr. Hunt is gone, I got no boss to answer to. But I'll be gone for a while. Got to attend to some personal business."

Kate looked him in the eye. "Will you be gone long, Mr. Brown?"

"No, not long. I'll be back when you need me."

"Then we are agreed that I take over the H bar H," Kate said. "I will tell Dr. Fullerton later. She needs to know these things."

"There are some things I need to say first, Mrs. Kerrigan," Brown said suddenly.

"Please feel free," Kate said, but she frowned a little again.

"There's close to ten thousand cattle headed this way, all of them with tick fever," Brown said. "If you let them get among your own, your cows will all be dead or mighty sick before its time for the spring gather. Ma'am, that could put you out of business."

Cobb looked at the puncher. "What do you suggest, Henry?"

"Get your cows the hell—begging your pardon, ma'am—out of the way. Drive the H bar H cattle all the way across the Mexico border if need be and the Kerrigan herd north where there's grass and water.

Mrs. Kerrigan, then you burn this cabin and the old Hunt place. Leave Savannah St. James nothing that she can use to get through the winter."

"Scorched earth," Count Andropov said with an air of great finality. "That is what we Russians did to Napoleon when he invaded the motherland."

"Will the St. James herd last through winter?" Kate asked.

"No, ma'am," Brown said. "The buzzards will grow so fat they won't be able to get off the ground."

Intrigued, she asked another question. "Does Savannah St. James know this?"

"My guess would be no. And if you told her, she wouldn't believe you."

"They haven't made a move this way yet," Cobb said.

"The stampede slowed them," Brown said. "But count on it. They're coming."

"What do you think, Frank? I mean about moving the herds," Kate said.

"What Henry says makes sense, Kate. Just get your cattle out of the way."

Kate nodded. "I'll take your advice into consideration, Mr. Brown. In the meantime, I'll ride out to the Hunt place tomorrow and take a look at the grass and the cattle."

"I'll ride with you, Ma," Trace said.

"No. You'll stay here in case the St. James woman makes a move against us." She smiled. "Trace, I'll take my derringer and a rifle, and I'll be quite safe. I don't really think we have anything to fear until the fall."

Henry Brown looked as though he was about to say something, but Cobb said, "Don't waste your breath, Henry. When Kate Kerrigan ties onto a thing, nothing you can say will change her mind."

Kate smiled. "Why, Frank, what excellent advice you give."

CHAPTER THIRTY-THREE

Kate Kerrigan crossed the Pecos shortly after sunup and then headed southwest onto the H bar H range. After an hour of riding, she saw her first steer, a big brindle that plodded in her direction for a few yards, then stopped, his nose lifted to the wind. After that more and more cattle appeared, all of them sleek and fat from grazing on good grass and what was at least a trickle of water in most streams.

The range looked just fine, the cattle healthy, and at no point did she see signs that squatters had moved cattle onto Hunt grass.

She rode along the bank of a dry wash for thirty minutes, looped around a stand of mesquite and juniper with tangles of brush and cactus in between, then latched onto a wide trail that aimed straight as an arrow due south.

As she expected, the trail led to the Hunt ranch house. The place was deserted. Devoid of the people that gave it life, its windows stared at her with dead eyes. Over by the bunkhouse a door banged open and shut in the wind. The day was hot, the sun burning bright in a blue sky, yet Kate shivered as she urged her horse toward the cabin, a place fit only for ghosts.

She rode past the empty corral and stepped out of the leather when she was still several yards from the door. She thought about taking her rifle but decided to leave it in the boot. The derringer in the pocket of her riding dress would suffice.

The interior of the cabin revealed the personality of the man who'd lived there: dark polished wood, steel-studded leather chairs, a rack of charred briar pipes on the mantel above a great round stove manufactured from riveted iron and brass. On one wall hung a picture of Robert E. Lee and on the opposite, a strange juxtaposition, a portrait of Abraham Lincoln draped in black crepe. A gun rack hung on the wall to the right of the door, but the rifles were gone, as was the petty cash from an upturned cashbox. Worn cow-skin rugs covered the wood floor and with great solemnity a massive grandfather clock ticked in a corner. Like Justin Hunt himself, the cabin was solid, steady, and seemingly indestructible.

Oddly depressed, Kate stepped out of the door back into the morning sunlight.

A tall, flashily handsome man in a frilled white shirt, riding breeches, and knee-high English boots sat his horse grinning at her. He had a Colt in his hand but holstered the pistol and swung gracefully out of the saddle. "Well, well, well, what do we have here?"

"My name is Kate Kerrigan. This is my property and you are on it."

"I beg to differ," the man said. He gave a deep bow. "Rueben St. James at your service."

Suddenly very conscious of how tightly her corseted riding habit fitted at the waist and bust, Kate said, "I've heard of you. What can I do for you, Mr. St. James?"

The man's grin was not pleasant. "There's a lot you can do for me, little lady."

"I have riders close," Kate said.

"Not close enough." St. James took a step toward Kate, another, then stopped. "I've claimed this ranch, but here's my deal. You can have it back after the spring roundup." The man's grin showed he was used to getting anything he wanted. "I expect you'll have a big belly by then and you'll have me to thank for it."

"Just don't hurt me," Kate said. "I'll give you anything you want, but don't beat me."

St. James's grin turned to a sneer. "Oh, but I plan to hurt you a lot."

"No, please . . ."

St. James grabbed her, his hands moving all over her body, squeezing hard. He forced his open mouth on hers and said, "Into the cabin."

"Yes . . . yes . . . just don't hurt me." Kate dropped her hand to her pocket and she thumbed back the hammer of the Remington. She tilted the little pistol and fired from there. The .41 caliber bullet ripped through the material of her dress and slammed into St. James's left side just under the ribs and plowed eight inches into his belly. He was a dead man and he knew it.

He screamed, a primal screech of rage, pain, and fear.

With his red eyes fixed on Kate, he took a step to his right, and brought his Colt up fast. The hammer of her derringer snagged in her pocket and she felt the spike of her own fear.

Blam!

The rifle shot that dropped Rube St. James shattered the silence of the morning like a rock through glass. Hitting between his left temple and the top of his ear, the .44-40 scattered his brains, and in an instant the dying man was a dead man.

Kate managed to yank clear the derringer and turned to see Trace sitting his horse, a smoking Henry in his hands.

"Sorry I was late, Ma."

Still shaken, she gave a little grunt. "You weren't late. You were just in time."

Trace dismounted and looked at the dead man. "Who is he?"

"That's Reuben St. James. He was a piece of filth who thought I was too scared of him to fight."

"Well, I reckon you taught him otherwise." Trace's eyes met his mother's. "Is it over now, Ma?"

"No, it's not. I have a feeling it's only beginning. This morning I lit the fuse."

"What do we do with him?" Trace said.

"Tie him on his horse and send him home to his sister," Kate said.

Trace sensed the steel in his mother. "I'll get it done."

"Good. I'll be right back." She went back to the cabin, sat at Jason Hunt's desk, and found pen, ink, and paper. The note she penned was short and to the point.

STAY OFF MY LAND.
~Kate Kerrigan

She went back outside where Trace had begun to rope Rube St. James across his horse. "Put this in his shirt pocket," she said, passing the folded note to her son. "I want Savannah St. James to know that it's me she's dealing with."

CHAPTER THIRTY-FOUR

The vaquero stood uncomfortably in the scented brass and red velvet interior of the *Emperor Maximilian*, his sombrero dangling from his brown, rope-scarred hands.

Savannah St. James frowned. "You mean all of them?"

"Sí, patrón. They are very sick."

Savannah's crimson robe slid from her crossed thighs, but the vaquero's news was so terrible she didn't notice or care. "Are you sure?" she asked, knowing what the answer would be.

"Sí, patrón. The cows have tick fever." The vaquero shrugged. "They will die, I think."

She kept pushing. "Will they last long enough for the Chisholm?"

"Maybe some, patrón. But you will not be allowed to drive sick cattle on the trail. It will become a matter for the Texas Rangers. You will be stopped and your cows will be shot."

Savannah rang the bell beside her, and when her

maid appeared, she said, "Leah, a bourbon. Make it a large one."

"Mr. Tweng replaced the cogwheels and repaired the steam pipe for the ice machine, Miss St. James," Leah said.

"How clever of him," Savannah said. "Then I'll have ice with my bourbon." She waved a dismissive hand at the vaquero. "That will be all for now. I will discuss the matter of the cattle with my brother when he gets back."

The man bowed and left and Savannah rubbed the temples of her suddenly throbbing head. The vaquero's news was devastating, but Reuben would find a way out of the unholy mess. He always did.

She accepted her drink from Leah and said, "Ask Mr. Tweng to come see me." She felt the need of someone to talk to. Leah was available, but she was a domestic and one didn't confide in servants.

Leah nodded and went in search of Tweng.

He appeared shortly, wearing his hooded leather coat, closed at the front by a row of eight brass buckles, his round hat, and ever-present goggles.

Savannah waved him into a chair. "I have bad news, I'm afraid."

"I am distraught, dear lady. Pray, what could the matter be?"

Savannah recounted what the vaquero had told her, then, "Since this is a matter of the greatest moment, I am open to advice."

Tweng sat up in the chair. "I have this to offer. We must avoid any involvement with the Texas Rangers or authorities of any kind. They may pry too closely into the origin of the herd. We can't explain away the fact that we lifted the cattle in Mexico and left eight or nine dead vaqueros in our wake."

"Indeed, Mr. Tweng. Once again, you have come to the crux of the problem," Savannah said. "But you offer no solution."

"There is one answer. Pick up and flee north into the territories."

"And spend the rest of my life in poverty? That I will not do."

"You could wed," Tweng suggested.

"And that is a typical male solution. Wed? Wed what? A pasty bank clerk? An army officer, only to find myself withering away in some dusty outpost of civilization? Perhaps you'd wish me to become a farmer's wife, pushing a plow, staring all day and every day at an ox's ass? Or perhaps I could wed a reverend and he could preach to me about the errors of my wicked ways?"

Tweng sat back. "I stand chastised, Miss St. James. My suggestion was ill-considered."

"I need a herd, Mr. Tweng. I must sell it and get out of this godforsaken wilderness forever."

"Then you must acquire another, healthier herd," Tweng said.

Savannah looked like she'd just been slapped. Then she clapped her hands. "Huzzah! Mr. Tweng, you have come up with the perfect solution! I will talk to Reuben when he returns and we'll make our plans. How wonderfully clever you are." She raised her glass and smiled. "And thank you for once again making my ice possible."

* * *

Jack Hickam and Pete Slicer found the dead man roped across his horse. The big stud grazed just a hundred yards from the western limit of the cattle herd, a sea of hide and horn that seemed to go on forever.

Hickam dismounted, grabbed the corpse by the hair, and yanked up the head. "Yeah, it's him all right. It's Rube St. James."

Slicer leaned forward in the saddle. "Looks like he's been shot, huh?"

"A couple times," Hickam said. "But a bullet through the head done for him."

"What's the paper in his pocket, Jack?" Slicer expertly rolled a cigarette and thumbed a match into flame. Through a cloud of smoke, he asked, "What does it say?"

Hickam took the paper and unfolded it. "It's got writing on it, Pete."

"Well, read it," Slicer said.

Hickam shook his head. "I don't have the knack, Pete. I never did learn how."

"Then let me see it." Slicer scanned the note. "Looks like he was shot by a gal named Kate Kerrigan. That's what I read into it."

"Must be a rancher hereabouts." Hickam gathered the reins of Rube's horse and swung into the saddle. "Well, let's get this back to his kin."

"I hope this ain't going to affect our wages," Slicer said. "Rube being dead an' all."

"Savannah has plenty of money, I reckon," Hickam said. "And if she don't, then we'll take it out in trade."

"Do her, you mean?"

"Well, it's a thought," Hickam said, grinning.

Savannah St. James's grief was a terrible thing to see. Racked by sobs, she threw herself on her brother's body and screamed and screamed. Her robe had fallen open and his dried blood stained her naked breasts and belly like rust. "My brother," she shrieked. "My friend, my beloved." She lifted her head to the blue, uncaring sky and her screeching cries rang through her bared teeth.

Hickam, Slicer, and the other guns stood in an impotent semicircle around the hysterical woman. It looked like they were frozen in place, their staring eyes wide like men who'd just seen a phantom in an abandoned graveyard. Even Marmaduke Tweng was shaken to the core and the hand that held his leather gauntlets shook.

Then her tone changed. Her screams became cries of rage, of the desire for vengeance, of her need to strike out and kill, kill, kill.

The face she turned to Hickam was a mask of fury. Her beautiful features twisted, distorted into the face of a demented demon. "Who . . . did . . . this?" Her voice was hollow as a funeral drum.

Hickam, a man with sand, felt a surge of horror not unmixed with fear. "Here," he said, quickly passing the note to Slicer. "You tell her."

"Somebody tell me!" Savannah screamed.

Slicer, as affected as the rest, swallowed hard. "The

note on your brother's body was signed Kate Kerrigan and it said to stay off her land."

Savannah St. James stood, heedless that her blood-stained body was on display under her open robe. "Find her. Find her and bring her to me." Distorted by hate, Savannah's face was the stuff of nightmares. "All of you go and as you bring her back, use her, use her often and hard. Break her, Mr. Hickam, break her." Finally aware of her nakedness, she closed her robe. "Every ship needs a figurehead and Kate Kerrigan will be mine." She pointed to the tangle of brass pipes and valves above the driver's cab of the *Emperor Maximilian*. "I will tie her up there and when I take possession of her land, she will be the first to know it. Then I will kill her. Only then will Reuben's soul be at rest."

Suddenly, Marmaduke Tweng was alarmed. "Miss St. James, hold off on that plan until I talk to you privately."

Savannah turned to him, her eyes glaring. "I have made up my mind, Mr. Tweng. The Kerrigan woman must die."

Tweng tried again. "Just a few minutes, I pray you. While your brother's body is prepared for burial."

Savannah tilted back her head and screamed. Then, she gave a shrieking yell. "No! I will not lay Reuben to rest in foreign soil. Mr. Tweng, you will use one of your infernal machines to burn him and I'll carry his ashes to his new home."

"Yes, yes of course," the little engineer said. "But first we must talk."

Jack Hickam spat. "The time for talking is done.

We'll ride, Miz St. James, and bring back that Kerrigan woman."

Tweng had spent most of his life tending to temperamental steam engines and was thus a patient man and slow to anger. But his rage flared, directed at Hickam, not Savannah. "You fool," he snapped. "Don't you think the Kerrigan woman will have her own armed men? You're headed into a gunfight that you might not win. Even if you do, it takes only one survivor to bring the Texas Rangers down on us. From what I've been told, they don't take kindly to men who abuse women. In Texas, that's a hanging offense."

"There's ten of us here," Hickam said. "Look at us— me, Slicer, Duke Lake over there, the rest of them—the fastest guns money can buy. I think we can take care of a few"—the big man searched for the most demeaning name he could use—"waddies. We'll kill them all. Don't worry about that. There won't be any survivors, man, woman, or child."

Savannah listened to the exchange in silence, staring at the body of her brother. Finally, she asked, "Have you anything else to say, Mr. Tweng?"

"Yes I have, Miss St. James." A cloud crossed the face of the sun and a dark shadow raced over the grassland. "You have ten thousand diseased cattle that you can do nothing with. Between now and spring they'll drift in all directions and infect any new herd you might acquire."

"And your point is?" Savannah's eyes never left Rube's body.

"My point is an urgent one. Use your men to help the

vaqueros drive the herd over the border into Mexico and let the cattle die off in the Chihuahua badlands. Only then, turn your attention to killing the Kerrigan woman and taking over her herd."

"Hell, no," Hickam said. "I say we get the Kerrigan gal first. The herd can wait."

"Look around you, man! They're already drifting east," Tweng said. "Three of the vaqueros quit yesterday. They don't want to be associated with sick cows and cattle ticks. The vaqueros that are left can barely hold the herd together. Miss St. James, for God's sake, use these men to drive the cattle into Mexico now before it's too late."

"I say this little man has a yellow streak," Hickam said. "First we have some fun with the Kerrigan lady and then take care of the goddamned herd."

Savannah was instantly angry. "Sir! Don't you dare use that kind of language while my brother lies cold on the ground! I can't take the slightest risk on anything that might imperil my future. We'll do as Mr. Tweng says. Revenge is a dish best served cold, and I can wait for a few more days."

Hickam was angry. "Damn it, lady, we're not cowpokes."

"I know that, but you will be amply rewarded once this enterprise is concluded. You have my word on that."

A realization struck her like a blow. For the first time, she realized that she no longer had the protection of Reuben's fast gun and his reputation as a man killer. She saw in Hickam's insolent eyes that he had become aware of that fact the moment he found her brother's body.

Despite her grief, despite her anger, Savannah knew she must use her feminine wiles. "Mr. Hickam . . . Jack . . . do this for me and I'll be so grateful. I will be in your debt." She smiled. "And I always repay what I owe with interest."

Hickam's eyes explored the woman's body and saliva formed at the corners of his mouth. "No limits?"

"No limits. None at all. I need a strong man at my side now that I've lost Reuben."

"Then we'll drive the herd into Old Mexico," Hickam said. "And when I get back, I'll demand my due."

"It will be waiting for you," Savannah said.

One of the guns sneered. "And what will be waiting for the rest of us? The answer is nothing. I ain't gonna nurse a bunch o' cows over the border unless I get Yankee gold money in my hand right now."

The speaker was a weasel-faced youngster with lank, pale hair that fell over the collar of his shirt. His name was Jim Clewiston, some said Crawford, and his main claim to a revolver rep was that he'd shot and killed Red Adams, the Killeen draw fighter. That scrape gave Clewiston a false sense of his own importance and an inflated idea of his shooting skills.

Hickam disabused him of both when he pumped two bullets into his chest.

Gray gun smoke trickled from Hickam's Colt as he looked straight at the rest of the gunfighters. "Anybody else say he ain't gonna nurse a bunch o' cows?"

He got no takers.

CHAPTER THIRTY-FIVE

Kate Kerrigan was well used to crying babies, but Jazmin Salas's daughter was the noisiest she'd ever heard, her little face bright red with a temper tantrum. As Jazmin prepared dinner, Kate sat in her chair by the fire, bounced the baby on her knee, and sang the old Irish Ballyeamon Cradle Song as she'd sung it a hundred times before.

> *"Sleep, sleep,* grah mo chree,
> *Here on your mamma's knee,*
> *Angels are guarding,*
> *And they watch o'er thee."*

Having none of it, the baby still fussed and bawled. Trace, Quinn, and Cobb had already beat a path to the door and Dr. Mary Fullerton suddenly remembered that she had some studying to do.

> *"The birdeens sing a fluting song,*
> *They sing to you the whole day long.*

*Wee fairies dance o'er hill and dale
For very love of thee."*

Jazmin pushed a pot off the hot plate and said, "I'll take her now, Mrs. Kerrigan."

"She just won't settle. She's very fussy."

"She's hungry." Jazmin sat opposite Kate, pulled down the neck of her blouse, and gave the child her breast. Immediately, there was a blessed silence.

"I really don't think she likes the cradle Marco made for her," Kate said.

Jazmin shook her head. "She doesn't. But he's very proud of it, and I don't want to hurt his feelings."

The cradle was an oval-shaped contraption made out of riveted steel and brass pipe that looked like a miniature ironclad. A system of gears and pulleys allowed the cradle to be rocked by a foot pedal and Marco was looking into a way to utilize steam power so that no human had to be present.

The baby hated it. Moses considered it a work of art and was forever polishing the brass.

Kate heard men talking outside and she rose from her chair and walked to the window. Because of the darkness she could see little, but she made out the shape of a horseman and heard Frank talk to the man. She stepped outside just as a young, good-looking man swung gracefully out of the saddle.

He saw Kate, swept of his hat, and bowed low. "John Wesley Hardin at your service, ma'am."

"I'm pleased to make your acquaintance, Mr. Hardin. I am Kate Kerrigan."

"Unfortunately, Wes is only passing through," Cobb

said. "We knew each other in the past, and I assure you he is a true gentleman of the South."

Kate decided to be a little flirtatious. Her eyelashes fluttering, she said, "And what makes a Southern gentleman, Mr. Hardin?"

"What makes any gentleman, Mrs. Kerrigan? He must know how to ride, to fence, to shoot, to box, to swim, to row, and to dance. If attacked by ruffians, a gentlemen should be able to defend himself and also to defend ladies from their insults."

Kate gave a little curtsy. "Then I am content to be in your company, Mr. Hardin. Our home is a humble one and the dinner prepared is plain in the extreme, but you are welcome to dine with us."

Hardin gave another bow. "I am honored, ma'am. It will be my pleasure."

Standing close by, Count Andropov smiled to himself in the gloom. It seemed that Queen Victoria's influence had finally reached the United States. People of a certain class didn't converse so much as dance a graceful minuet with words.

After dinner and profuse thanks to Kate, the words John Wesley Hardin spoke to Frank Cobb were direct and to the point. "Saw some sights, Frank. I didn't want to mention them in front of the ladies."

"You see a big herd, Wes?"

"Sure did. It looked like it was being driven south toward Old Mexico."

"South? You sure about that?"

"That's what it looked like to me. Them boys were having a time keeping the herd together."

"What other sights, Wes?" Cobb asked.

"Maybe we should move away from the cabin," Hardin said.

Once they'd put distance between themselves and the cabin and were in moon-laced shadow, Hardin leaned closer and said, "I never saw the like before and I ain't likely to see it again."

Cobb waited until Hardin tied into his story.

"I rode out of some mesquite and there standing in front of me was a man and a woman. The man was a little feller, dressed real strange, and he had a leather mask on his face. He was holding what I took to be a rifle, a kind of brass thing with pipes all over it. The little feller had a pack of some kind on his back, connected to the rifle with a leather hose."

"Strange kind of rifle," Cobb said.

"Stranger still was what come out of the barrel. It shot flame, Frank, streams of scarlet fire like water coming out of a hose."

"My God, what was he doing with such a thing? Hunting?"

"Hell no. He was burning human bodies, two of them. They'd been stripped and were charred black, like how you'd see steaks left in the pan for too long. And the stink of burning flesh was real bad. Hell, I can still smell it."

Curious, Cobb asked, "Then what happened?"

"What happened was, they saw me." Hardin slapped the Colts in their shoulder holsters. "I was wearing these so I wasn't scared none, but I was spooked, that feeling you get in a graveyard at night, but I didn't let it show. 'What are you folks up to?' says I. And the woman shows me this painted pot and she says, 'I'm burning my brother's body so I can collect his ashes in this urn and take them back east for burial.' She points to the other body and says, 'He's the one who shot him. His ashes can lay where they fall.'"

Hardin offered Frank his cigar case and when both men were smoking he said, "I'd give all I own or will ever own for one night with that woman, Frank. Man, she was a sight to see. Anyway, I was kinda wary of the little man in the mask with the fire gun, so I didn't put any kind of suggestion to her."

"What did you do?"

"They didn't seem inclined to talk so I asked if I was on the right trail for the Kerrigan Ranch. I said a friend of mine was working there and I wanted to get reacquainted. The woman pointed the way and then she said, 'Tell that gal Kate Kerrigan that I'll be coming for her.'"

"Just that?" Cobb asked.

"Ain't it enough? The lady looked real mean when she said it."

"It don't make any sense. The woman who made the threat is Savannah St. James, but she's driving her herd south, away from the Kerrigan Ranch."

"Frank, nothing made sense back there," Hardin said. "They got a big carriage, looks like a steam locomotive with part of a car attached. But it doesn't ride on rails. It's got six wheels, each taller than me, two in the front and four at the back."

"What the hell is it?"

"Damned if I know. But it's a monster." Hardin touched his hat brim. "I'm on the scout, Frank, so I got to be moving on. I'll look you up again sometime." He made to swing into the saddle, then stopped. "Hell I almost forgot. I saw Henry Brown over to Fort Davis way. He'd just killed a man and was one day ahead of the Rangers and a few hours in front of a hemp posse of the dead man's kin. We got to talking about me coming here and he said for you to look out for him."

"Henry's always welcome at this ranch." Cobb touched his hat brim. "Ride easy, Wes. It was good to see you again."

Hardin swung into the saddle. "Yeah, and you too, Frank. You too."

Chapter Thirty-six

The young Rurales captain sat his horse on a rise and watched through his field glasses as ten thousand head of cattle passed below him. The herd seemed to cover the entire desert, a harsh, arid land dominated by yucca, creosote, mesquite, and thornbush, hemmed in by high mountain ranges. It was not cattle country and could not sustain such a vast number.

As far as he could tell, vaqueros and white men pushed the herd, though the billowing dust cloud made it difficult to tell.

Behind the captain was a ten-man detail, dressed in the Rurales field costume of wide sombreros and crossed ammunition belts. Each man carried a model 1866 Winchester and one or more revolvers. They were a tough, hard-bitten bunch and more than a match for any bandito south or north of the border.

What he witnessed was an invasion of Mexican territory, and the captain saw his duty clear. The herd must go back to where it had come from.

The captain waved his men forward and led the way down the rise, his horse kicking up plumes of sand from the surface of the slope. Imagining that he was dealing with wayward Texas punchers, he didn't reach for the rifle slung on his back.

It would prove to be a fatal mistake.

"Yeah, I see them," Jack Hickam said to Pete Slicer. "Go round up the boys. Leave the vaqueros to drive the herd." Hickam kneed his horse forward fifty yards out of the dust and waited for the Rurales, his hands on the saddle horn.

The Mexicans arrived when the captain drew rein and his Rurales formed up in line behind him. Following the lead of their officer, they didn't unship their Winchesters.

"Ah, señor, a good day to you." the captain said in perfect English.

"And to you," Hickam said. "What can I do for you, General?"

The officer smiled. "Alas, I am a mere captain."

Hickam grinned, aware that Slicer and the others had ridden up and were behind him. "Well, a nicely set-up young feller like you should be a general."

The captain's smile slipped a little. "You are most gracious, señor. It seems that you've lost your way. You have crossed the border into Mexico."

"Well, dang me. Is that a fact?" Hickam asked.

"Yes, it is a fact, señor. You must turn your herd and

return to Texas. There is nothing out here for cattle, no water or grass. They will all die very quick, I think."

Hickam's grin widened. "Well, see, that's the plan, general. This is a diseased herd and we want them to die . . . as you say, very quick."

"Not on Mexican soil." Unlike his men, the captain wore a tan-colored uniform tunic with his rank on the collar. The day was hot and dark arcs of sweat had formed in his armpits. "I order you to turn this herd, señor."

"And if I don't?" Hickam said.

"Then I will arrest you and take you to Chihuahua City for trial."

Hickam sneered. "On what charge?"

"An armed invasion of the sovereign state of Mexico, señor. Such an offense carries the penalty of death by firing squad."

"Well, soldier boy, that ain't gonna happen."

The captain saw it then, the fierce, killing light in Jack Hickam's eyes. He knew he didn't have time to unlimber his rifle and went for the Colt in a flap holster on his hip. His fingertips barely touched leather before Hickam shot him off his horse.

The surviving guns earned their wages.

The Rurales line broke under a barrage of fire. Skilled draw fighters were deadly at close range and half the Mexicans were killed in the first volley. The rest managed to draw their own revolvers and return fire. Two of the Texans went down. Slicer, shooting a pair of Colts off the back of his rearing horse, killed three of the Mexicans and Hickam and the others took care of the rest.

Dust and gun smoke drifted across the battlefield and Hickam let out a rebel yell that was echoed by a couple other guns. He swung out of the saddle, slid his Winchester out of the boot, and stepped to the wounded captain. The young man raised a hand in supplication, begging for mercy. Hickam, holding the rifle like a pistol, scattered his brains with a single shot. He stepped from body to body, put three of the wounded out of their misery, then slid his rifle back into the boot.

"Vaqueros have lit out," Slicer said, nodding in the direction of a rapidly diminishing dust cloud to the south.

"Let 'em. The herd is already drifting all over the place. Let 'em die here." Hickam motioned Slicer closer. "The two of ours who went down?"

"Both dead," Slicer said.

"We shed the blood and Savannah St. James takes the profit."

"Seems like, Jack."

"Well, it ain't gonna happen, lay to that," Hickam said. "I want the woman, sure, but I also want the money the cattle will bring in Abilene."

"We have to steal them first," Slicer said. "And the money gets divided among those of us who are left."

"Oh, yeah, that's gonna be the way of it." Hickam stared hard at Slicer. "You don't look too good, Pete. The sight of all them dead men bother you?"

Slicer grimaced. "Belly hurts bad. Got the taste of blood in my mouth."

Hickam's laugh was cruel. "Who gets your share of the money, Pete?"

Hickam and the others returned to the *Emperor Maximilian* with eleven horses and the weapons of the dead Rurales. Their own dead they left to rot in the desert sun with the Mexicans.

CHAPTER THIRTY-SEVEN

"So Savannah St. James says she's coming for me." Kate Kerrigan moved around the table.

Cobb nodded. "That's what Wes Hardin just told me."

"And she expects me to cower in my cabin and wait for her. Is that it?"

"It would seem that way, Kate."

"Well, she's got another thought coming. Kate Kerrigan cowers from nobody." Her little chin stubborn, she said, "The very idea!"

Suddenly, Cobb was wary. "Kate . . . what do you have in mind?"

Mary Fullerton placed her coffee cup on the saucer. "Frank, aren't you afraid to ask?"

Cobb looked from her to Kate and back to Mary. "I sure am."

"Well, afraid or not, here's my answer. I'm going out to meet that young lady and I'll say, 'Well, here I am. What are you going to do about it?'"

No surprise there, Cobb thought. "No, Kate. That's a good way to get yourself killed."

"It's also a good way of showing Miss St. James that I'm not afraid of her or her hired gunmen," Kate said stubbornly.

"I can't let you do that, Kate," Cobb said.

Mary's eyes grew wide. "Oh dear."

"Frank, don't ever tell me what I can and cannot do. My mind is made up and there's an end to it. I will hear no more." Kate glared at Mary. "And that includes you, Dr. Fullerton."

Mary raised her teacup to her lips and smiled into the rim. "I'm not saying a word."

"At least let me come with you," Cobb said.

Kate shook her head. "No, Frank. It's all too obvious that you are a man well practiced with the revolver. I intend to use words, not bullets. But I'll take Mose with me if that makes you feel better."

Trace Kerrigan crumbled a sugar cookie in his fingers and watched the crumbs drop onto his plate. Without looking up, he said, "Ma, this will be settled by bullets, not words."

Kate smiled. "Can the Irish not charm the birds out of the trees? I think Miss St. James will listen to reason."

"And if she doesn't?" Cobb asked.

Not giving an inch, Kate said, "Frank, let's not build houses on a bridge we haven't crossed yet."

Kate drew rein under a blue sky as the morning came in clean and the sun already burned like a gold coin. Around her and Moses, the grasslands stretched into hazy distance. She put a spyglass to her eye and scanned the land ahead. "Mose, I see tents and the great steam machine Mr. Hardin mentioned. But I see no cattle. Where is the herd?"

"I don't know, Miz Kerrigan. It's gone."

"I know it's gone, Mose, but gone where?"

Moses shook his head and said nothing.

"Well, let's talk with Miss St. James. I'm sure she can solve the mystery."

Unconvinced, Moses said, "Miz Kerrigan, I don't think we should do this, no."

"Keep your revolver handy, Mose. Words have been known to fail." She thought about taking her Henry from the boot but decided that could be construed as downright unsociable. She left the rifle alone and kneed her horse forward.

Kate wore her English riding habit, a top hat with green gauze around the crown and on her left shoulder a small enamel brooch that displayed the ancient Kerrigan crest and motto, *My God, My King, My Country*. She decided, wrongly as it turned out, that her costume was more than a match for anything Savannah St. James might wear.

As Kate and Moses rode closer, five men left their tents and watched them. All wore a gun like they were born to it.

Kate drew rein and said in as a commanding voice as she could muster, "My name is Kate Kerrigan. I'm here to speak to the woman who calls herself Savannah St. James."

Pete Slicer, very ill, his face ashen, gave a little bow.

"That can be arranged, ma'am. If you'll just set and bide awhile."

That was unnecessary. A door of the *Emperor Maximilian* opened and Savannah stood in the doorway. Beside her, Kate heard Moses's sharp intake of breath.

The woman wore an over-the-bust corset of fine red leather, cinched at the waist with six straps on each side, fastened with ornate bronze buckles. From one of the lower straps hung a gold pocket watch. Her black boots reached to the middle of her thighs and were decorated with metal butterflies. In her left hand, she carried a riding crop, in the other a Remington derringer, engraved and gold-plated. She spoke to Slicer. "Who is this person?"

"My name is Mrs. Kate Kerrigan. I know yours and judging by the goods you have on show, I know what you are." Kate smiled sweetly.

"You are most gracious, Mrs. Kerrigan. Or may I call you Kate?"

"Please do. Come anywhere near my ranch and I'll kill you . . . ah, Savannah."

"Not before I tear your eyes out, my dear. May I offer you tea?"

"That would be nice. I'd like to poison yours, you know."

"And I yours. Is oolong to your taste?"

"You're a trollop, Savannah, and you dress like a jezebel. Why yes, oolong would be divine."

"Then please come inside, but do trip and break your damned neck, *por favor*," Savannah said, smiling.

Kate dismounted and stepped into the *Emperor*.

A large man sprawled on a leather couch gave her an insolent grin. "So this is Kate Kerrigan? I reckon one day soon I'll have some fun with you."

"Get out, Jack," Savannah ordered.

Hickam scowled. "That's no way to talk to—"

"Get out, I said. We'll pick up where we left off later."

With an ill grace, Hickam rose, slipped his suspenders over his shoulders, and picked up his hat and gun belt. "I'm leaving, but I'll be back."

"Jack, Mrs. Kerrigan consorts with Negroes. See that the one outside gets a cup of coffee or something." After the big man left, Savannah said, "Please sit, Kate, though as a rule, I don't allow the Irish anywhere near my table." She motioned to the urn on the table. "You don't mind if my brother Reuben joins us? He did love taking tea with the ladies."

"You are most kind to ask, Savannah. I don't mind at all, but what a sorry piece of white trash you are."

Savannah rang a bell and when her maid appeared, she said, "Tea for two, Leah. Oolong if you please, but don't use the best china."

After the maid curtsied and left, Kate said, "I love your perfume, Savannah. French, isn't it? I know it's used mostly by those who work at night."

"Then you must try some, Kate." Savannah rang the bell again. "Leah, the *Eau de Minuit* please. I know it's the cheap stuff, but my guest won't know the difference."

Leah curtsied, left, and quickly returned with the perfume.

Savannah dabbed it onto Kate's neck. "There, just where the pulse is, my dear. It brings out the musky bouquet and smells heavenly on you. I so look forward to putting a hemp noose around that pretty neck and hearing it go"—she snapped her fingers—"*snap!*"

Kate sniffed. "Really? I don't like this perfume at all, Savannah. It makes me smell like you, a cheap woman. Ah, here is Leah with the tea, at last."

Savannah poised sugar tongs over Kate's cup. "One lump or two? Why did you kill my brother?"

"Just one, Savannah, thank you. Because he was a lowlife who tried to rape me."

"Do make a trial of the oolong, my dear," Savannah said. "I value your opinion. And Leah's sponge cake is simply delicious. As though anyone could rape a red-headed Irish trollop like you. How many men have you had, Kate? Dozens? Scores? No doubt, you told Reuben it was available and you killed him when he tried to get at it. Ah, how is the sponge cake?"

Kate kept up her end of the conversation. "Almost as good as my own. You are a most thoughtful host. Your brother was an animal, Savannah. He needed killing. By the way, the oolong is just perfect."

"I'm told that oolong comes all the way from Cathay and that its name means Black Dragon. Isn't that most interesting? I'm going to kill you, Kate, and take everything that's yours. But not today, my dear. Revenge is a dish best served cold, and I'll come when you least expect it. More tea?"

"Please. From this day forward, I'll always expect you, Savannah."

"Let me add sugar for you," Savannah said. "There, one lump. Perhaps if you hadn't murdered my brother, I might have taken just your herd. But now that's quite impossible. You must die, dear Kate."

"May I have another piece of sponge cake?" Kate asked.

"Please do. I like to watch the crumbs fall from your mouth."

"You are most generous, Savannah. Where is your herd?"

"Gone." Savannah waved an elegant hand. "In Mexico somewhere. The cattle were diseased and few would have lasted through the coming winter. Of course, that is why I'm taking yours."

Kate took a sip from her cup. "The tea is most enjoyable. So you're a thief as well as a trollop."

"You're most welcome, Kate. Do you know that you're trespassing on my land? You're a common squatter. Pray, do you henna your hair that color?"

"It's my natural red, Savannah. Of course, you wear a wig, don't you? And how can I squat on open range?"

"Because, my dear, I have a land grant from the late Emperor Maximilian of Mexico giving me all the range between the Pecos and the big fork of the San Saba. It's all quite legal, I assure you. And no, I don't wear a wig, but I'm used to the petty jealousies of envious women. Can't I tempt you to more tea?"

"No. I must be going. A Mexican land grant is worthless in the state of Texas. Doesn't such a tight corset pinch your fat when it pushes your bosoms up like that?"

"I know the grant is worthless, but before you can contest it, the spring will be here and I'll be gone with your cattle. And by then, you'll be dead. No, the corset is quite comfortable, though flat-chested women like you may find it hard to understand."

Kate rose to her feet. "Well, Savannah, thank you for the lovely tea and I look forward to our next meeting. I doubt we'll be so friendly then."

Savannah glanced out the window. "A mist is coming down, Kate. Are you sure you don't want to stay for dinner and spend the night? I believe Leah has prepared a potato dish. Isn't that what poor Irish peasants eat?"

"Once again, you are most gracious, Savannah, but I won't spend the night in a brothel."

Savannah glanced at the watch attached to her corset. "La, how time flies, even when one is bored." She rang a bell and when Leah promptly appeared, said, "Mrs. Kerrigan is leaving. Make sure you wash the cups well." She smiled at Kate. "I'll see you to the door."

Kate stepped outside. Moses still sat his horse and the mist, gray as a ghost, rose to the animal's belly. There was no sign of Hickam and the other guns, though she heard ribald laughter from one of the tents.

Moses dismounted and assisted Kate into the saddle.

"Next time we meet, I'll kill you, Kate," Savannah said. "Now please ride carefully. One just can't tell what dangers may be hidden in a fog."

"People have tried to kill me before, but I'm still here, Savannah."

"Then I'll succeed where others have failed." Savannah said to Moses, "Guard your mistress well, boy. Her life is very important to me."

Kate looked beyond the woman and saw Hickam walk toward them. "Your male friend is coming, Savannah. He must miss you."

For a moment, Savannah St. James dropped her flinty façade and seemed almost dejected. "He wants my body and what I can give him. All my life, I've sold myself to gentlemen, and now I must give it freely to a sweating, stinking hog." She smiled. "Your death is costing me dearly, Kate Kerrigan."

CHAPTER THIRTY-EIGHT

Moses Rice was concerned. "Mist is getting thicker, Miz Kerrigan. I can't see no farther than my hoss's ears."

"Are we still headed east, Mose?" Kate said, a shadowy figure in the murk.

"I got no way of telling. Even the hosses don't know which way is which." Moses looked around him. "It sure is quiet though."

"I've never seen a fog this thick. We'll find a place to shelter until it drifts away. It's going to be dark soon, so the sooner we stop the better."

"Miz Kerrigan, this is flat country. There ain't a place to shelter, no," Moses said. "All we can do is git off'n these hosses and sit right where we're at. I'd sure hate to fall into a ravine or some such."

Although Mose couldn't see her, Kate nodded. "Dismount, Mose. We'll wait it out."

She and Moses sat together, holding the reins of their horses. Visibility was down to a few yards. With no wind, the mist just hung there, unmoving, surrounding them like mother-of-pearl walls.

The deathly quiet made Moses whisper, "I could sure use a cup of coffee."

"Didn't they offer you one at the St. James place?"

"No, ma'am. That big feller said he wouldn't give coffee to a nigger man. It's what he said, all right. Left me there with no coffee. Made me feel bad."

Kate felt a surge of sympathy. "Mose, when we get home you can have all the coffee you want."

"And them sugar cookies that Miz Salas bakes, huh?"

"All you can eat."

"Then dang, Miz Kerrigan, I sure wish this fog would lift in a hurry."

The mist was so thick Moses couldn't see Kate's smile.

Ten minutes later, like a firefly in the mist, Kate saw a lantern bobbing toward them.

"I see it, Miz Kerrigan," Moses said, his eyes round as coins. "I got my revolver ready."

Kate stood and slid her Henry from the boot. Fingers of fog clutched at her. Despite the murk, coyotes in the distance yipped their hunger, hunting by smell.

"See anything?" Moses asked quietly.

"Only the lamp. It's coming straight toward us."

"Evil things in the fog, Miz Kerrigan. Things that ain't for good Christian folks to see."

"I think we'll see them soon enough, Mose." Kate waited until the lantern drew closer and was transformed from a firefly into a halo of orange light, then yelled, "Halt! Who goes there?" She turned to Moses. "Silly thing to say, huh?"

She was answered almost immediately. "My name is Marmaduke Tweng and I'm a steam engineer. I have a man with me."

"Who is he?" Kate called.

"Just a sickly fellow looking for a private space to kill himself."

"Come on in and don't let me see you with a gun in your hand," Kate ordered.

Another man's voice spoke. "Lady, in this fog, you couldn't see a fallen star in my hand. Name's Pete Slicer."

Kate was alarmed. "Are you one of Savannah St. James's gunmen?"

"I was. Now I'm just looking for a place to die."

"Well, you've chosen the right spot," Kate said. "Come in slow."

The light bobbed closer and then the mist parted to reveal a small, gnome-like man in a leather coat and a top hat with goggles on the front of the crown. He carried a lantern at the end of a willow branch that bent under the weight. Beside him, Pete Slicer stood by his horse, the reins in his gun hand.

Slicer bowed. "I'm sorry to intrude, ma'am. But we didn't expect to meet fellow travelers in the fog."

"Earlier I was at Savannah St. James's locomotive . . . whatever you wish to call it. I believe you saw me there."

"I don't doubt it," Slicer said. "I have been sick in my

tent from a cancer deep in my belly. The pain has gotten so bad I've decided to end it."

"I told Mr. Slicer that because of the *Emperor Maximilian*'s tendency to bog down in places, I know the lay of the land around these parts," Tweng said. "I offered to find him a suitable place to self-destruct and promised to say a prayer over his remains."

Kate was skeptical. "Did Savannah order you to do this?"

"Oh dear, no. Miss St. James has no hold over me. I'm an engineer. I plan to build a steam-engine flying machine that could have carried Mr. Slicer and myself above the fog, but I haven't perfected it yet. Thus, we were forced to set out on foot." Tweng turned to Slicer. "Shall we continue on our quest?" He consulted the huge iron watch that hung around his neck. "It's almost midnight. *Tempus fugit* and all that."

"Mr. Slicer, you are no friend of mine, but I will not see a man, even an enemy, blow his own brains out. There is a fine doctor at my ranch. Let Dr. Fullerton examine you before you make a final decision."

Slicer nodded. "That is most thoughtful, ma'am, but I'm afraid it's too late. The cancer has taken its course."

"Let the doctor determine that. If she says the cancer has no cure, then you can scatter your brains with my blessing, Mr. Slicer."

Tweng smiled a wispy smile. "One of the great pleasures in my life is to meet intelligent women. What you say makes a great deal of sense, Mrs. Kerrigan. I toyed with the idea of operating on the patient while he was under the influence of morphine, replacing his cancerous stomach with one made of bronze and glass. I calculated the valves and cogwheel gearing, but the power source still eludes me. How does one make a steam engine the size of a silver dollar? And what about proper lubrication and maintenance?" He shook his head. "For now I implore you to give the doctor a try, Mr. Slicer. You have nothing to lose."

Kate frowned. "You mentioned my name, Mr. Tweng. Do you know me?"

"We haven't been formally introduced, dear lady, but I provided the steam that warmed the water for your tea. Miss St. James has spoken of you often, Mrs. Kerrigan, and I fear she means you ill."

"She's made that pretty obvious," Kate muttered. She turned to Slicer. "What's your decision, Mr. Slicer?"

"When the fog lifts, if I'm still breathing, I'd like to be examined by your doctor."

Marmaduke Tweng clapped his gloved hands. "Excellent! And now on a more pleasant note I have here"— he reached into the pocket of his leather coat—"an excellent bottle of cider of my own making, a delightful combination of ripe California apples and a steam press. I suggest we all sit down and enjoy this nectar."

"Not for me," Slicer said. "Drinking hurts my belly."

"Give me the bottle," Kate Kerrigan said, reaching out a hand. "After the day I've had, I could sure use a drink."

Chapter Thirty-nine

In the afterglow of his wild mattress time with Savannah St. James, Jack Hickam accepted her order that he check on the Hunt cattle and search the house for anything of value. After that, he was to burn all the ranch buildings so that Kate Kerrigan would not have a refuge should she by bad luck escape the initial slaughter at her place.

"Leave the herd where it is," Savannah said. "We can't take a chance on the grass around here. It's probably covered in ticks."

Hickam merely touched his hat brim and nodded. "I'll be back. I hope you'll be looking for me."

With practiced ease, Savannah smiled. "Of course I will, big boy. I'll count the hours."

Like hell I will, you filthy, rutting hog.

The fog cleared just before sunup and the morning light that showed the way to the Kerrigan Ranch also lit the trail for Hickam and his four remaining gun hands.

It was way down in the summer and the sun was less hot, the long grass beginning to recapture its greenness. The sky was blue as an upturned Wedgwood bowl and the air, washed clean by the night's mist, smelled of piñón and late blooming wildflowers.

Hickam noticed none of these things. His intent stare was concentrated on the man who stood outside the Hunt ranch house, watching him.

When Hickam rode within hailing distance, the man grinned and called out, "Jack, my ver' good fren'. How good it is to see you again."

The man was a large Mexican, his sombrero pushed back on his head. A yellow bandana worn over his black ringlets was tied at the nape of his neck. He was dressed in the brocaded finery of a well-to-do vaquero. Two pearl-handed Colts rode his hips and a wallet-sized painting on metal of the holy Virgin of Guadalupe hung by a thick steel chain from his neck.

Hickam drew rein. "Surprised to see you here, Arturo. I heard the Rurales had strung you up in the town square at Veracruz. I heard you died like a pig."

Arturo Baxa's grin widened. "Then you heard wrong, my fren'." He shrugged. "For here I am with my compadres." He waved to the half dozen men standing behind him, their hands close to their holstered guns."

Hickam nodded. "I see Gustavo Oliveros skulking there. Heard you robbed a bank down Uvalde way last month, Gustavo, and killed a woman teller. She had four young *niños*, or so I was told."

Oliveros was a tall thin man with dead eyes. "How come I haven't killed you by now, Jack? That is a situation I must remedy as soon as possible."

"Come, come," Baxa said. "There is no need for harsh words. We are all compadres here, brothers under the skin. Is that not so, Jack?"

"Whatever you say, Arturo. Why are you here?"

"Cattle, *mi amigo*. Here there are cows for the taking and I will drive them across the border and sell them in Chihuahua or Piedras Negras, maybe so."

"The cows are mine, Arturo." Hickam ordered his men to dismount.

"Ah, perhaps a mistake has been made," Baxa said after a while.

"You made it, Arturo."

The Mexican thought about that. After a few moments, he said, "Half, Jack. I will take half the cows, and then, as always, we part *buenos amigos*."

Hickam shook his head. "No deal, Arturo. The cattle stay right here."

Baxa spat into the dirt. "Jack, you are making Arturo very angry. You are his good fren' and he doesn't wish to be angry with you. We are both banditos, are we not? I will take just two hundred cows.

"You will take nothing, amigo," Hickam said. "Now you and your boys git on them horses and ride."

For a moment, it looked like Arturo Baxa would back down. He made a half turn as though he was about to speak to his men, but then his hands dived for his guns.

Jack Hickam was way too fast. He saw the metal plaque on Baxa's chest jump as his bullet went through it. Then a ball burned across his right shoulder and a second cracked close to his ear as Oliveros fired at him. Hickam swung on the man but the four draw fighters were shooting and the Mexican went down. The gunmen kept up a steady fire, their trigger cadence as fast and regular as a snare drum in a regimental band. The tune they played was death and before the smoke cleared six men lay dead on the ground and Arturo Baxa was dying. The only casualty on the American side was Hickam's burned shoulder.

Hickam stepped to Baxa and looked down at the man, but the Mexican seemed not to notice. He held the plaque to his face and stared at it in strange disappointment. Hickam's ball had put a neat hole through the Virgin of Guadalupe. Baxa looked up at Hickam and an incredulous smile touched his bloodstained lips. Then he fell back and died.

"You're hit, Jack," one of the gunmen said.

"It's a scratch. Round up their horses and guns." Hickam grinned. "Hell, at this rate we're gonna get rich off dead Messkins." He looked around at his gunmen. "Anybody see a cow?"

"I did," a man said.

"How did it look?" Hickam asked.

The man shrugged. "Like a cow."

"Good, then we've inspected the herd. Now we'll burn this place to the ground and throw Arturo and his boys into the fire. We ain't got time to bury a bunch of damn greasers."

CHAPTER FORTY

"You don't have stomach cancer, Mr. Slicer," Dr. Mary Fullerton said. "You have a bleeding ulcer that's very far advanced."

Pete Slicer's face showed relief and anxiety. "And what does that mean, Doc?"

"It means you're going to have to change your behavior if you expect any kind of cure. What do you eat?"

Slicer shrugged. "Whatever I can get."

"Bacon and beans. Greasy stews. Burned steaks?"

"Yup, all o' them."

"Alcohol?"

"Sure. Whiskey, rum, gin, beer, whatever is available. Saloons ain't always well-stocked."

"And you smoke?" Dr. Fullerton asked pointedly.

"Cigars, cigarettes, a pipe, whatever—"

"Is available. Yes, I know." The doctor's lovely face grew stern. "All that ends of right now, Mr. Slicer. No smoking, no drinking, and you will watch your diet."

Slicer grinned. "And if I don't?"

"If the ulcer is untreated it can cause severe bleeding

and such a hemorrhage can be fatal. An ulcer can also turn cancerous. That will kill you more slowly but much more painfully." Dr. Fullerton smiled. "Do I make myself perfectly clear?"

Slicer swallowed hard. "What do I do, Doc?"

"I already told you Mr. Slicer. No smoking, drinking, or unhealthy food."

"Hell, Doc, what do I eat? Begging your pardon for my language."

"I'll make up a diet sheet for you and you must stick to it. Soft boiled eggs with a little toast, oatmeal—"

"You mean the stuff I feed my hoss?"

"Made with water and salt, oatmeal is quite tasty and you can add milk if you like. Cornmeal mush, custards, plain boiled rice, chicken broth cooked without skin . . . it's all on the diet sheet. And one other thing, Mr. Slicer, you must avoid all worry and anxiety."

Slicer was incredulous. "Doctor, I sell my gun. You know how worrisome it is to draw down on a man and wonder if he's finally the one that's half a second faster on the draw than me?"

"If you wish your ulcer to heal, then you must avoid those situations," Dr. Fullerton said. "One thing more. Once you stop drinking and eat properly you'll lose weight, and that is never a bad thing." She smiled. "That will be two dollars. I'd like to see you again in a week."

"Doc, you're the only thing standing between me and death," Slicer said. "I'm not going anywhere. Where can I find a couple boiled eggs?"

* * *

"I suppose he's quite good-looking in a rough and ready sort of way," Kate Kerrigan said to her friend.

"He's a patient, Kate. That's all," Mary Fullerton said. "And he's one of Savannah St. James's men, remember."

"The way he's been mooning around your surgery, it seems that Mr. Slicer has turned a new leaf. Not that I trust him."

"Slicer, I don't trust you," Cobb said. "And when I don't trust a man, bad things can happen."

"Hell, Frank, I'm not even wearing a gun. Doc Fullerton said I have to give up revolver fighting until my ulcer heals." He took out a large bronze pocket watch that he'd bought from Count Andropov. He consulted the time. "I've been on a special diet now for . . . forty-five minutes."

"How many men have you killed, Pete?" Cobb asked.

"Too many. Let it go at that."

"I don't want you around here. I want you far away from the Kerrigan Ranch."

"That's not how it's gonna be, Frank. I'm staying close to the doctor. She's the only one that can save me."

"If I decide to kill you, Pete, Mary won't be able to save you."

"I'm not gonna fight you, Frank." Slicer's face twisted in pain. "Now you're making me nervous and my ulcer is starting to hurt. Doc Fullerton said that's what would happen."

Cobb shook his head. "You don't have a nerve in your body, Pete. Now listen up real good because here's how hard times could come down on you. You make any kind of move against Kate Kerrigan, I'll kill you. Make any kind of move against any member of her family, I'll kill you. Make any kind of move—"

"I get the picture, Frank," Slicer said, irritated. "I don't intend to make any kind of move against anybody."

"Then see you keep that picture in your head, Pete. I'm not a patient or forgiving man."

"You won't catch me wearing a gun," Slicer said.

"I don't care, Pete. Gun or no gun, I'll kill you just the same."

"Frank, I saw you talking with Pete Slicer," Kate said.

"Just passing the time of day, Kate."

"You don't lie very well, Frank. I can see it in your eyes."

"I don't trust him," Cobb said. "He hired on as a gun with Savannah St. James and he runs with Jack Hickam, a man even meaner than he is."

Kate changed the subject. "I want to talk to you about something, Frank."

"Does it concern Slicer? If it does, I'll—"

"No, it's not about Slicer. It's about us, all the people here at the ranch. How many gunmen does Savannah St. James have?"

"I don't know. But I reckon what she has are the best."

"And who do we have?"

Cobb hesitated only a moment. "Me. Trace is good with a rifle and he'll stand. We can depend on Moses Rice and in a pinch Count Andropov, even though he's as crazy as a bedbug. Quinn is young, but he can shoot pretty good. And there's Marco Salas, but he's not gun savvy."

"And me," Kate pointed out.

"And you. But I'd rather keep you out of it."

"If my sons are in the fight, I'll be right with them. Do we stand a chance against hired guns, Frank?"

"No."

"Then what do we do?"

"You won't like my answer, Kate."

"Try me."

"Savannah St. James will be gone come next spring," Cobb said. We pull out, all of us, and winter in San Antone. Then, in the early summer—"

"We come back and start all over again."

"Yeah. That's what we do, Kate."

"Turn tail and run." She didn't like it one bit.

"That's the way of it. Hurt pride, but still aboveground."

"I won't do it. I won't cut a hole in the wind, running away from what's mine. I'll stay right here on my own ground and fight, even if it's just me and my sons."

"That's a helluva thing to say to me, Kate."

She lowered her head, not wanting Frank to see the tears in her eyes. "I know it is. And I'm sorry, Frank. I didn't mean a word of it."

Cobb lifted up her chin with his bent forefinger. "We'll stick together and we'll get through this, Kate."

Kate rubbed her tears away with the back of her hand. "It's the waiting that's getting to me. Having to stand helplessly by until Savannah St. James decides to make her next move."

"She'll come soon and then one way or another it will be over."

"When the smoke clears, we'll be the ones still standing. Won't we Frank? I need you to tell me that we'll all be alive."

Cobb nodded. But he didn't say a word.

BOOK THREE
The Reckoning

CHAPTER FORTY-ONE

Hack Rivette had murdered three people since Frank Cobb had run him off the Kerrigan Ranch. He was lying on his belly on the grass, contemplating killing another.

The big man who went in and out the door of the strange steam carriage seemed to be the bull of the woods. And the way the shapely woman in the scarlet robe fawned on him confirmed that impression.

The woman herself made Rivette's mouth water. His needs were few and simple—he wanted the woman in the scarlet robe and all that went along with her.

The money he'd netted from killing the preacher and his wife up near Fort Worth was all spent. In Johnson County, he'd shot a sodbuster off his horse and found just eighty cents in his pockets. He'd later sold the horse to a slaughterer for five dollars. Hard times all right. But Rivette figured things were shaping up.

He rose and untied his horse from a mesquite bush. He dusted himself off and climbed into the saddle. It was time to make his move and whatever came next could only be a change for the better.

* * *

A pistol fighter looking for work? Jack Hickam watched the big man ride closer and decided that was the case. Bad times were coming down all over West Texas and Reconstruction had cast up a tide of flotsam and jetsam. The huge, uncurried brute with the belt gun was obviously one of them.

A careful man, Hickam called out his boys and waited for the rider to get closer. He spoke when the rider reined in. "Howdy,"

Rivette nodded, not liking what he saw. *Hell, does this part of Texas grow nothing but draw fighters?*

"Looking for work? Name's Jack Hickam. I do the hiring around here."

Hell's fire, more bad news. Jack Hickam had a big rep and was a gun to be reckoned with. Rivette decided he'd better back up and talk pretties. "Yes, sir, looking for work." He grinned. "They call me Hack Rivette and I've been riding the grub line this past three-month. I'm feeling mighty gaunt."

Hickam's eyes flicked to the Colt on the big man's hip. It was well cared for, with a long Texas barrel and expensive leather. "You're carrying iron, Mr. Rivette. Can you do anything with it?"

"I get by," Rivette said. "I was fast enough to put the crawl on Frank Cobb a spell back."

Hickam shook his head. "Never heard of the gent."

"He's a gun. Or at least he thinks he is."

"Plenty of them around." Hickam nodded, making up his mind. "Light and set. Two hundred dollars when the job is done. There's bacon and beans in the pot over by the tents and horse lines."

"What's the job?" Rivette asked.

"You'll find out soon enough."

"I saw him through the window and didn't like the look of him. Is he to be trusted?" Savannah St. James asked Hickam.

"Yeah, I think he's to be trusted, and if you didn't like the look of him neither will Kate Kerrigan. With all that hair and beard, he'd scare any woman. Besides, if he don't work out, I'll kill him."

He and Savannah lay in bed, a foldout cot that doubled as a sofa. Naked as a seal, her hair damp with sweat, Savannah watched the rise and fall of Hickam's hairy chest as he breathed and she smelled the rank odor of the man. Marmaduke Tweng had constructed a network of jointed steam pipes under the mattress to heat the bed in winter. But in the waning days of summer they were not needed. The interior of the *Emperor Maximilian* was hot and close and Savannah was irritable.

"I've reached a decision," she said.

"What's that?" Hickam asked.

"Kate Kerrigan has lived long enough. I'm going to end it."

"Just set the day." Hickam grinned. "I'm looking forward to it."

Savannah's arms waved in the air like snakes. "Yesss! We strike and then there's no more prissy, stuck-up

Mrs. Kerrigan and her spawn. I'm sure she dyes her hair, you know."

Hickam leaned up on an elbow. "When do we go, Savannah?"

"Sunday. I'm sure we can catch her on her knees praying and that is just so exquisite. Then she's all yours, Jack."

"Two days from now. That sets just fine with me. You won't be jealous if you see me use another woman?"

"Not so long as you kill her afterward."

"You got no worries on that score." Hickam flexed the thumbs and fingers of his huge hands. "Just leave that to me."

Savannah smiled. "That's why I love you so much, Jack. You're so . . . so masterful."

CHAPTER FORTY-TWO

Moses Rice saw Kate Kerrigan in the little cemetery on the rise behind the cabin and was troubled. She stood very still and stared west, her red hair and bright green skirt streaming in the high wind.

Terrible dreams had disturbed Moses's sleep the last few nights and he'd wakened in the darkness very much afraid, the dying coals of Marco Salas's forge casting a scarlet hell-light around him. Should he tell Miz Kerrigan that in his dream, he'd seen her dead body and the bodies of her children and that the wheels of a great machine that belched steam crushed them into the ground? It had been a dreadful dream.

Moses stood undecided about what to do. Miz Kerrigan was still on the rise and maybe she should know. She had the gift, as he did, but maybe her dreams were more pleasant and that would reassure him. His mind made up, he walked toward the rise. He had the reassuring weight of the Colt's Dragoon in his waistband and the white clouds that scudded across the blue sky were a good sign. But still, he carried a heavy burden and the memory of the dreams gave him no peace.

Kate heard footsteps behind her. She turned and smiled. "Mose, what are you doing up here?"

"Saw you, Miz Kerrigan, but I didn't want to disturb you, no."

"You're not disturbing me, Mose." Her eyes searched his face. "But you look troubled and you brought your pistols."

Mose stared at his shuffling feet. "I'm having bad dreams, Miz Kerrigan. I see everybody, all of us, dead."

Kate said nothing.

"You have the gift. Have you dreamed a terrible dream?"

Kate smiled and took the black man's hand. "Yes, I've had dreams and like you I've seen things. There, where the cabin stands, I saw a great mansion with four white pillars outside. I've seen gardens around the house and fat cattle in the pastures. I see my sons grown to manhood, tall and straight, and my daughters as pretty as a field of bluebonnets. And I see you, Mose, in an armchair on the porch telling my grandchildren what the land was like in the olden days when Texas was wild. I see all those things and I will make then happen, Mose. And you will help me."

"Is that really how it's going to be, Miz Kerrigan, just like you dream it?"

"Yes, Mose. That's exactly how it will be."

Moses considered that. "I don't think I'll have bad dreams no more, Miz Kerrigan."

Kate smiled. "Let's go back to the cabin and get some coffee."

Marco Salas stepped out of his shop and called to Kate and Moses before they entered the cabin. "I have something to show you, Mrs. Kerrigan."

She stepped into the shop and Marco waved to an object that stood behind the forge. "What do you think?"

"What is it?" Kate asked.

"It's a cannon, Mrs. Kerrigan."

"It's a small cannon," Moses said.

Marco shrugged. "Well, I only had so much iron."

The black cannon barrel was about three feet long, banded by three shining steel hoops. Brass cogwheel gears cranked by a wooden handle apparently adjusted for elevation and the cannon itself was fixed to a round iron platform about the size of a large dinner plate, though it was at least three inches thick. Inlaid into the barrel were the ornate brass initials *KR*.

"This is what the cannon fires, Mrs. Kerrigan." Marco dropped a heavy iron ball about the size of a walnut into her hand. "Thanks to Count Andropov, I have gunpowder and fuse," the blacksmith said. "But only enough for one shot."

"You haven't tested it?" Kate asked.

"No. The count had only a little piece of fuse in his wagon." He grinned. "But I don't need to test the cannon. I will shoot it against our enemies."

"Marco, make sure you stand well back if you ever try to touch that thing off," Kate cautioned.

"It is a fine cannon," Marco said. "See, it says KR on

the barrel for Kerrigan Ranch, and that means it won't fail."

Despite her misgivings, Kate smiled. "Thank you, Marco. It is indeed a fine cannon."

On their way to the cabin Moses said, "I think that is a dangerous thing Marco has built."

Kate nodded and smiled. "Thank God we'll never have to use it."

"Well, maybe next Independence Day," Moses said.

"No. Not even then," Kate said positively.

CHAPTER FORTY-THREE

"The woman lives," Hack Rivette said. "I want her."

"Miss St. James wants her dead and that's the name of that tune," Jack Hickam said. "You don't agree, Rivette, then get on your horse and ride."

Rivette sat in a tent with Hickam and the four Texas guns. He knew it was not the time to push, but he asked, "Who gets her, the St. James woman?"

"She's mine," Hickam said. "You stay away from her."

"Hell, we should all get a taste." Rivette looked around at the guns, seeking their approval, but they avoided eye contact.

"Leave Savannah be or I'll kill you, Rivette." Hickam's eyes telegraphed his thoughts. He was ready to draw if he had to.

Rivette read the signs and said, "I made a joke, Jack. That was all."

Hickam's eyes didn't change any. "Then see you don't make another one. And the Kerrigan woman is mine, at least for a while. You can have her after I finish."

"And then kill her?"

"Yeah. And then you kill her."

"A big waste, Jack. Kill a fine-looking gal like that."

"It's what Savannah St. James wants. How many times do you need to hear that?"

Rivette shrugged. "I got your drift."

Hickam took a swig from the bottle the men in the tent had been passing around. "Go check the horse lines, Rivette. There are still Comanches about."

"Why me?" Rivette asked churlishly.

"Because you're the new man and you haven't proved yourself. Now git and do what you're told."

Hack Rivette stepped out of the tent on a slow burn. He knew he couldn't shade Hickam on a drawdown, but he planned to kill the man and take his woman. *Women,* he corrected himself. That thought made him grin.

He had no intention of walking up and down the horse lines. He wandered close to the *Emperor Maximilian* hoping for a glance of Savannah St. James. The woman was not in sight, but a little man in a leather coat and top hat with goggles in front stood at the rear of what Rivette considered the railroad car. "What the hell are you?"

The little man straightened up. He held the brass handle of a wooden bucket in his hand. "I'm a steam engineer. My name is Marmaduke Tweng."

"Who the hell has a name like that?" Rivette said, deciding to take out his viciously bad mood on the little gnome.

"I do," Tweng said. "My name dates back five hundred years to the First Baron Tweng, a soldier of great distinction in the Scottish Wars of Independence. He fought on the English side, of course, since his name was not Marmaduke MacTweng." He smiled. "A little steam engineer humor there."

"Like I give a damn." Rivette nodded to the bucket. "What you got in your poke?"

"Charcoal for the furnace. The *Emperor Maximilian* will be on the move Sunday—"

"That's the day after tomorrow."

"Yes it is. Very good. I'm firing up the furnace to heat the boiler for the steam, and though charcoal is in short supply around these parts, I can use mesquite in a pinch. It burns very hot and clean but is quite difficult to ignite."

"How come you got all them big pocket watches on your coat?" Rivette asked. "You're a strange cove and no mistake."

Tweng smiled and pointed to his watches one by one. "Austin . . . New York . . . London . . . Berlin . . . Peking . . . and Melbourne, Australia. When I manufacture my steam-powered flying machine, I'll need to know times around the world."

Rivette's big hands bunched into fists. "Flying machines? What the hell are you talking about? You trying to make a fool out of me? I'm gonna beat that smile off your face, you little runt."

"No, you won't."

Rivette turned and saw Savannah standing outside the *Emperor*, the door behind her ajar. She held her gold-plated Remington derringer in her hand.

The big man grinned. "Hell, missy, I was just gonna have a little fun."

"Mr. Tweng is my steam engineer and I set store by

him. Now be off with you." She wore a wasp-waisted leather corset that left little to the imagination.

Rivette walked toward her, grinning. "Maybe it's time you and me sat down for a little talk, missy."

Savannah raised the derringer to eye level. "I believe I can put two shots into your face at this range. You want to roll the dice, mister?"

Hack Rivette was a bully and a braggart, but there was no bottom to him, no real sand. He knew the woman could do exactly as she said and had probably done it before. "You go to hell." He turned on his heel and walked away, his face working. Now he had another score to settle.

"Mr. Tweng, are you quite all right?" Savannah called.

"Just fine," Tweng said, waving a hand.

Savannah smiled. "Maybe I should have shot him."

Tweng nodded. "Maybe you should have, at that."

CHAPTER FORTY-FOUR

"If I remember my military history correctly, a flanking shot can take down a whole row of soldiers," Count Boleslav Andropov offered. "The same principle applies to hired gunmen."

"Then we place my cannon here." Marco Salas jumped, startled. "What was that?"

"Just an owl," the count said. "Wondering who we are."

"It's so dark out here away from the cabin," Marco said.

"Then bring the lantern closer to us." Andropov looked over both shoulders. "Too many ghosts of dead Indians around here."

"Grab an end," Marco directed. "We'll lift the cannon onto the rise."

The count grunted as he lifted. "Damn. It weighs a ton."

Marco said, gasping, "Here, Count, right here."

Andropov groaned.

"Wait a minute. Do you think it's in the right place?"

"Yes, yes, it's in the right place," Andropov said. "Ahhh . . . I hurt. This is yet another ailment I must relate to Dr. Fullerton. Poor, poor Count Andropov, a man of suffering."

The rise stood only three feet above the flat, but Marco's plan was to hide behind the hillock and then, when Savannah St. James's gunmen were in the right position, touch off the cannon.

"When the time comes, I think we will do great execution, Marco. The Cossacks will go down in droves and Mrs. Kerrigan's ranch will be saved."

Marco's teeth flashed white in the darkness. "It is a mighty cannon."

The count didn't think it was a mighty cannon, but to spare the sturdy little Mexican's feelings he said nothing, glad the gloom hid his expression of doubt.

"Count Andropov, we must be vigilant," Marco said. "At the first sign of invaders, we will run here and man the cannon."

"A fine plan," the Russian said. "We will be the first line of defense, though first lines have an unhappy habit of being wiped out."

"Then you must bring your rifle, Count, and sell your life dearly."

Andropov blinked. "Falling for the flag is not quite what I have in mind, Mr. Salas."

But the Mexican wasn't listening. He sighted carefully along the top of the cannon, then clapped his hands. "This is going to be grand."

"Indeed," Count Andropov said, fervently wishing that he'd never left Mother Russia.

* * *

The cabin lamps were lit against the evening darkness as Kate Kerrigan said, "Mose, I have instructions for you that you must carry out to the letter. Do you understand?"

He nodded. "I surely do, Miz Kerrigan."

"Very well then. Now, at the first sign of approaching trouble you will get Ivy and Shannon and take them west on good horses into the brush country."

"But Miz Kerrigan—"

"There you will hide and only come out of hiding when you hear me call out for you. The girls are old enough to appreciate the danger we are in, so they will cooperate."

"But I want to—"

"If you don't hear my voice, then you will know I am dead. You will then use the money I'll give you to get out of West Texas. And no, Mose, you cannot stay here and fight. I need you to save my daughters. They trust you."

"It's a hard thing to leave you in danger, Miz Kerrigan," Moses said. "What about your house?"

"It's only a cramped little cabin with a fancy door, Mose. No great loss."

"You don't mean that, Kate," Frank Cobb said from across the room.

Kate smiled. "Not a word of it, but the lives of my girls must be my first consideration."

Cobb looked at Moses. "Seems like you got it to do, old fellow.

Moses sighed. "I know where my duty lies. It begins and ends with the pretty lady sitting there in her chair."

"Thank you, Mose," Kate said. "I feel better now that you'll take on the job. Ensuring the welfare of two young lives is a heavy responsibility."

Moses nodded and his face split into a smile. "Heaviest I've ever had, I reckon."

"Tonight I'll say a rosary for you, Mose."

"That will surely help, Miz Kerrigan," Moses said.

CHAPTER FORTY-FIVE

"The *Emperor Maximilian* is building steam nicely, Mr. Hickam. He will be ready to go first thing tomorrow morning," Marmaduke Tweng said.

"You sure Savannah will be safe in there once the lead starts flying?" Jack Hickam asked skeptically.

Tweng nodded confidently. "The glass is tempered and will deflect bullets. Now listen to this." He removed a small panel from the side of the *Emperor* near the back wheels and opened a valve. "Hear that?"

"Yeah, I thought I heard water running," Hickam said.

"You heard correctly. At great pressure, the water is forced through copper pipes by steam power and as it goes, it activates little levers that lock the windows in place. Once the *Emperor* starts to roll, I will do the same for the doors. No one can enter until I close the valve and cut off the water."

"Or leave," Hickam pointed out.

"Miss St. James will be quite safe until this dreadful business is over, I assure you."

"Savannah says you have a fire gun," Hickam said.

"Yes, a device of my own invention. Though I'm told that Professor Wilkins of Oxford College in England has made a similar device that's mounted on a gun carriage. He calls it an infernal machine."

"Your gun burns bodies."

"To ash."

"Then make sure you bring it tomorrow, Tweng. You'll have plenty of work for it."

"Will there be many bodies, Mr. Hickam?" Tweng was a timid man at heart.

"A lot. Depend on it." Hickam grinned. "Who burns better, women or men?"

"I'm afraid I don't know," Tweng said, horrified.

"Well then, you'll find out tomorrow, won't you?" Hickam walked away, laughing.

Hack Rivette decided to make his play that day. His shifty eyes were busy. For a while, he stood and watched Marmaduke Tweng shovel charcoal into the *Emperor Maximilian*'s furnace, then use his gloved hand to clang the flap shut again. Over by the tents, Jack Hickam was talking to a man and the man kept nodding, agreeing with whatever Hickam was telling him. Rivette saw a flicker of movement behind one of the *Emperor*'s windows and he swore that Savannah St. James had been naked. All that led to thoughts he shared with no one.

He smiled to himself. The woman would be his soon enough, once Hickam was out of the way. He was living the last few hours of his life, and that gave Rivette a great deal of satisfaction.

Hickam went into the tent and the man he'd been

talking with walked in Rivette's direction. He had field glasses hanging from a strap around his neck. "Mount up. We got a job to do."

"What kind of job?" Rivette asked gruffly.

"We're gonna scout the Kerrigan place, make sure they don't have any unpleasant surprises in store for tomorrow."

"Who says?" Rivette looked at him closely, remembering that they called the man Lefty.

"You know who says. The boss, Jack Hickam."

"He ain't gonna be the boss too much longer," Rivette muttered.

"Well, that's between you and him, I guess." The man was small and thin and wore his Colt on his left hip. "Let's get saddled up."

Rivette decided to go along with it. He planned to kill Hickam in the evening, make one less for dinner. Until then, he'd nothing better to do.

He glanced at the window where he thought he'd seen Savannah, but there was no sign of her.

Count Ivan Boleslav Andropov put his telescope to his eye and studied the advancing riders. He didn't know who or what they were, but he was sure they were up to no good. When the smaller of the two scouted the land ahead of him with field glasses, it confirmed the count's suspicions . . . they could only be a pair of the notorious Savannah St. James's hired gunmen.

Faithful to his promise to Marco Salas, Andropov had taken up a perch in the cemetery above the Kerrigan cabin. Although his .42 Berdan infantry rifle had an effective range of three hundred yards, such a shot was beyond his skill as a marksman. His great fear was that the riders would spot the cannon and ruin their plan for an ambush.

For a few moments, Andropov kneeled in thought, soft grass under him and the late August sun warm on his shoulders. He had no time to raise an alarm. By then, the spies might be gone.

Crouching low, he made his way across the rise and dropped down to the flat on the other side. He ran, still crouched, staying to the thin cover of mesquite and wild oak. A dip in the ground ahead gave him respite. He dropped into the hollow, regained his breath, then bellied up the slope and peered through the long grass.

The two men had moved forward a hundred yards and were very close to the cannon. Andropov felt his heart lurch in his chest. All they had to do was turn their heads a little to the left and they'd see it, but both seemed fixated on the terrain that lay ahead of them, peaceful enough, dotted here and there with grazing cattle.

Andropov nodded to himself as he watched the pair search for improvised defenses that the Kerrigans might have thrown up in haste to guard the cabin and its inhabitants. Then he had a moment of sheer horror. The man with the field glasses swung his horse around and rode directly for the cannon.

Andropov bit his lip hard. *My God, had he seen it?*

The rider drew rein and leaned forward in the saddle. He shaded his eyes with his hand and gazed intently at the shallow rise where the cannon was only partly hidden.

Andropov made up his mind. Desperate times required desperate measures. He pushed the Berdan in front of him and sighted on the small man who had dismounted and was walking toward the rise. The big man on the horse watched him.

Andropov, as he'd been taught, took a breath, let some of it out, then squeezed the Berdan's trigger. The rifle slammed against his shoulder, and at the same instant, he saw the little man drop like a sapling felled by an axe.

His fingers fumbling, the Russian worked the bolt and dropped a paper cartridge into the Berdan's chamber. He slammed the bolt home and his narrowed eyes searched for the big gunman. To his surprise, the man had turned tail and ran, his horse already vanishing into its own dust cloud. Andropov rose to his feet, threw the rifle to his shoulder, and snapped off a shot, but he knew even as he pulled the trigger that it would be a miss. He was right. The man was gone, galloping fast into the distance.

His rifle dangling in his left hand, Andropov stepped to the man he'd shot, who was dead as a cigar store Indian. The Russian looked down at the man and placed his hand on his bloody chest. He shook his head. "Damned Cossack, why did you make poor Andropov kill you?"

The only answer was the sigh of the wind as it rippled the long grass. He heard footsteps behind him and turned, expecting to see Frank Cobb, but it was Marco Salas, his face concerned.

Marco glanced at the dead man. "Is my cannon all right?"

Andropov gave a little nod. "Yes it is. And so am I. Thank you for your concern."

Marco gave a little bow. "I am glad you are unhurt, Count. Who is he?"

"One of the St. James gunmen, I believe. There were two of them, but the other ran away. They were using field glasses to spy on the cabin."

Marco stepped to the cannon and inspected it closely. "It is undamaged, thank God."

Andropov nodded to the dead man. "This one may have seen it. He was walking toward it when I shot him."

"And the other? Did he see it?"

"I don't know. I don't think so. Let's get this one on his horse."

Marco nodded. "Yes, we must take him back to the house."

"No. I'll drop him off at the cemetery and we can bury him later. There's no point in upsetting the ladies."

"But he might still be alive," Marco said.

Andropov cursed in Russian. "Marco, his chest is shot through and through, he's not breathing, his heart is not beating, and his eyes are staring at nothing. I'm pretty sure he's dead."

The Mexican crossed himself. "Then may he rest in peace."

"Amen. Now let's get him on the horse."

CHAPTER FORTY-SIX

Hack Rivette was in a seething, killing rage as he drew rein near the clanking, steaming *Emperor Maximilian* and swung out of the saddle.

"Where the hell is Lefty Wilder?" Jack Hickam yelled above the racket.

"He's dead."

"What happened?" Hickam was joined by the three surviving gunman.

Savannah stood at a window and looked on.

"He got bushwhacked by a hidden rifleman," Rivette said. "Probably Frank Cobb."

Surprised, Hickam asked, "You mean he was laying for you?"

Rivette's anger snapped. "Of course he was laying for us. Probably him and others. They know we're coming."

"How many?"

"Hell, I don't know. Enough to drop us all before we get anywhere near the damn Kerrigan spread, lay to that."

Hickam didn't believe it. "Are you sure? Are you certain it was Cobb?"

"Yeah, I'm sure. You calling me a liar?"

"How come you didn't get hit?" one of the other gunmen asked snidely.

"Because I lit out of there," Rivette said. "Damned if I was gonna stay put and swap lead with sharpshooters I couldn't see."

Savannah opened one of the *Emperor*'s doors and stepped outside. Her lustrous hair was piled on top of her head in a cascade of glossy waves and curls, and she wore a pearl blouse, black taffeta skirt, and lace-up boots with high heels. An antique brass hand magnifier hung around her neck, and a gold mechanical watch hung from a chain around her waist.

Rivette thought her breathtaking and wanted more than ever to possess her.

The woman waved the men away from the *Emperor*. When they were sufficiently distant from the roar of Marmaduke Tweng testing the steam engines, she said, "I couldn't hear from inside. Jack, what has happened?"

"Lefty Wilder is dead, shot down by Frank Cobb." Hickam read the question on her face. "He's a former lawman and good with a gun."

"I reckon he's doing that Kerrigan gal," Rivette said, grinning.

"Crudity does not become you, Mr. Rivette," Savannah said. "There is a lady present."

"Keep that in mind, Rivette," Hickam ordered.

The gunman apologized, his face working. "Sorry, Miss St. James." *But soon you'll be the one that's sorry.*

"Rivette says the Kerrigan crowd is laying for us,

Savannah. They got riflemen in position to defend the place."

"They know we're coming and they can pick us off at a distance," Rivette put in. "I was lucky to get away with my life."

Savannah's laughter was light as a spring rain. "There's no need for your concern, gentlemen. Mr. Tweng assures me that the *Emperor Maximilian* is the most powerful weapon on earth. It will crush anyone and anything in its path. The late Mexican emperor Maximilian feared assassination above all else and that is why his great land carriage is made of the finest steel and the windows of reinforced glass. Both will turn aside bullets. All the windows and doors can be locked and no enemy can force his way inside."

"So we just drive it over folks," Hickam said.

"Yes, Jack. Over folks and through buildings," Savannah said. "The *Emperor* will pulverize everything in its path, human and animal, crushing and destroying. When the enemy is demoralized, I mean Kate Kerrigan and her minions, Mr. Tweng will open the doors and we will leave the *Emperor* and shoot down those who are still standing." She laughed again. "There won't be many of those."

She saw doubt in Hickam's eyes and said, "The terrain around the Kerrigan place is perfectly flat. The *Emperor* will be in its element."

Hickam nodded and grinned. "It can be done, by God."

"Of course it can be done, Jack, and it will be done," Savannah said. "Someone as insignificant as Kate Kerrigan will never get her men to stand against a modern, steam-powered fighting machine like the

Emperor. By this time next year, Kate Kerrigan will be long dead and we'll be living in London, Paris, or Rome."

The latter part of that speech angered Rivette. Savannah St. James would be in his bed in London or wherever, not Jack Hickam's. The man had to die today . . . before tomorrow's attack.

CHAPTER FORTY-SEVEN

"Kate, I think you should get the girls out today," Cobb said. "If Savannah St. James's men were scouting the place like Andropov says, an attack could happen anytime."

Kate looked at Moses Rice. "Mose, what do you think?"

The black man nodded. "Mr. Cobb speaks the truth, Miz Kerrigan. I've been smelling the wind and it just ain't right. There's something wicked coming."

"Then that settles it." Kate wrapped her knuckles on the table. "Ivy, Shannon, you're going with Mose." She smiled. "It's the beginning of a great adventure."

Ivy was eleven, old enough to know what was happening. "We want to stay with you, Ma. We can help you."

"Attend to your mother, young ladies," Cobb said, doing his best, and failing, to make his voice stern.

"It's all right, Frank. I understand how Ivy feels. I would have felt the same at her age." Kate drew her daughters closer to her chair and kissed them both. "The best way you can help is to go with Mose. He'll need you to take care of him."

"That's right, Miz Kerrigan, I sure will." Moses nodded his grizzled head.

"Ma, suppose you die?" Shannon asked carefully. "I don't want my ma to die."

"I won't die. We'll all be together again real soon. You'll see."

"Moses, Kate packed up some grub, and I've saddled the horses," Cobb said. "Best you head out before dark."

"Ma, please . . ." Ivy said, tears in her eyes.

Kate smiled back her own tears. "It will be only for a few days and then I'll come for you. Now, go with Mose, and be polite to him like I taught you."

"Ma"—Shannon hesitated—"you'll come for us?"

Still holding back tears, Kate nodded. It was a long time before she managed to say, "You know I will."

All walked slowly outside, Ivy and Shannon clinging to their mother.

The girls mounted their horses, then reached across the distance to hold hands.

Cobb, his face grim, stood beside Moses' paint and said in a whisper, "Mose, we're up against some mighty rough men, men without a conscience. Do you understand what I'm saying?"

Moses nodded. "Got me my Dragoon, Mr. Cobb."

"I'm sorry, Mose, but it had to be said."

"I know it had. And I'll pray that it don't never come to that."

Moses Rice and the girls rode out under an amber

sky. Only when they were out of sight did Kate lay her head on Cobb's chest and let the tears come.

"We'll defend only the cabin," Cobb said. "Trace, you and Quinn will take up positions at the front and rear windows. Your mother is a good rifle shot. She'll fight and there's no use trying to talk her out of it."

"What about Doc Fullerton?" Trace asked.

"She'll be in the cabin with Marco Salas's wife and children. God help you, it's going to be cramped in there."

Quinn asked, "What about Marco and the Count?"

"They've volunteered to acts as pickets and keep watch. At the first sign of trouble, they'll fall back and join you in the cabin."

"And you, Frank?" Trace questioned.

"I can fight better off a horse."

Trace didn't question that. Frank was a mounted pistol fighter in the Texas guerrilla style, and his revolver skills would be wasted in the close confines of the cabin.

Cobb looked around the table. "Any questions?"

Trace shook his head. "I guess not. You, Quinn?"

The boy nodded. "Only one. The cabin's timbers are bone dry and it would catch fire real easy. What if they torch it?"

"Then you all get out of there in a hurry and take up a position in the blacksmith's shop," Cobb directed. "God willing, I'll be there to help you."

"It's pretty bleak, Frank," Trace said.

Cobb nodded. "That's the word for it, all right. *Bleak.*"

Trace thought of another question. "How many men does Savannah St. James have?"

"If she's been hiring guns, she'll have plenty," Cobb said.

"All the more for us to shoot," Quinn pointed out.

Cobb grinned. "You'll do, Quinn. You'll do."

Kate Kerrigan walked up the rise behind the cabin to the cemetery. She stood beside the fresh grave of the boy Count Andropov had killed and said a rosary for his immortal soul.

By the time she was finished, the day had begun to shade into evening. As far as her eyes could reach, she could see the healthy longhorns and the white faces of the Herefords grazing on her broad acres. Indeed, it was a land worth fighting for, the Kerrigan Ranch, her present and her future and her family's future.

Lithe and beautiful as an Irish warrior queen, Kate walked down the darkening hill. Lamps were lit in the cabin and she smelled the tang of baking bread and roasting meat.

Chapter Forty-eight

The light was fading, coyotes yipped, and Hack Rivette steeled himself to take his shot. If he was to be the bull of the woods and own Savannah St. James and all she represented, it was time to get rid of Jack Hickam. Rivette stood in shadow near the horse lines and watched the gunman move back and forth in front of the fire. He had already spent an hour or more inside the *Emperor Maximilian* and that rankled. Hickam was getting what Rivette wanted and that had to stop.

He stepped out of the shadows and walked toward the tents where the fire burned and bacon and beans cooked in a sooty pot. Hickam had his back turned and stared into the fire, a cigar in his teeth. Rivette drew his gun and held it down by his leg. His mouth was dry and fear fiddled a tune in his belly. Suppose his revolver misfired? Suppose his target turned at the last moment and drew? He forced those doubts out of his head.

Jack Hickam was already a dead man. He just didn't know it yet.

Moving quietly for such a big man, Rivette moved

closer . . . ten yards . . . five . . . he slowed his pace . . . spitting distance. *Now!*

He raised his Colt and fired a shot into Hickam's back and then he almost screamed. Hickam didn't drop!

Jack Hickam was among the best of the best. As sudden as a striking cobra, he drew and fired.

Rivette took the ball in the center of his chest and knew he was a dead man. Both men dropped to their knees swaying, but facing each other. Rivette tried a shot and scored a hit. Hickam, roaring his outrage, absorbed the ball and fired twice. He hit Rivette in the chest a second time and his third shot took the big man smack between the eyes.

He toppled over on his side and lay still. Hickam, snarling like a wolf, emptied his gun into him. The last thing Jack saw in this life was Savannah walking toward him. She didn't look sad. Just angry as hell.

"What happened?" she asked the three guns who were staring slack-jawed at the dead men.

No one said anything for a moment.

Finally one of them, built like a rain barrel, said quietly, "The new man walked up and shot Jack in the back. Then Jack turned and done for him."

"Are they both dead?" Savannah asked.

"As they're ever gonna be, ma'am," Rain Barrel said.

"Damn. That means you boys will need to haul extra freight."

A towhead said, "This is a bad luck outfit, lady. I'm outta here."

As the other two muttered agreement, Savannah put

her hands on her generous hips and said, "What will it take to keep you boys here? Just name it."

Rain Barrel shook his head. "Ma'am, what you got we all want, but the price is too high."

Savannah looked at them coldly. "You damn scum. You signed on to stay until the job is over. Well, it isn't over until my herd is in Kansas."

"It's over," the towhead said, his eyes glittering in the firelight. "But you owe me and I'm gonna claim my due."

Rain Barrel grinned. "And that goes fer me as well."

The men advanced on her, naked desire in their eyes.

Savannah drew her derringer and shot Rain Barrel in the face. The squat man screamed and fell. The other two hesitated for just a moment and that was their death.

Two rifle shots rang out and both men were hit. The towhead fell immediately, but the second staggered a few steps, then pitched forward, his face in the fire.

Marmaduke Tweng walked out of the gloom, a Henry .44-40 fitted with a strange brass and copper sight as long as the rifle itself.

Savannah took a deep breath. "Thank you, Mr. Tweng."

"Some things I just can't let happen, Miss St. James. The violation of a woman is one of them." After a moment's hesitation, he asked, "What will you do now?"

She frowned. "What do you mean?"

"Will you hire more men?"

"With what? My money is all gone."

"Can I take you somewhere?" Tweng offered.

"Of course you can. We attack the Kerrigan Ranch in the morning just as I planned."

Tweng frowned. "You mean using only the *Emperor Maximilian*?"

"You told me it is a weapon of war." Behind her a circle of firelight pooled scarlet in the darkness.

"It can be used as such." Tweng nodded .

"I want the Kerrigan Ranch destroyed and every living thing dead, Mr. Tweng, especially Kate. Can you do that?"

"As an engineer, I'm anxious to discover if an armored vehicle can be used in war," Tweng answered. "Of course, I'll be killing people, but it's all in the cause of advancing science. Yes, by the Lord Harry, I'll do it."

"I want them all dead, Mr. Tweng. I mean every last one of them, adults and their spawn. Crushed, pounded, pulverized to death. I want to watch Kate Kerrigan's blood and guts spurt from under the wheels."

Tweng nodded. "Yes, yes, I believe the *Emperor* has that capability. As always, steam will see us through."

Savannah's smile was slow, seductive. "To seal our bargain, may I do something nice for you, Mr. Tweng?"

"Alas, dear lady, as much as I admire them for their intelligence and wit I am not drawn to the charms of womankind. I much prefer mankind, if you understand my meaning."

"You're a queer little man, Mr. Tweng."

"No, Miss St. James. I am a steam engineer."

CHAPTER FORTY-NINE

Kate Kerrigan could not sleep. Frank Cobb's plan for the defense of her ranch kept playing over and over in her head. To fight expert gunmen from the confines of a cabin that could be burned to the ground in minutes was a recipe for disaster.

She rose quietly and threw her cloak over her night attire. She took the Henry from the rack on the wall and stepped outside. All was quiet and a horned moon rode high in the sky. The menfolk were asleep in the blacksmith's shop except for Count Andropov, who always bedded down in his rickety general store.

Kate walked away from the ranch buildings and moved west onto the flat grassland. Coyotes, attracted by a fresh grave, prowled the cemetery on the rise and yipped their eternal hunger.

Driven by the will to survive, she walked a mile into the prairie and then stopped, her rifle by her side. Here, on this ground, was where the Kerrigan Ranch would make its fight.

Trace and Quinn were good rifle shots, as was Count

Andropov. And so was she. Frank would stay mounted, as was his training and inclination. Kate stared into the shrouded darkness. Even at the charge, Savannah St. James's mounted gunmen would be out in the open and they could be stopped by accurate rifle fire. It all depended on . . .

Ahead of her, the clouds parted and a lone horseman walked his horse into sight. Kate racked a round into the Henry, a sharp, mechanical sound that carried far.

The rider stopped and sat his saddle in silence.

"I can drop you from here," Kate called. Jesus, Mary, and Joseph her voice sounded too high, as though she was frightened—which she was.

The man in the distance laughed. "Who else in West Texas would have an accent as Irish as the pigs o' Docherty?"

Kate thought she recognized the voice. "Who are you?" she called, her words echoing.

"Well, I could be President Ulysses S. Grant, but I'm not. You know me, Mrs. Kerrigan. I'm Henry Brown, late in the employ of the deceased Mr. Jason Hunt."

Kate felt her heart leap, but she remained cautious. "Ride closer and let me take a look at you."

The horseman rode forward.

She recognized him and let her rifle fall to her side. "It's delightful to see you again, Mr. Brown. Where have you been?"

"Here and there. I'm riding the owlhoot, but what brings you out onto the big grass in the middle of the night?"

Kate ignored that and asked her own question. "Mr. Brown, did you see any sight of armed men?"

"Sure didn't. But in the distance I saw lights in the windows of what looked like a railroad car. Heard it too. Somebody build a railroad since I was last here?"

"No. It's not a railroad. I have some things to tell you, Mr. Brown."

He stepped out of the saddle, walked his horse forward, and smiled. "Tell away, Mrs. Kerrigan."

Using as few words as possible, Kate told of the events leading up to the impending attack on the Kerrigan Ranch. "I couldn't sleep and came out here to study the ground."

Brown nodded. "I agree with you that this is the best place to make our fight."

"*Our* fight, Mr. Brown?"

"I told you I'd come back when you needed me. I'm many things, Mrs. Kerrigan, not all of them honorable, but I do keep my word."

"I'm so glad you'll be with us, Mr. Brown. I think we're going into a fight badly outnumbered. And Savannah has that strange machine I told you about."

"Then we'll just have to even the odds. Now let me get you back to the cabin so you can get some rest." He looked at the star-scattered sky. "We'll be back here before sunup."

"You think they'll attack in the morning?" Kate asked.

"Judging by the noise that steam carriage was making, that would be my guess. If not tomorrow, then the day after." He walked Kate to her cabin and then went to the cluttered blacksmith's shop in search of Frank Cobb.

He found him in his blankets, his head wedged between the feet of the anvil. Brown shook Cobb awake, and for his trouble got the cold muzzle of the man's Colt jammed between his eyes.

"Don't shoot. It's me, Henry Brown."

Cobb swore. "I could've blowed your damn fool head off, Brown."

"We need to talk."

"What time is it?"

"Midnight. Thereabouts."

"You don't wake up a Christian white man at midnight or thereabouts," Cobb griped.

Brown grinned. "I do it all the time."

"Then it's a wonder you're still alive." Still grumbling, Cobb rose to his feet and followed him outside and a distance from the forge. "Well, what's so all-fired important? Make it good, Henry, because I'm seriously considering putting a ball into you."

"Frank, I met Mrs. Kerrigan tonight."

Suddenly, Cobb was wide-awake. "Met her where?"

"Out on the grass. She plans to make our stand there."

"*Our* stand? Are you planning to stay around this time?"

Brown grinned. "I sure am. I like Mrs. Kerrigan and you, too, Frank, since you're such an affable feller."

"My plan is to defend the cabin," Cobb argued.

"I know. She told me. She thinks it's a lousy plan and so do I. You'll be trapped like rats in the cabin. But out on the flat we can pick off the bad men before they even get close."

"They come in a rush and they'll come fast," Cobb pointed out.

"So? We'll just need to shoot fast is all."

Cobb shook his head. "Kate is the boss. She does as she pleases."

"And this time she happens to be right. What about the machine Savannah St. James has?"

"It's a steam carriage. We've nothing to fear from that. She and her hired guns will come mounted."

Brown shook his head. "We got a fight on our hands, Frank. Damn, I'm looking forward to it."

"That's because you're a crazy man, even crazier than Wes Hardin. I'm going back to my blankets."

"Mrs. Kerrigan wants us out on the flat before sunup. I hope I see you there."

"Brown, when the fight starts your horse's nose will be up my horse's ass."

"That's my brave boy," Brown said, grinning.

Frank Cobb badly wanted to shoot him.

CHAPTER FIFTY

Savannah St. James rang for her maid, who appeared in her nightgown, her hair in curling ribbons and her dark face shining with night cream. "I'm sorry to call you so late, Leah. You must think me most inconsiderate."

"Not at all, Miss St. James," the maid said. "It is no trouble."

"Please sit, Leah." Savannah motioned to the sofa.

The woman sat on the edge.

"How long have you been with me, Leah?"

"Fifteen years, Miss St. James. Ever since you were a lovely young thing living in London town."

"You've been a good and faithful servant, Leah."

"Thank you." The woman looked puzzled.

"You know I attack the Kerrigan woman and her vile clan tomorrow morning, don't you?" Savannah asked.

"Yes, ma'am. And a wicked, wicked woman she is, murdering poor Mr. St. James like that."

"Indeed she is. Leah, I asked you here because I want

to give you this." She pulled a bloodred ruby ring from her finger. "It's the only thing of value I have left."

Leah looked stricken. "Miss St. James, are you dismissing me?"

"Yes I am, Leah. All my money is gone and I can no longer pay you." Savannah laid her derringer on the table beside her. "When this is over and I watch Mrs. Kerrigan die, I will use that weapon to take my own life."

"But why, Miss St. James?" Leah couldn't understand. "You will have the herds."

Savannah smiled. "Ah, yes, the herds. But I have no money to pay cowboys to see cattle through the winter and round them up come spring. No money to drive them north." Savannah smiled. "I very much doubt that I have enough pennies in my purse to see myself through winter. I'd probably starve to death. I rolled the dice, you see, and I lost."

"Your brother could have saved us," Leah said loyally.

"Yes, he could, but now he's dead, and the only thing remaining to me is to avenge his murder. How I long to kill that Kerrigan woman."

Leah shook her head. "I'm not leaving you, Savannah. I love you as though you were my own child. If we die, we die together."

"No, Leah, you must leave. Save yourself."

"This is the first command from you I have refused to obey. I will not leave. I will remain at your side until the end. If we both must die of starvation, then so be it."

Savannah rose from her chair and took Leah in her

arms. "You are all I have left. Later, we'll talk about the old times and we'll laugh and cry and remember."

"Perhaps we'll find a way," Leah said. "You'll find a way to live and love again."

"I can't be young again. And I won't let you suffer with me." Savannah reached behind her and found the derringer. "Farewell, Leah. I love you so much."

The derringer roared and Leah died instantly.

Savannah lay the woman out on the couch and sat back in her chair. She sat in silent vigil over Leah's body until sunrise, when Marmaduke Tweng called out for her.

"I thought I heard a shot in the night, Miss St. James," Tweng said. "Was it the Kerrigan woman?"

"No, Mr. Tweng," Savannah said. "Leah took her own life. I wanted to dismiss her, but she couldn't bear to be parted from me."

"Where is she? Oh, I see her," Tweng said. "She looks so peaceful lying there."

"Yes, she's at peace now. We will bury her in the spot where the Kerrigan cabin stands and put Kate Kerrigan at her feet."

"Poetic justice." Tweng wore his goggles. His leather coat was buckled to the neck and he wore a pair of leather gauntlets.

"I want everyone dead," Savannah reminded him.

Annoyed, Tweng said, "Yes, and I assured you that the *Emperor Maximilian* has that capability. I have not changed my mind since. I believe that, properly handled, it will cause great slaughter."

Savannah went back inside and dressed for war. She wore her tight leather corset, Mexican army officer's campaign pants, and high boots. Across her chest hung a bandolier of .44-40 rifle shells for the Henry she'd propped against her chair.

Tweng appeared at the door again. "I will lock the doors and windows and open them again when we're ready to finish off the wounded."

Savannah nodded. "Can I depend on you, Mr. Tweng? Can you kill?"

Tweng smiled. "Dear lady, I am only the engineer. The *Emperor* will do the killing, and very efficiently. Remember, he is invulnerable to gunfire."

"Then let's get it done."

A few moments later, she heard the *click-click* of the doors and windows locking in place and then a great bellow from the drive train as Tweng gave full throttle to the steam engines. His cabin was in front, fully enclosed by reinforced glass, and on each side of his seat was a system of heavily oiled levers that guided the *Emperor*.

Marmaduke Tweng was very excited. Hitherto, he'd considered the *Emperor* as merely a conveyance, but finally it would prove its worth as a weapon of war.

He smiled. Steam would see him through.

CHAPTER FIFTY-ONE

Long before dawn, Kate Kerrigan and Jazmin Salas had coffee on the boil, bacon frying, and biscuits in the oven to feed the hungry men.

They stood around outside and ate in silence, each busy with his thoughts. Frank Cobb started out surly, still angry at being wakened by Brown when he was dreaming about Kate, but coffee helped. By the time he was ready to move onto the grass, he was almost cheerful.

Kate wore a canvas riding skirt, then becoming fashionable, boots, and a man's shirt. On her head was a battered hat and black gloves covered her hands to reduce the impact of the Henry's recoil. Even at that early hour of the morning, she was dazzlingly lovely. The gallant Count Andropov declared her to be "a vision of Celtic beauty."

Marco Salas carried no weapon since he was proficient with neither rifle nor pistol. He wore his leather blacksmith's apron and a pair of goggles as eye protection should his cannon decide to blow up on him.

An unexpected recruit to Kate's little army was Pete Slicer. Although still gaunt and in constant pain, he insisted on joining in the defense of the ranch.

Cobb was not impressed. "Pete, I see you make one fancy move, I swear to God I'll gun you."

"I'll stick," Slicer said. "I'm not doing this for you or for Kate Kerrigan. It's for Dr. Fullerton. She saved my life and now I'm going to help save hers."

Henry Brown grinned. "Sweet on her, huh?"

"You could say that." Slicer glared. "But don't say it again."

"You're a mite touchy on that subject, Pete," Cobb said.

"Yeah, well, I don't think Mary is sweet on me," Slicer grumbled.

"Oh, I don't know," Brown said. "Stranger things have happened."

Slicer glared again. "You're a pushy man, sonny. It's gonna get you shot one day."

Kate and the others were in position while it was still dark, strung out across twenty-five yards of prairie. The only people not in the firing line were Marco, who left to tend to his cannon, and Dr. Fullerton, who held herself in reserve to treat the wounded.

Cobb had decided to stay on the ground and join in the rifle fire. He lay on the grass next to Kate, Trace on her other side.

"Do you see anything, Frank?" Kate asked.

Cobb shook his head. "Not a thing."

"Trace, you and Quinn have young eyes," Kate said. "Keep a sharp watch."

Count Andropov turned to Henry Brown at his side. "This reminds me of the Russian 345th Regiment of Foot waiting for the French cuirassier cavalry charge at the Battle of Borodino."

"Did the Russians win?" Brown asked.

"No. They were wiped out to a man."

Brown stared. "Count, go lie down beside somebody else, huh?"

Marco Salas kneeled beside his cannon and for the third time in a few minutes checked that the fuse was still in place. Not trusting commercially made lucifers to light when needed, he'd made his own matches that were about as unstable as sticks of sweating dynamite.

He could see nothing in the darkness around him but ten minutes after he'd taken up his position he heard a distant rumble. Something was coming and Marco prepared himself. He said a prayer to Our Lady of Guadalupe, then polished the iron cannon barrel with an oily rag. The cannonball nestled inside the breech ready to inflict great damage to the enemy cavalry, and Marco's hands trembled with excitement as the hour of battle drew closer.

"Ma, can you hear that?" Trace questioned.

"Yes I can." Kate pushed a wayward curl off her forehead. She turned to Cobb, "Frank, what is that?"

"It sounds like horses. But, damn it, could Savannah St. James have that many? It sounds like a cavalry regiment."

"The Cossacks are drawing closer, Mr. Brown," Andropov said. "We must meet their charge with bravery and determination before they wipe us out."

"Count, git the hell away from me."

The distant rumble became a roar and in the distance, still far off, the beams of four large reflector lamps probed the darkness.

Kate was the first to recover from the shock. "That's not horses. It's a machine. It's Savannah's steam carriage."

"Traveling in style, isn't she?" Cobb said sarcastically.

Filled with a sense of foreboding, Kate said, "I hope that's all it is."

CHAPTER FIFTY-TWO

Marmaduke Tweng halted the *Emperor Maximilian* to let the morning light catch up with him. He was well pleased with *Emperor*'s performance on flat ground. It was more nimble than he'd thought, with a top speed as fast as a man on a galloping horse. Fitted with fire guns, the great machine would be a formidable weapon indeed. When this nasty Kerrigan business was settled, he'd work on arming the *Emperor* with guns fore and aft and perhaps on the sides.

The speaking tube above Tweng's head hissed into life. Savannah's voice sounded tinny as she said, "Why have we stopped, Mr. Tweng?"

"Waiting for the light, Miss St. James."

"I think we should press on, Mr. Tweng."

"If I can't see 'em, I can't mash 'em, Miss St. James. We'll only be a few minutes. The darkness is already fading."

"A soon as possible, Mr. Tweng." *Thunk.* Savannah replaced her end of the speaking tube.

Tweng sighed. How little people knew about the plight of the steam engineer. Even the great, sooty ironclads that patrolled the world's oceans did not fight in the dark. Come sundown, they were blind as bats.

As it was, the morning light arrived with agonizing slowness and it was almost thirty minutes before Tweng drove the *Emperor* forward. He adjusted his goggles and settled his top hat more firmly on his head. Hissing, clanking, throbbing in every bolt, the mighty *Emperor Maximilian* was going to war.

"Leah, when I kill the Kerrigan woman, I'll prop you up at a window so you can see." Savannah smiled. "Would you like that, dear?"

Leah's dead eyes stared at her, her head bobbing with every movement of the *Emperor*.

"Yes, I thought you would. You're such a treasured friend." Savannah reached for the speaking tube and blew into the mouthpiece. "Mr. Tweng, can you hear?"

"Loud and clear, Miss St. James."

"When will the killing start? Miss Leah is most anxious to know."

"Soon, Miss St. James. The *Emperor* is on the scent."

Savannah sang, "A-hunting we will go, a-hunting we will go . . ." She stopped. "The morning seems fine, Mr. Tweng. It will be a sunny day."

"That is also my opinion, Miss St. James."

Savannah's voice continued to carry through the speaking tube. "Did you hear that, Leah, darling? It's a fair day for killing Mrs. Kerrigan. Mr. Tweng, will she scream much when crushed under the *Emperor*'s wheels?"

"That entirely depends on where she's crushed, Miss St. James," Tweng said. "The head now, that would kill her instantly."

"Well, we don't want that, do we, Leah?" Savannah said. "Avoid the head at all costs, Mr. Tweng."

"I certainly will," Tweng said. "This is proving to be a most interesting experiment."

As it rolled across the prairie, the *Emperor Maximilian* was a beautiful sight, an engineering masterpiece of steel, glass, bronze, copper, and green and gold paint. Its massive wheels, each as wide as an axe handle, were the height of a tall man and driven by massive pistons. As it neared Kate Kerrigan and her band, the *Emperor* looked more predator than machine, a fiery nightmare dragon from another age.

Forward in the driver's cabin, looking like a malevolent gnome, Marmaduke Tweng heard a *Ping!* as someone tried a long-range rifle shot. He immediately checked his dials and gauges and ascertained that no damage had been done. He smiled. It would take more than rifle fire to turn the *Emperor* from its just and rightful course.

CHAPTER FIFTY-THREE

Marco Salas and his cannon were positioned a hundred yards in advance of Mrs. Kerrigan and her engine. He heard the crash of rifles and saw puffs of smoke, but the terrible machine came on at speed. It was less than a mile away and closing fast.

The cannon had a short fuse that Marco would light when the machine was almost abreast of it. He figured that a broadside hit might hit something vital and stop the machine in its tracks. The trick was to know just when to light the fuse.

He crouched behind the shallow rise with his matches at the ready. He knew he wouldn't have to wait much longer.

The riflemen were kneeling, taking their shots, but the machine seemed impervious to their fire. It seemed like an inexorable force of nature that nothing could stop.

Cobb didn't like it. "Kate, run back to the cabin,

saddle a horse, and get the hell out of here. Look for Moses and the girls."

Kate snapped off a shot, racked the lever. "I most certainly will not. My place is here, defending my ranch."

"Damn it, woman. There's no stopping that thing. It will soon roll right over us."

"Then we'll all die together, Frank. I'm not leaving." She looked around her. "Where is the Count?"

Cobb grimaced. "He ran away. If I survive this, I'll kill him."

But Andropov had not made a run for it. He returned mounted on one of Kate's best horses, a stick of dynamite in his hand. "It's the only one I have," he yelled at Kate. "But it will get the job done."

Before anyone could object, Andropov yelled something in Russian, kicked his horse into motion, and charged directly for the oncoming *Emperor*.

He had covered half the distance when disaster struck. His horse wanted nothing to do with the noisy, smelly machine and reared, throwing Andropov from the saddle. For long moments, the Russian lay still on the ground as the *Emperor* drew closer to him, its enormous studded wheels throwing up massive clods of dirt.

But Andropov rose unsteadily to his feet and charged directly for the machine, lighting the dynamite as he ran.

"Get back here!" Cobb yelled.

But the Russian couldn't hear him. He ran directly for the driver's cabin, tossed the dynamite underneath, then tried to jump clear. His coat caught on a projecting steam valve and he fell heavily on his right side.

An instant later two things happened. The dynamite exploded under Marmaduke Tweng's cab and the front left wheel of the *Emperor* rolled over Andropov's chest and crushed it to a scarlet, jellified nightmare of blood and bone. Killed instantly, Count Ivan Boleslav died without sound, far from his native Moscow.

The dynamite didn't even slow the *Emperor*. Remorselessly, the snarling machine came on as though no mortal power on earth could stop it.

Kate Kerrigan witnessed the count's terrible death and whispered, "Oh my God in heaven, help us." Her hand left her rifle and took her rosary from her pocket.

Cobb saw and quickly said, "Later, Kate. When the shooting is done." He rose to his feet and yelled, "Everybody aim for the cab. Shoot the driver. Kill the son of a gal!"

Bullets rattled against the reinforced glass of Marmaduke Tweng's windshield and one well-intentioned round actually starred the glass, but none penetrated. Tweng grinned. He'd spotted another target . . . and it was out in the open. He swung the *Emperor* into a turn.

CHAPTER FIFTY-FOUR

Marco Salas was horrified. The devil machine was driving straight at his cannon. He stood and tried to wave the monster away, but it didn't waver or slow its speed. Wearing goggles and a top hat, the little man in the cabin was hunched over the controls. On his present course, he'd mangle the cannon into a pile of scrap iron in just a couple minutes.

Marco was fast running out of time, but he took one of his matches from his pocket and struck it on the filed chunk of iron he kept for that purpose. The wood was thin and brittle, and the match broke. He was stricken. *"Madre de Dios!"*

He glanced fearfully at the looming machine, so close he saw the driver's bared teeth. He tried a second match, holding the stick close to the blue head. It fired and he quickly lit the fuse. To distract the driver, Marco jumped to his left, away from the cannon, and waved his arms. He saw the grinning driver make a slight adjustment to a set of levers and the *Emperor* moved away

from the cannon, bringing it almost on top of him. The
roar of the machine deafened Marco. He felt its heat and
smelled its stinking breath . . . the rank odor of death.

Marco jumped for the rise. Too late! The same
bloody wheel that had crushed Andropov to death
caught the blacksmith's left leg and pulped it flat from
the knee down, grinding bone and muscle deep into the
earth.

Kate Kerrigan and the others ran toward Marco Salas.

The machine began to drive past him and Marco
realized he'd failed. The cannon had not fired.

A wave of terrible pain hit the little Mexican . . . just
as the cannon roared and jumped three feet into the air.

The iron cannonball took an errant course. It shot
high, missed the side of the *Emperor* and veered right.
For a few moments, it seemed that the machine had
again escaped unscathed as it rolled onward, seeking
other victims. In fact, the tiny ball had caused massive,
unseen destruction, like an insignificant iceberg tearing
out the bottom of a great steamship.

The range was short and the cannonball had retained
most of its velocity. It punctured the bottom of the front
plate of the furnace, dangerously thin to save weight.
The cannonball deflected upward and punched another
eight-inch hole in the metal just above the original
damage. A jet of red-hot flame immediately shot into
the interior of the *Emperor* and an instant later the boiler
exploded, blowing out the walls and roof of the quarters
that had once housed Leah. Everything in the living
areas of the *Emperor*—furniture, wall panels, flooring,
and ceiling tiles—burned readily. Scarlet lance-heads of

fire and clouds of boiling hot steam ravaged through the great machine from stem to stern, setting alight everything in their path.

The *Emperor Maximilian* shuddered to a halt . . . and Savannah St. James began to burn.

Kate ran to Marco.

The little blacksmith's left leg was crushed, and he was in excruciating pain but still conscious. He smiled as he said, "I done for it, didn't I, Miz Kerrigan?"

Kate smiled and pushed Marco's hair from his forehead. "You surely did. You were very brave."

Marmaduke Tweng knew the *Emperor* had suffered a mortal wound.

The array of dials in front of him fluctuated wildly, the pointers moving like wagging fingers. The steam valves above his head hissed like snakes and dripped hot water when they should have carried cold.

Suddenly, the speaking tube squawked to life and Savannah's hysterical voice screamed, "Mr. Tweng, let me out!"

"Right away, Miss St. James." Tweng jerked on the small lever that locked and unlocked the doors. Nothing. The lever moved slackly in his hand.

"Please Mr. Tweng!" Savannah shrieked. "Unlock the doors."

Unnerved, Tweng opened his door and jumped. When he got up he ran . . . into the lowered rifle of a man with cold eyes and his finger on the trigger.

Tweng raised his hands and yelled, "Please don't shoot! I'm an engineer!"

The fire found Savannah and she began to scream.

Behind Kate, Cobb watched. "Oh, my God." Red flames reflected on his face. Beside him Trace looked horrified.

Kate looked at the burning *Emperor* and saw what Frank and Trace saw. She gently laid Marco's head on the grass and rose to her feet.

Savannah stood behind the glass, her face close to the pane, long fingernails tearing at the unyielding reinforced surface in futility. She had always envied Kate's red hair but no longer had cause for envy. Her hair was red as it burned away on her scalp.

Kate made to move closer to the window, but Cobb stopped her. "No. It's too dangerous."

She had no option but to stand and watch the woman burn.

Just before the end, Savannah pushed her blackened face close to the glass and stared out, her face twisted, her teeth still white in her mouth.

At first, Kate thought the expression was one of pain. She realized she was wrong and saw it for what it was . . . a look of pure, unadulterated hatred. It was the face of a demon one could expect to meet in the lower levels of hell.

Kate crossed herself, and then Savannah St. James was gone. A sudden flare of fire marked the spot where her body fell.

CHAPTER FIFTY-FIVE

That afternoon, Dr. Mary Fullerton, who'd never attempted such surgery before, amputated what remained of Marco Salas's leg below the knee. She used all the morphine she had for the operation and had none left.

"Marco will have to depend on whiskey to ease his pain during his recovery," Mary said to Kate. "We'd better lay in a good supply."

"Yes . . . yes, I'll see to that," Kate said distractedly.

Mary put a hand on Kate's shoulder. "Don't let that awful woman still torment you after her death, Kate. You must let it go."

Kate looked at Mary with haunted eyes. "You didn't see her face. Even as she burned to death, she hated me."

"Well, she doesn't hate you now, does she?" Mary pointed out somewhat carefully.

Kate shuddered. "I close my eyes and still see her face. She looked evil, like a devil."

"Hate is an evil emotion, and most times it destroys

the hater, just as it destroyed Savannah St. James." Mary smiled. "Soon you'll see your daughters again and the faces of Ivy and Shannon will be the ones you see when you close your eyes at night."

They heard a short knock and the door to the doctor's tiny cabin opened.

Pete Slicer stepped inside, smiled at Mary, and touched his hat. "Good evening, doctor."

"Have you come to see me, Pete?" Mary asked.

"Unfortunately, no. I have a question for Mrs. Kerrigan."

"Ask away, Mr. Slicer," Kate said.

"I'm the one that captured the driver of that damned—beggin' your pardon, Dr. Fullerton—machine. Do you want I should shoot him?"

Kate smiled. "No, leave him for the Texas Rangers."

Slicer frowned. "He says he's an engineer. Is that a good thing?"

"I suppose there are good engineers and bad engineers," Kate said. "Marmaduke Tweng happens to be a bad one."

Slicer was puzzled. "But you don't want me to plug him?"

"No, Mr. Slicer. I don't want you to plug him," Kate repeated.

Slicer looked as though he was about to leave, but he hesitated. "I'm sorry about the count, Mrs. Kerrigan. I know you set store by him."

"Yes, he was a nice man. He made me laugh, especially when he proposed marriage to me every other day."

"Me and your son Trace and Frank Cobb made a box

for him. It's not much, but then there's not much of him left to bury."

Dr. Fullerton said, "Yes, thank you, Pete. You can leave us now."

After Slicer left, Mary produced a bottle of whiskey and two glasses. "I don't know about you, Kate, but I could use a drink."

"I think I could use two or maybe three. I'd like to forget this day ever happened."

"Why didn't you shoot me, Mr. Slicer?" Marmaduke Tweng asked.

"Because Mrs. Kerrigan told me not to. She says to keep you for the Rangers."

Tweng was chained to one of the blacksmith shop's roof supports. He shook his manacles. "Is this really necessary?"

Slicer nodded. "It sure is. Mrs. Kerrigan says you're a bad engineer."

"On the contrary, I'm a fine engineer. That's why I won't hang, Pete. In these modern times, good engineers are hard to find. The whole world runs on steam and I'm one of the few who know how to tame it. The government will not stand idly by and see me hang."

"You killed a man, Tweng, and crippled another," Slicer said. "You'll swing all right."

"I wouldn't be too sure about that," the little man said. "This great nation of ours needs steam-powered airships, steam-powered underwater craft, steam-powered horseless carriages. Only engineers like me can supply those things."

Slicer shook his head. "Airships and horseless carriages. You talk a lot of nonsense, Tweng. If the Rangers hear you speak like that, they'll string you up for sure."

Frank Cobb and Trace Kerrigan stood outside the burned-out hulk of the *Emperor Maximilian* in the waning day. A scorched door hung open on its brass hinges and from inside the stench of burned flesh was a palpable thing.

"It's still too hot, Frank."

Cobb shrugged. "It's got to be done. Kate will expect a coffin."

"I don't want to do this, Frank." Trace's face bore an expression of trepidation and horror.

"I don't want to, either. But we can't leave it to the womenfolk." Cobb smiled briefly. "This is what your mother calls men's work."

Trace frowned. "She says that about cowpunching."

"She says that about a lot of things. Tighten your belt a notch and let's get it done."

Perhaps to make up for his hesitation and lest Frank think him a coward, Trace stepped through the open door first. The heat was intense, the odor rank.

Having nothing to prove, Cobb stood outside the door and said, "What do you see?"

Trace made no answer.

"Move aside there, Trace. I'm coming in." Cobb stepped inside.

A slender column of carbonized flesh and white bone lay on the floor. The skull was intact; its empty eye sockets revealed nothing, but the white, perfect teeth grinned.

Cobb grimaced. "This is what hell must look like. I'm going to start saying my prayers."

"I-think-that's-another-one-over-there," Trace said then he bent over and vomited violently.

Cobb gave him a push. "Go outside, Trace. Get some fresh air."

Trace wiped his mouth with the back of his hand. "I'll stick."

"It's a body all right." Cobb nodded. "Hard to tell, but I think it's another woman."

"Who was she?"

"I don't know. Maybe Kate can tell us. We'll make a pair of small coffins and come back and shovel this up."

"I'm going out." Trace hurried outside.

Cobb lingered a little longer. He would not have wished a death like this on anybody, even Savannah St. John.

CHAPTER FIFTY-SIX

A week later, in response to a telegram sent by Frank Cobb, the Texas Rangers took Marmaduke Tweng away. Before they left, their sergeant told Kate that Tweng would most probably go to trial and that she and the other eyewitnesses could expect to be called to give evidence.

Three weeks after the Rangers, a pair of middle-aged army captains showed up and spent several hours inspecting the wreckage of the *Emperor Maximilian*. They seemed less than impressed.

Captain Forbes, an officer with impressive handlebar whiskers and a whiskey nose, said to Kate, "I know how distressing my questions must be for you, dear lady, but did anyone take cannons out of the machine?"

"There were no cannons, Captain," Kate said. "More sponge cake?"

The officer brightened and held out his plate. "I fear I'm imposing on your hospitality, ma'am. As bachelor officers, I'm afraid Captain Hale and myself do not often experience the exquisite joy of sponge cake, especially when served by such a beautiful lady."

Kate smiled at the compliment. "You are not imposing in the least, sir. I do enjoy seeing men eat."

Captain Hale had soulful brown eyes and no doubt, a hidden sadness. "The army has long been interested in a steam-driven fighting machine that can carry cannon, but the one that attacked your ranch falls very short of our expectations." He smiled under his mustache. "The *Emperor Maximilian* was a clever clockwork toy, no more than that."

Kate wanted to say that it was a clockwork toy that killed one man and maimed another, but she held her peace. The minds of the officers were made up and nothing she, a mere civilian, could say would change their opinion.

The officers left with a sponge cake for the trail and Kate thought that was the end of it. But a month later, on a cold fall morning, two silent Pinkertons in bowler hats and long wool coats arrived.

Like the army officers, they inspected the wreckage but ventured no reason for their visit and didn't reveal their conclusions. They arrived and were gone in less than thirty minutes.

That night, Cobb reported to Kate on conditions on the range. The grass was plentiful and the cattle seemed in good shape. "Mose said they look like the fat kine in the Bible . . . but he's always saying stuff like that."

"Mose says we need to get rid of the wreckage on our pasture." Kate poured more coffee in his cup. "He says two women burned to death in there and that it's an evil thing. Did you notice that the cattle don't go near it?"

"I guess we could hire somebody to take it away, Kate. But it's going to be an expensive proposition."

"I don't care, Frank. I want it gone. I swear the ghosts of Savannah St. James and Leah still haunt the awful thing."

Cobb nodded. "I'll see to it."

"Please do. It brings back some terrible memories."

Cobb brought in several contractors who inspected the massive heap of scrap iron, rubbed their chins, then refused the job.

"The word has gotten around about what happened here," one man said. "None of my men will work on this hulk."

And that's where the matter might have remained . . . but during the first days of winter, the government arrived and everything changed.

The Federals arrived with a dozen heavy freight wagons, fifty men bearing an assortment of cutting tools, and an escort of an army infantry company.

Despite the show of power, the man in charge was a lowly clerk in the War Department, accompanied by a stern, middle-aged female secretary who would later lecture Dr. Fullerton on the laxative virtues of prune juice.

The clerk's name was Atwood Mitchell and he proved to be affable enough. Sitting in Kate's parlor, he told her the wreck would be cut into pieces and loaded onto the wagons. "It will then be taken by rail to Washington for further study."

"The government's interest surprises me, Mr. Mitchell. Especially since the army showed no interest."

"Ah, yes, but we're acting on a recommendation by the Pinkertons, Mrs. Kerrigan. The Pinkertons, more than most, realize that we're living in a technological age driven by the power of steam. It drives our factories, our great oceangoing ships, our powerful locomotives, and soon it will govern every aspect of our lives." Warming to his subject, Mitchell took a quick gulp of coffee and said, "There is already talk in Europe, yes, and in Washington, that the lower orders could be locked in their factories while steam power supplies their every need by way of food, clothing, and rudimentary accommodation. Think of it, Mrs. Kerrigan, the working class need never leave its workbenches except to eat and sleep."

"I don't think I would wish to live in the kind of future you envision, Mr. Mitchell," Kate said, her eyes frosty.

"Well, of course, not, Mrs. Kerrigan. You are a lady of means and beef production is a necessary part of the plan. The masses must be fed, you know. No, I was talking only about the working poor." He smiled. "Or, as the modern term in Washington has it, the factory poor."

Oblivious to Kate's mood, Mitchell rose to his feet. "A thousand thanks for your hospitality, dear lady. Now I must see to my workmen."

Cobb, who had been listening intently to Mitchell's speech, felt a mean little pain in his belly. "You know if the man who invented that steam monstrosity outside has been hung?"

"Oh dear no, sir. Indeed he has not. That is, if you're referring to Mr. Tweng . . . or should I say *Sir* Marmaduke Tweng since Queen Victoria has seen fit to knight him for his services to steam engineering." Mitchell smiled. "My dear sir, you don't hang engineers of Sir Marmaduke's caliber."

"You do know he killed a man and crippled another," Kate pointed out rather coolly.

"Water under the bridge, gammon and spinach, as Mr. Dickens says. Sir Marmaduke is back in Washington even as we speak, working on a steam-powered balloon that can carry an entire ballroom, including an orchestra and two hundred waltzers under its belly." Mitchell's voice took on a reverent tone. "He's a genius indeed, is Sir Marmaduke."

CHAPTER FIFTY-SEVEN

Kate Kerrigan and Frank Cobb stood at a distance and watched the *Emperor Maximilian* cut to pieces. The day was chilly and for the first time in a year, Cobb wore a sheepskin and shotgun chaps. Kate had on a pioneer bonnet and a heavy wool cloak.

The wagons were fully loaded and the machine all but gone except for a few scraps of metal and charred wood when Mitchell bent at the waist, picked up something, and examined it closely. After a few moments he stepped to Kate and said, "I found this on the ground, Mrs. Kerrigan. Did you lose it, perhaps?" In the palm of his hand was a gold ring with a massive, bloodred ruby stone. "If it had been in the steam vehicle when it burned, I'm sure the gold would have melted."

Instinctively, Kate shrank back from the ring. "It's not mine. It belonged to a woman called Savannah St. James. She died in the fire."

"Ah, then perhaps you'd like to have it as a keepsake," Mitchell offered.

Kate looked ready to object but Cobb said, "I'll take it. Mrs. Kerrigan is a little overwrought at the moment."

Mitchell nodded. "Yes, I can understand that. And now, Mrs. Kerrigan, I must bid you adieu. Thank you once again for your hospitality."

"You are most welcome, Mr. Mitchell," Kate said, giving him a little curtsy as etiquette demanded. In fact, she thoroughly disliked the man.

As the short day shaded into evening, she and Cobb watched the wagons leave.

Kate turned to him, her back stiff with anger, "Why did you say I was overwrought and why did you take the ring?"

"As to the first, I thought you seemed upset," Cobb said.

"Well, I wasn't, Frank. I was glad to see that horrible thing leave. And as to the second?"

Cobb shook his head. "I don't know, Kate, I really don't."

"How could you possibly think I wanted a ring that once was on the finger of Savannah St. James?"

"I . . . I didn't. I don't know what I thought."

"Chicken and dumplings for dinner tonight, Frank. Are you looking forward to it?"

Cobb smiled. "I sure am."

"Well, you won't get any until you get rid of that ring."

"I'll chunk it away first chance I get."

"No, I have a better idea. Come with me."

A cold north wind swept the cemetery on the rise as Kate and Cobb made their way to the most recent graves. Savannah St. James's grave was a little way from the rest.

Kate could not abide the thought of her resting near Count Andropov. She shivered. "This is where we laid her. One day I'll get a marker for her. Let me have the ring, Frank." When Cobb passed it to her, she laid it on the grave. "It was hers. Now she's got it back."

"Do you think she knows?"

Kate nodded. "She knows. Wherever she is, she knows."

"She was beautiful, you know."

"Yes, you said that when we buried her. And you were right. Savannah was a beautiful women." Kate raised her pert nose and smelled the air. "Ah, chicken and dumplings are in the wind."

"Good. I'm starving."

"Frank, that future Mitchell was talking about. Will it come to pass?"

"Kate, it's already here."

"But it won't be our future."

"Not a chance." Cobb waved a hand. "Our future is out there on the grass with the cattle. The Kerrigan Ranch is our future."

"Will we have peace now, do you think?"

"Kate, it will soon be 1870. Modern times. Savannah St. James was the last of the old-timey outlaws."

"I hope so."

"I know so." Cobb took Kate's hand and they walked to the cabin, hungry for chicken and dumplings, and the warmth of the family and the fire in the grate.

EPILOGUE

Over the next couple years, Kate Kerrigan prospered as her land and herds grew and she became the most important rancher in West Texas. She soon abandoned the little cabin and built herself a fine house. It was not yet as large as it would become, but two of its eventual four pillars were already in place.

Marco Salas forged himself an ornate peg leg of steel and brass that even had a slot for his favorite pocket watch. He expanded his blacksmith's shop and boasted to all that would listen that he had the finest artificial leg in Texas.

Dr. Mary Fullerton left to study surgery in Germany, but she and Kate corresponded regularly. Pete Slicer sold his guns and followed her.

Henry Brown later rode with Billy the Kid, became a lawman, and was lynched after a botched bank robbery.

Peace came to the Kerrigan Ranch but even as 1870 arrived, dire and powerful men cast envious eyes on Kate's green pastures and fat cattle. Once again, her sons and Frank Cobb at her side, she would be forced to take up the gun and fight for what was hers.

TURN THE PAGE FOR AN EXCITING PREVIEW

THE KERRIGANS
A Texas Dynasty

The Family That Tamed the Wild West!

*In a sprawling new saga that embodies the pioneer spirit,
the masters of the Western introduce the Kerrigans,
a rough-and-tumble clan of pioneers,
making their own way across darkest America,
led by a woman as ferocious as the Texas sun.*

A strong, beautiful mother of five, Kate Kerrigan
has made do since losing her husband in the bloody
Battle of Shiloh. Now, two years after the Civil War,
there's nothing left for them in Tennessee but poverty
and bad memories, so Kate decides a better life awaits
them in far-off West Texas. Thus begins a 1,000-mile
trek through some of the harshest and most dangerous
territory on the frontier. By pulling together,
the Kerrigans discover the conviction to overcome
the unimaginable hardships and the strength of
spirit that will help them build one of the largest
cattle empires in the history of the American West.

THE KERRIGANS
A Texas Dynasty

BY WILLIAM W. JOHNSTONE
with J. A. Johnstone

On sale now, wherever Pinnacle Books are sold.

CHAPTER ONE

"You had to do it, Miz Kerrigan," Sheriff Miles Martin said, hat in hand. "He came looking for trouble."

Kate Kerrigan stood at her parlor window, stared into moon-dappled darkness, and said nothing.

"I mean, he planned to rob you, and after you fed him, an' all," Martin said.

Kate turned, a tall, elegant woman. Her once flaming red hair was now gray but her fine-boned, Celtic beauty was still enough to turn a man's head.

She smiled at Martin.

"He planned to murder me, Miles. Cover his tracks, I guess."

"Where is Trace?" Martin said.

"Out on the range, and so is his brother," Kate said.

"And Miss Ivy and Miss Shannon?"

"My segundo's wife is birthing a child. Doc Woodruff is off fly-fishing somewhere, so Ivy and Shannon went over to Lucy Cobb's cabin to help. Lucy has already had three, so I don't foresee any problems."

Then as though she feared she was tempting fate, Kate said in the lilting Irish brogue she'd never lost, "May Jesus, Mary, and Joseph and all the saints in heaven protect her this night."

"He was a city slicker," Martin said.

The sheriff, a drink of water with a walrus mustache and sad brown eyes, stood in front of the fire. He had a Colt self-cocker in his holster and a silver star pinned to the front of his sheepskin.

The fall of 1907 had been cold and the winter was shaping up to be a sight worse.

"He had the look of one," Kate said.

Martin looked uncomfortable and awkward, all big hands and spurred boots. He chose his words carefully, like a barefoot man walking through a nettle patch.

"How did it happen, Miz Kerrigan? I need to ask."

"Of course, Miles," Kate said. "Why don't you sit and I'll get you a brandy. Only to keep out the chill, you understand."

The big lawman sat gratefully in the studded leather chair by the fire.

"I'm right partial to brandy," he said. "Warms a man's insides, I always say."

Kate poured brandy in two huge snifters, handed one to Martin, and settled herself in the chair opposite.

The lawman thought she sat like a queen, and why not? Kate's range was larger than some European kingdoms.

Martin played for time.

He produced the makings and said, "May I beg your indulgence, ma'am?"

"Please do. My son Quinn is much addicted to cigarettes, a habit he learned from our vaqueros, who smoke like chimneys."

"Doctors say it's good for the chest," Martin said.

"So I've heard, but I do not set store by what doctors say."

Kate sipped her brandy, and then stooped to poke the logs into life. She didn't look up.

"I've killed men before, Miles."

"I know, Miz Kerrigan, but I was trying to spare you a lot of fool questions."

The woman's emerald green eyes fixed on Martin's face.

"I'll tell you what happened here earlier this evening and you can ask your questions as you see fit."

The lawman nodded.

"I'd given the servants the night off, and I was alone in the house when I heard a horse come to a halt outside."

"What time was that, Miz Kerrigan?"

"It was seven o'clock. I was here, sitting by the fire eating the cold supper the cook had prepared for me, and heard the grandfather clock chime in the hallway. A few moments later a knock came to the door."

Kate's blue silk day dress rustled as she sat back and made herself more comfortable.

"I answered the summons and opened to a man, an ordinary looking fellow wearing an old dark jacket that was several sizes too large for him. He had no overcoat; the evening was cold and he shivered.

"He said he was hungry and could I spare him a bite

of food? Since I'd no kitchen staff available, I opened the door and let him come inside."

"That was a mistake, Miz Kerrigan," Martin said.

Kate smiled.

"Miles, over the years I've let many men into this house. Geronimo once sat where you're sitting. We had tea and cake and he wanted to talk about old Queen Vic."

The lawman stirred uncomfortably in his chair and glanced over his shoulder, as though he expected to see the old Apache's ghost glowering at him from a corner.

"Well, I led the way to the kitchen and the man followed me. He said his name was Tom and that he was looking for ranch work. He had the most singular eyes, rather mean and foxy, like those I used to see in some Texas gunmen back in the old days. I must admit, I did not trust him."

"You did right," Martin said. "Not trusting him, I mean."

"Thank you, Miles. I'm sure your approval will stand me in good stead should you consider hanging me."

"Miz Kerrigan! I have no intention . . . I mean . . . I wouldn't . . ."

Kate gave the flustered lawman a dazzling smile.

"There, there, Miles, don't distress yourself. I'm certain the facts of the case will speak for themselves and banish all doubt from your mind."

"Yes, yes, I'm sorry. Please proceed."

Martin was fifty years old and Kate Kerrigan could still make him blush.

"I fixed the man some beef sandwiches, and indeed,

he was as wolf hungry as he professed," Kate said. "It was after he'd eaten heartily that things took a dangerous turn."

"Was the sugar scattered all over the kitchen floor part of it?" Martin said.

"Indeed it was. A small sugar sack had been left on the counter by a careless maid and Tom, if that was really his name—"

"It wasn't," Martin said.

Kate looked at him in surprise.

"Please go on, Miz Kerrigan," the lawman said.

"Well, the man jumped up, grabbed the sugar sack, and threw the contents over the floor. He shoved the empty sack at me and said, 'You, fill this. The jewels you're wearing first.'"

"'Mister,'" I said, "'I've been threatened by more dangerous bad men than you.'"

Martin reached into the pocket of his coat and withdrew a revolver.

"Then he drew this on you."

Kate glanced at the gun.

"Yes, that's it, a Hopkins & Allen in thirty-two caliber. He said to fill the sack or he'd scatter my brains."

"Oh, Miz Kerrigan, you must have been terrified," Martin said.

Kate shook her head.

"Miles, you've known me how long? Thirty years? You should remember by now I don't scare easily." She frowned. "And for God's sake, call me Kate. You never called me anything else until I got this big house and eight hundred thousand acres of range to go with it."

Now it was the lawman's turn to smile.

"Kate it is, and you're right, you never did scare worth a damn, beggin' your pardon."

"I also used to cuss, Miles, before I became a lady."

"You were always a lady, Kate. Even when all you had to your name was a cabin and a milk cow and a passel of young 'uns."

Kate nodded.

"Hard times in Texas back in those days after the war."

"We'll wind it up," Martin said. "It's growing late and I'm only going through the motions anyhow."

"The fact remains that I killed a man tonight, Miles. It's your duty to hear me out."

Kate rose, poured more brandy from the decanter into the lawman's glass and then her own.

She sat by the fire again and said, "When the man pointed the gun at me, I took off my necklace and bracelets and dropped them in the sack. He wanted my wedding ring, but I refused. When he looked at it and saw it was but a cheap silver band, he demanded the expensive stuff.

"I told him I kept my jewelry in my bedroom and he told me to take him there. He also made an extremely crude suggestion and vowed he'd have his way with me."

"The damned rogue," Martin said, his mustache bristling.

"In my day I've heard worse than that, but right then I knew I was in real danger."

Kate's elegant fingers strayed to the simple cross that now hung around her neck.

"There's not much left to tell, Miles. I played the petrified, hysterical matron to perfection and when we went upstairs I told the robber that my jewels were in my dresser drawer."

Kate smiled.

"How often men are undone by their lusts. The wretch was so intent on unbuttoning the back of my dress that he didn't see me reach into the dresser drawer and produce—not diamonds—but my old Colt forty-four."

"Bravo!" Martin said, lifting his booted feet off the rug and clicking his heels.

"I wrenched away from him, leveled my revolver, and ordered him to drop his gun. His face twisted into a most demonic mask and he cursed and raised his gun."

"The murderous rogue!" Martin said.

"I fired," Kate said. "John Wesley Hardin once told me to belly shoot a man and I'd drop him in his tracks. I followed Wes's advice—the only bit of good advice he ever gave me or mine—and hit the bandit where a respectable man's watch fob would have been."

"But he got off a shot," Martin said. He reached into his pocket again and held up the spent .32. "Dug it out of your bedroom wall."

"Yes, he got off a shot, but he was already a dead man. He dropped to the floor, groaned for a few moments, and then all the life in him left."

"Kate, you've been through a terrible ordeal," Martin said.

"I've been through it before, Miles. The man who came here was intent on raping and robbing me. I fight to keep what is mine, whether it's a diamond ring or a single head of cattle. I've hanged rustlers and other men who would threaten Ciarogan, and as God as my witness I'll do it again if I have to."

Sheriff Martin's eyes revealed that he believed every word Kate had just said.

He'd known some tough, fighting ranchers, but none even came close to Kate Kerrigan's grit and determination.

She'd built an empire, then held it against all comers, an amazon in petticoats.

Martin built a cigarette and without looking up from the makings, he spoke.

"His name was Frank Ross. He'd served five years of a life sentence in Huntsville for murder and rape when he killed a guard and escaped. He later murdered a farmer and his wife near Leesville and stole three dollars and a horse."

Martin lit his cigarette.

"Then he came here."

"Miles, why didn't you tell me all this before?" Kate said.

"After what you've gone through, I didn't want to alarm you."

Martin read the question on the woman's face and shrank from the green fire in her eyes. She had an Irish temper, did Kate Kerrigan, and the sheriff wanted no part of it.

"I got a wire a couple of days ago from the Leesburg marshal and he warned that Ross could come this way," he said. "I never thought it could happen the way it did."

"It did happen," Kate said.

"Yes, Kate, I know, and I'm sorry."

Martin rose to his feet.

"I'll be going now. One of my deputies took the body away. You should know that. I'll see myself out."

The big lawman stepped to the door, his spurs chiming.
He stopped and said, "My respects to your fine family."
"And mine to Mrs. Martin."
Martin nodded.
"I'll be sure to tell her that."

Kate Kerrigan had defended herself and her honor,
just another battle to stand alongside all the others that
had gone before.

But the killing of Frank Ross hung heavy on her, and
she felt the need for closeness, to hold something her
husband, dead so many years, had touched.

All she had was the ring on her finger . . . and the
letter that had begun it all.

Kate walked to her office, unlocked the writing
bureau, and took the worn, yellowed scrap of paper
from a drawer.

She returned to the parlor, poured herself brandy, and
sat again by the ashy fire.

After a while, she opened the letter and read it again
for perhaps the thousandth time . . . the letter that had
founded a dynasty.

CHAPTER TWO

In April 1862, on the eve of a battle that would pass into American legend, a barefoot Johnny Reb handed a sealed letter to another.

"You'll give it to her, Michael, give it into the hand of my Kate," Joseph Kerrigan of Ireland's green and fair County Sligo said.

"And why would I, Joseph Kerrigan?" Michael Feeny said. "When you'll be able enough to give it to her yourself."

Kerrigan, a handsome young man with eyes the color of a Donegal mist, shook his head.

"That I will not," he said. "Did you not hear it yourself in the night, out there among the pines?"

"Hear what?" Feeny said, his puzzled face freckled all over like a sparrow's egg.

"The banshee, Michael. She screamed my name. Over and over again, coming from her skull mouth, my name . . . my name . . ."

"Jesus, Mary, and Joseph and Saints Peter and Paul,

it cannot be so, Joseph. You heard the wind in the trees, only the wind."

"You'll give my Katherine the letter," Kerrigan said. "She's a strong woman, and after she reads it she'll know what to do. And tell her this also, that her husband fell fighting for a noble cause and brought no disgrace to his name."

"And it's an ancient and honorable name you bear, Joseph Kerrigan, to be sure," Feeny said. "You say you heard the banshee, and I will not call you a liar, but she screams for someone else, not you. Many men will die this day and the next."

"And I will number among them," Kerrigan said.

He shoved the folded letter into Feeny's hands.

"As you see it is sealed, Michael. Captain O'Neil used his own candle and impressed the molten wax with the signet off his finger. And why not, since I have no ring of my own and the captain's bears the crest of Irish kings?"

The two young soldiers marched together, the swaying, shambling, distance-eating tramp of the Confederate infantry.

Their regiment, the 52nd Tennessee, was part of Braxton Bragg's Second Corps of the Army of the Mississippi, and there wasn't a man who shouldered a rifle that day who didn't believe that he could take on the entire Yankee army by himself and send them running all the way across the Potomac.

"I'm charging you with a great duty, Michael," Kerrigan said. "That letter you bear so carelessly tells Katherine what she and our children must do to go on without me, and, if need be, where she can find help to do it."

Michael Feeny thrust the letter back toward Kerrigan.

"No need for it," he said. "Give it to her from your own hand when all this is done."

"When all this is done, I will be done as well," Kerrigan said. "Think you, Michael, that the banshee cries for no reason?"

"A man knows not the hour of his death, Joseph. If he could, what man would walk blindly into the path of a galloping carriage or cross a railroad track at the wrong moment?"

Feeny doffed his kepi and wiped sweat from his brow with the back of his hand.

"The banshee is a demon, but God is with us, Joseph. Ah man, you will bear whatever message you have to your Katherine upon your own lips."

"It will not be, Michael. I have no desire to die on the field of honor, but I am confident that is my fate. But even so, I hope so very powerfully that I am wrong and you are right. Death is no boon companion whose company I seek."

Feeny grinned, and placed the kepi at a jaunty angle back on his head.

"Remember this one?" he said.

He tilted back his head and sang.

"Oh, my name is George Campbell
and at the age of eighteen
I fought for old Erin her rights to maintain,
And many a battle did I undergo,
Commanded by that hero called General Munroe."

A big, grizzled soldier with corporal's stripes tapped Feeny on the shoulder and grinned.

"And didn't we English stick his honor's head on a pike at Lisburn castle?"

"Aye you did, and be damned to ye," Feeny said. "You should be marching for the Tyrant, Englishman, and not for the South."

The big man laughed and said no more.

"Well, that's taken the song from my lips," Feeny said. "Let us then keep hope before us instead. Make no prediction of your own doom, Joseph. Walk bold and tall into whatever soldiers' hell is ahead for us, and come out alive on the other end. Perhaps both of us will come out together."

"Aye, perhaps. But I cannot presume upon providence when my conviction is so strong. So I ask you to bear this letter on your body through the fight ahead. I have another copy of the same inside my own jacket, in case you should be taken away in battle along with me. Sometimes those letters are found and sent on to the families after the dead are carried from the field."

"All this woeful talk falls far shy of prudence, Joseph Kerrigan. My sainted old grandmother told me that the things we speak go to God's ear, and He sometimes causes them to come to pass. So talk of life, not death."

"Very well. If God is kind to both of us, we will rejoice. But if I should die and you live, then I ask you to go, as first opportunity allows, to Nashville and present it to my beloved and tell her my spirit will watch over her all her days. I don't trust the army to get the letter to her. You, I do trust."

Feeny was ready to argue further with Kerrigan. He

did not, though, instead merely laying his hand briefly on the other's shoulder. "I give you my promise, good Joe. I expect never to be called on to fulfill it, but if fate brings ill to you and I survive, I pledge to you that your wife will receive from my own hand what you've given me. I vow it on the grave of my sainted mother."

Kerrigan turned to his companion, shifting his rifle sling as he did so.

"Your mother is alive and well, Mike."

"And so she is, hale and hearty and as fond of the gin as ever. But her grave, or the place it will be, exists somewhere, empty for now, and it is that grave on which I vowed."

"You are an odd old crow, Mike. An odd crow, or the devil take me."

"I am odd, and know it. But also trustworthy. You can count on me to carry that letter to Nashville if it falls to me to do it."

"I know it will not be easy, my friend. The federals took Nashville in February. Travel in these times is no Sunday stroll."

"Aye. Even so, Joe. Even so."

Joseph Kerrigan nodded and blinked fast, hard-fought emotion struggling inside him. He managed to choke it back and respond with a simple: "Thank you, Mike."

"Think nothing of it. There will be nothing for me to do, because we will live through this fight, you and I. Let me hear you say it, Joseph."

"We will . . . will live through this fight. Both of us."

"Aye indeed, and come out the other end heroes, with a gold medal on our chests."

"That's how it will be, Michael, lay to that." But there was no conviction in Kerrigan's voice.

All Joseph Kerrigan would experience of the famed Battle of Shiloh, which commenced early the next morning, was a series of events that entered his consciousness in a troubling jumble, running together, bleeding one into the other in a welter of confusion it would require much time to untangle.

No such time would be given him.

In the brief period he had left to know anything at all, Joe Kerrigan would be immediately conscious of only a few things, beginning with the feeling of his own heart pounding as if trying to exit his chest when the call came from the orderly sergeant to check armaments and prepare to advance.

Kerrigan would be aware, in a distant, numbed way, of standing and advancing into a rising crackle and blast of rifle fire and artillery beyond the cannon-blasted forest ahead of him. The foe had awakened and was beginning to resist the advancing Bonnie Blue Flag.

Mike Feeny was still at Kerrigan's side, and said, "Joe, I'm going to make another vow to you. One day you and I will return to this very bit of woods and enjoy a picnic here with our wives and children. These are pretty woods, except for what is happening here. It would be an ideal place for children to play, don't you think?"

"It would, Mike, of a truth. But I will make no plans

until I know if what the banshee fated for me is truth or deception."

"Live, my friend. Live. Let death take others, but us live."

They advanced, drawing closer to gunfire unseen but loudly heard ahead of them.

Even now Kerrigan could see nothing he could make sense of, though the sound of the fight heightened and the screams of dying men grew louder.

Then he heard a puzzling rustling and rattling in the trees, a repeated tick-tick-tick sound, followed by a shower of leaves and small twigs.

The ticking, like the sound of rain dripping from eaves after a summer thunderstorm, came from soft lead Minié balls striking trees, the clattering and crackling and downfall of greenery from bullets clipping branches and twigs, denuding trees already struggling to fight off the barrenness of the winter past and clothe themselves for spring.

A man walking to Kerrigan's left grunted and fell, blood streaming down the front of his leg, pouring from a fresh wound. A big grizzled Englishman, he collapsed, groaning, and made only one effort to rise. A second Minié ball caught him in the chest and sent him flat to the ground, a red rose blossoming in the middle of his butternut shirt.

"Holy Mother Mary bless us and save us!" Feeny said, horrified, as he watched the corporal fall.

Kerrigan glanced at Feeny as two other men near them dropped, one wounded in the shoulder, the other shot through the chest and dead.

"This is hot work, Michael," he said. "But such a fire cannot last for long."

But the hail of gunfire sheeting toward the advancing Confederate line increased.

The thumping of lead hitting trees and men was now so steady as to drown out the sound of twigs and branches being clipped, though they drifted to the ground in an unceasing shower.

A command from somewhere just behind the line then ordered the soldiers to take shelter from the fire.

"They're killing us, boys!" the officer yelled. "Down on your bellies."

Kerrigan recognized the fine Irish voice of Captain O'Neil, but it was hoarse and broken by shouting, in-human stress, and fear.

He, Feeny, and several others around them took cover behind the white, skeletal trunk of a fallen oak and there breathed the gasps of terrified men.

But at least they could still breathe, and for that Kerrigan voiced a silent prayer of thanks.

He turned on his back and reloaded his rifle; sur-prised the hand working powder, ball and ramrod was steady.

"This ain't really safe," said a deeply southern voice on the far side of Feeny. "This here log humps up on the bottom side so there's a space between it and the ground, see? Get down low enough and you can look right under. A bullet hits that gap and it's going to sail right through and—"

The man said no more.

His words about the protective deficiency of the warped log had been prophetic. He took a bullet through the face, its destructive course angling down from his forehead through sinuses and throat, lodging finally somewhere in his chest.

"Jesus, Mary, and Joseph," Feeny wailed. "Will you look at poor Anderson all shot through and through?"

He fingered a black rosary, blessed by a cardinal, and sounded like a man about to burst into tears.

"You were right, Joe . . . we will die here," he said.

Kerrigan's earlier morbid convictions about death had been all but forgotten after the first shots were fired.

He was scared, no question, but above and beyond that he was angry, filled with a biting fury at the very idea that men he did not know, and against whom he had done no violence, were trying to kill him.

A vision of his beautiful wife, Kate, rose in his mind and he vowed to her image that, dire premonitions be damned, he would fight to live, and return to her side.

Feeny, battling terror, proved that he had sand. And besides, as he was well aware, did not his name mean "brave soldier" in the ancient Gaelic?

He moved upward a little, leveled his rifle across the top of the log, and took aim in the general direction of the federals.

The action inspired Kerrigan to do the same, though neither of them had a precise target sighted.

Kerrigan defied fate and lifted his head above the protective height the log provided, readying to fire.

Then, in a single instant of time . . . there was nothing.

In darkness and without pain, Kerrigan collapsed partially on top of Feeny, the Minié ball that had shattered his skull lodged deep inside his brain.

He had not heard the blast of his own rifle or known whether he had even managed to fire it.

Nor did he feel himself die.

There had been no time to feel or know anything.

Joseph Kerrigan had merely stepped through a doorway into eternity.

"Joseph? Can you hear me?" Feeny said.

He knew there would be no answer.

More alone in the midst of a roaring battlefield than he had ever felt in his most solitary moments, Feeny was used up. Every man has a limit, and he'd reached his.

His panic became mindless and he pushed Kerrigan's mutilated corpse away from him.

Against all the dictates of logic and common sense, Feeny turned to run as if he could outpace the flying bullets chasing him.

He could not, of course.

Feeny felt something like a sledgehammer crash into the small of his back, and he pitched forward, momentum slamming his face hard into the bloodstained earth. He groaned, tried to stand, and felt a searing pain in his right leg. Looking down, he saw a nightmare of blood and shattered bone before he collapsed onto the ground.

Then all went quiet and still and he neither saw nor heard.

For Michael Feeny, late of County Mayo, Ireland, the Battle of Shiloh, just aborning into history, was over.

CHAPTER THREE

Kate Kerrigan rose from her chair and returned her husband's letter to her writing desk.

It had been brought, no, the word was smuggled, to her by Michael Feeny, who arrived in Nashville more dead than alive from a wound received at Shiloh.

She'd been poor then, and all the poorer for her husband's death, but Kate had a family to care for and playing the weeping widow and living off the charity of others had never entered her thinking.

Still, it had been a long, long time since she'd filled a bucket with water, soap, and a scrubbing brush.

The blood of the dead robber and would-be rapist still stained her bedroom rug and she could not abide the thought of it remaining there.

She was at the foot of the grand staircase, bucket in hand, when someone slammed the brass doorknocker hard . . . once, twice, three times.

Kate's revolver was in the parlor and she retrieved it, then returned to the door as a man's hand—for surely a woman would not have knocked so loudly?—hammered the knocker again.

"Who is it?" Kate said, her voice steady. The triple click of her Colt was loud in the quiet. "I warn you I put my faith in forty-fives."

A moment's pause, then, "Miz Kerrigan, it's me, ma'am, Hiram Street, as ever was."

Kate recognized the voice of one of her top hands and unlocked the door.

"Come inside, Hiram," she said.

Street was a short, stocky man with sandy hair and bright hazel eyes.

He was a good, steady hand with a weakness for whiskey and whores, but Kate did not hold that against him.

"I was on my way back from town and met Sheriff Martin on the trail and he told me what happened," Street said. "I rode here as fast as I could to see if you needed help."

Kate pretended to be annoyed.

"Running my horses again, Hiram?"

"Well, I figgered this was an emergency, Miz Kerrigan, begging your pardon."

The cowboy wore a mackinaw and a wool muffler over his hat, tied in a huge knot under his chin.

He looked frozen stiff.

"Were you drinking at the Happy Reb again?" Kate said.

"I can tell you no lie, ma'am. I sure was, but I only had

but two dollars and that don't go far at Dan Pardee's prices."

"Come in and I'll get you a drink, Hiram. You look as cold as a bar owner's heart."

"Dan Pardee's anyway," Street said as he stepped inside.

He looked around at the marble, gold and red velvet of Ciarogan's vast receiving hall and said, "I ain't never been in the big house before, ma'am. Takes a man's breath away."

Kate smiled.

"It wasn't always like this, Hiram, back in the day."

"You mean when you fit Comanches, Miz Kerrigan. I heard that."

Kate nodded.

"Comanches, Apaches, rustlers, claim jumpers, gunmen of all kinds and ambitions, even Mexican bandits raiding across the Rio Grande. Yes, I fought them all and killing one never troubled my sleep at night."

"Maybe that's why I'm a mite uneasy about that there iron you got in your hand, ma'am," Street said.

"Oh, sorry, Hiram." Kate smiled and let the revolver hang by her side. "Please come into the parlor."

Street, with that solemn politeness punchers have around respectable women, and with many a "Beggin' your pardon, ma'am," asked if he could remove his hat and coat.

"And should I take off my spurs, Miz Kerrigan?" he said. "I don't want to scratch your furniture, like."

"My sons don't take them off, so I don't see why you should," Kate said.

"Ciarogan is sure quiet tonight, ma'am," Street said,

accepting a chair and then a bourbon. "That's why that no-good saddle tramp came here."

"As you know, my sons are out on the range and Misses Ivy and Shannon are helping Lucy Cobb give birth. I also gave the servants the night off."

"Got fences down everywhere, but Mr. Trace told me to stay to home on account you'd be here alone," Street said. "I'm real sorry I left, Miz Kerrigan."

"How were you to know what would happen this evening, Hiram? Though I'll make no fuss about your lapse this time, don't do it again."

"Never, ma'am, I swear it."

"Then we'll let the matter drop. I'll tell Trace that I sent you into town on an errand."

"I appreciate that, ma'am. He has a temper, has Mr. Trace."

"Ah, he takes after me," Kate said.

Street hurriedly took a sip of his whiskey and said nothing.

Then, "Miz Kerrigan, I haven't been riding for Ciarogan long, but I'd like to hear about how it all started." Street smiled. "You got the only four-pillar plantation house in Texas, I reckon."

"I doubt that," Kate said. "But I started with a small cabin and a thousand acres of scrub," Kate said.

Street spoke into the silence that followed.

"Ma'am, I'd like to hear the story of how you got here."

"Really, Hiram? Do you want to hear my story or do you like being close to the Old Crow bottle and warm fire?"

Street's smile was bright and genuine.

"Truth to tell, both," he said. "But I'm a man who

loves a good story. I figger to get educated some day and become one of them dime novel authors."

"A very laudable ambition, Hiram," Kate said.

She thought for a few moments, then said, "Very well, I won't sleep tonight after what happened and the servants won't be back until late, so I'll tell you the story of Ciarogan and what went before."

Kate smiled. "But you have to sing for your supper, Hiram."

"Ma'am?"

"There's a bucket of water and scrubbing brush at the foot of the stairs, and I have a rug in my bedroom that needs cleaning."

Street had the puncher's deep-seated dread of work he couldn't do off the back of a horse, but Miz Kerrigan was not a woman to be denied.

"Follow me," she said.

Street grabbed the soapy, slopping bucket and followed Kate up the staircase, his face grim, like a man climbing the steps to the gallows.

Wide-eyed, the cowboy stared at the bloodstained rug.

"Him?" he said.

"Him."

"Gut shot, ma'am?"

"I didn't take time to see where my bullet hit."

"But look at the rug, Miz Kerrigan."

"I see it, Hiram. That's why you're here."

"But, ma'am, it looks like Miles Martin and his deputies tramped blood everywhere. The tracks of big policeman feet are all over the rug."

"Then you have your work cut out for you, Hiram. Have you not?"

Street made a long-suffering face, like a repentant sinner.

"This is because I rode off and left you alone, Miz Kerrigan. Ain't it?"

Kate smiled.

"Why Hiram, whatever gave you that idea?"

After an hour, many buckets of water, and a good deal of muttered cursing, Hiram Street threw the last bucketful of pink-tinted water outside and returned to the parlor.

"All done, Miz Kerrigan," he said.

Kate put aside the volume of Mr. Dickens she'd been reading and rose to her feet.

"I'll take a look," she said.

Kate cast a critical eye over the wet rug and said, "There, Hiram, in the corner. You missed a spot."

"Sorry, ma'am," Street said.

He got down on his knees and industriously scrubbed the offending stain with the heel of his hand. The spot was only the size of a dime, but Kate's eagle eyes missed nothing.

"Very well, Hiram," she said. "Now, we'll let the rug dry. I'll use one of the guest rooms for a few days."

Once the chastened cowboy was again sitting by the fire, a glass of whiskey in hand, Kate smiled at him.

"Do you still wish to hear the story of Kate Kerrigan, her life and times?"

Street settled his shoulders into the leather and nodded.

"I sure do, ma'am."

"I'll tell you of my early days, when just staying alive was a struggle. To relate all that's passed in the last forty years would be too long in the telling."

Kate flashed her dazzling smile and continued to do so.

"I'm sure there's enough material in the story of my younger days for a hundred dime novels," she said.

"Beggin' your pardon, Ma'am, but I'm eager to hear the tale of Kate Kerrigan," Street said.

"Then, Hiram, you shall at least hear some of it."

J. A. Johnstone on William W. Johnstone
"Print the Legend"

William W. Johnstone was born in southern Missouri, the youngest of four children. He was raised with strong moral and family values by his minister father, and tutored by his schoolteacher mother. Despite this, he quit school at age fifteen.

"I have the highest respect for education," he says, "but such is the folly of youth, and wanting to see the world beyond the four walls and the blackboard."

True to this vow, Bill attempted to enlist in the French Foreign Legion ("I saw Gary Cooper in *Beau Geste* when I was a kid and I thought the French Foreign Legion would be fun") but was rejected, thankfully, for being underage. Instead, he joined a traveling carnival and did all kinds of odd jobs. It was listening to the veteran carny folk, some of whom had been on the circuit since the late 1800s, telling amazing tales about their experiences, that planted the storytelling seed in Bill's imagination.

"They were mostly honest people, despite the bad reputation traveling carny shows had back then," Bill remembers. "Of course, there were exceptions. There was one guy named Picky, who got that name because he was a master pickpocket. He could steal a man's socks right off his feet without him knowing. Believe me, Picky got us chased out of more than a few towns."

After a few months of this grueling existence, Bill returned home and finished high school. Next came stints as a deputy sheriff in the Tallulah, Louisiana, Sheriff's Department, followed by a hitch in the U.S. Army. Then he began a career in radio broadcasting at KTLD in Tallulah, which would last sixteen years. It was there that he fine-tuned his storytelling skills. He turned to writing in 1970, but it wouldn't be until 1979 that his first novel, *The Devil's Kiss*, was published. Thus began the full-time writing career of William W. Johnstone. He wrote horror (*The Uninvited*), thrillers (*The Last of the Dog Team*), even a romance novel or two. Then, in February 1983, *Out of the Ashes* was published. Searching for his missing family in a postapocalyptic America, rebel mercenary and patriot Ben Raines is united with the civilians of the Resistance forces and moves to the forefront of a revolution for the nation's future.

Out of the Ashes was a smash. The series would continue for the next twenty years, winning Bill three generations of fans all over the world. The series was often imitated but never duplicated. "We all tried to copy the Ashes series," said one publishing executive, "but Bill's uncanny ability, both then and now, to predict in which direction the political winds were blowing brought a certain immediacy to the table no one else could capture." The Ashes series would end its run with more than thirty-four books and twenty million copies in print, making it one of the most successful men's action series in American book publishing. (The Ashes series also, Bill notes with a touch of pride, got him on the FBI's Watch List for its less than flattering portrayal of spineless politicians and the growing power of big government over our lives, among other things. In that respect, I often find myself saying, "Bill was years ahead of his time.")

Always steps ahead of the political curve, Bill's recent thrillers, written with myself, include *Vengeance Is Mine, Invasion USA, Border War, Jackknife, Remember the Alamo, Home Invasion, Phoenix Rising, The Blood of Patriots, The Bleeding Edge*, and the upcoming *Suicide Mission*.

It is with the western, though, that Bill found his greatest success. His westerns propelled him onto both the *USA Today* and the *New York Times* bestseller lists.

Bill's western series include *Matt Jensen, the Last Mountain Man, Preacher, the First Mountain Man, The Family Jensen, Luke Jensen, Bounty Hunter, Eagles, MacCallister* (an Eagles spin-off), *Sidewinders, The Brothers O'Brien, Sixkiller, Blood Bond, The Last Gunfighter*, and the new series *Flintlock* and *The Trail West*. May 2013 saw the hardcover western *Butch Cassidy: The Lost Years*.

"The western," Bill says, "is one of the few true art forms that is one hundred percent American. I liken the Western as America's version of England's Arthurian legends, like the Knights of the Round Table, or Robin Hood and his Merry Men. Starting with the 1902 publication of *The Virginian* by Owen Wister, and followed by the greats like Zane Grey, Max Brand, Ernest

Haycox, and of course Louis L'Amour, the western has helped to shape the cultural landscape of America.

"I'm no goggle-eyed college academic, so when my fans ask me why the western is as popular now as it was a century ago, I don't offer a 200-page thesis. Instead, I can only offer this: The western is honest. In this great country, which is suffering under the yoke of political correctness, the western harks back to an era when justice was sure and swift. Steal a man's horse, rustle his cattle, rob a bank, a stagecoach, or a train, you were hunted down and fitted with a hangman's noose. One size fit all.

"Sure, we westerners are prone to a little embellishment and exaggeration and, I admit it, occasionally play a little fast and loose with the facts. But we do so for a very good reason—to enhance the enjoyment of readers.

"It was Owen Wister, in *The Virginian*, who first coined the phrase 'When you call me that, smile.' Legend has it that Wister actually heard those words spoken by a deputy sheriff in Medicine Bow, Wyoming, when another poker player called him a son of a bitch.

"Did it really happen, or is it one of those myths that have passed down from one generation to the next? I honestly don't know. But there's a line in one of my favorite westerns of all time, *The Man Who Shot Liberty Valance*, where the newspaper editor tells the young reporter, 'When the truth becomes legend, print the legend.'

"These are the words I live by."